THE MAN IN THE IRON MASK

THE MAN IN THE IRON MASK

by

ALEXANDRE DUMAS

ABRIDGED

A BANCROFT

CLASSIC

BANCROFT BOOKS

LONDON

BANCROFT BOOKS
49–50 Poland Street
London W . 1 A 2 LG

First published in the "Bancroft Classics" 1967
This impression 1973

430 00087 1

CONTENTS

CONTENTS

Chapter 1

TWO OLD FRIENDS

WHILST every one at court was busily engaged upon his own affairs, a man mysteriously entered a house situated behind the Place de Grève. The man we have just alluded to walked along with a firm step, although he was no longer in his early prime. His dark cloak and long sword plainly revealed one who seemed in search of adventures; and, judging from his curly moustaches, his fine and smooth skin, which could be seen beneath his sombrero, it would not have been difficult to pronounce that the gallantry of his adventures was unquestionable. In fact, hardly had the cavalier entered the house, when the clock struck eight; and ten minutes afterwards a lady, followed by a servant armed to the teeth, approached and knocked at the same door, which an old woman immediately opened for her. The lady raised her veil as she entered; though no longer beautiful or young, she was still active and of an imposing carriage. Hardly had she reached the vestibule, than the cavalier, whose features we have only roughly sketched, advanced towards her, holding out his hand.

"Good-day, my dear Duchesse," he said.

"How do you do, my dear Aramis," replied the Duchesse.

He led her to a most elegantly furnished apartment, on whose high windows were reflected the expiring rays of the setting sun, which filtered through the dark crests of some adjoining firs. They sat down side by side.

"Chevalier," said the Duchesse, "you have never given me a single sign of life since our interview at Fontainebleau, and I confess that your presence there on the day of the Franciscan's death, and your initiation in certain secrets, caused me the liveliest astonishment I ever experienced in my whole life."

"I can explain my presence there to you, as well as my initiation," said Aramis.

"But let us, first of all," said the Duchesse, "talk a little of ourselves, for our friendship is by no means of recent date."

"Yes, madame; and if Heaven wills it, we shall continue to be friends, I will not say for a long time, but for ever."

"That is quite certain, Chevalier, and my visit is a proof of it."

Aramis bowed over the Duchesse's hand, and pressed his lips upon it. "You must have had some trouble to find me again," he said.

"Yes," she answered, annoyed to find the subject taking a turn which Aramis wished to give it; "but I knew you were a friend of M. Fouquet's, and so I inquired in that direction."

"A friend! oh!" exclaimed the Chevalier. "I can hardly pretend to be that. A poor priest who has been favoured by so generous a protector, and whose heart is full of gratitude and devotion to him, is all that I pretend to be to M. Fouquet."

"He made you a bishop?"

"Yes, Duchesse."

"A very good retiring pension for so handsome a musketeer."

"Yes, in the same way that political intrigue is for yourself," thought Aramis. "And so," he added, "you inquire after me at M. Fouquet's?"

"Suffice it to know that I learnt you had returned from Vannes, and I sent to one of our friends, M. le Comte de la Fère, who is discretion itself, in order to ascertain it, but he answered that he was not aware of your address."

"So like Athos," thought the bishop; "that which is actually good never alters."

"Well, then, you know that I cannot venture to show myself here, and that the Queen-Mother has always some grievance or other against me."

"Yes, indeed, and I am surprised at it."

"Oh! there are various reasons for it. But, to continue, being obliged to conceal myself, I was fortunate enough to meet with M. d'Artagnan, who was formerly one of your old friends, I believe?"

"A friend of mine still, Duchesse."

"He gave me some information, and sent me to M. Baisemeaux, the governor of the Bastille."

"And so Baisemeaux indicated to you——"

"Saint-Mandé, where I forwarded a letter to you."

"Dear Duchesse, pray arrive soon at the circumstance which brought you here; for I think we can be of service to each other."

"Such has been my own thought. I need a sum of money to restore Dampierre."

"Ah!" replied Aramis coldly—"money? Well, Duchesse, how much would you require?"

"Oh! a tolerably round sum."

"So much the worse—you know I am not rich."

"In that case you have a friend who must be very wealthy.—M. Fouquet."

"M. Fouquet! He is more than half ruined, madame."

"So it is said, but I would not believe it."

"Why, Duchesse?"

"Because I have, or rather Laicques has, certain letters in his possession, from Cardinal Mazarin, which establish the existence of very strange accounts."

"What accounts?"

"Relative to various sums of money borrowed and disposed of. I cannot very distinctly remember what they are; but they establish the fact that the Surintendant, according to these letters, which are signed by Mazarin, had taken thirteen millions of francs from the coffers of the State. The case is a very serious one."

Aramis clenched his hands in anxiety and apprehension. "Is it possible," he said, "that you have such letters as you speak of, and have not communicated them to M. Fouquet?"

"Ah!" replied the Duchesse, "I keep such little matters as these in reserve. The day may come when they may be of service; and they can then be withdrawn from the safe custody in which they now are."

"You must be in sad want of money, my poor friend, to think of such things as these—you, too, who held M. de Mazarin's prose effusions in such indifferent esteem."

"The fact is, I am in want of money."

"And then," continued Aramis in cold accents, "it must have been very distressing to you to be obliged to have recourse to such a means. It is cruel."

"Oh! if I had wished to do harm instead of good," said Madame de Chevreuse, "instead of asking the general of the order, or M. Fouquet, for the five hundred thousand francs I require——"

"Five hundred thousand francs!"

"Yes; no more. Do you think it much? I require at least as much as that to restore Dampierre."

"Yes, madame."

"I say, therefore, that, instead of asking for this amount, I should have gone to see my old friend the Queen-Mother; the letters from her husband, the Signor Mazarini, would have served me as an introduction, and I should have begged this mere trifle of her, saying to her, 'I wish, madame, to have the honour of receiving you at Dampierre. Permit me to put Dampierre in a fit state for that purpose.'"

"It is a snare," thought the Bishop; "it is impossible that Anne of Austria could listen to such a woman as this."

"Well?" said the Duchesse.

"Well, madame, I should be very much astonished if M. Fouquet had five hundred thousand francs at his disposal at the present moment. And the Queen will certainly do for you what the Surintendant is unable to do."

"Oh! certainly."

"And so, you are now going to denounce M. Fouquet to the Queen," said Aramis.

"'Denounce!' Oh! what a disagreeable word. I shall not 'denounce,' my dear friend; you now know matters of policy too well to be ignorant how easily these affairs are arranged. I shall merely side against M. Fouquet, and nothing more; and, in a war of party against party, a weapon of attack is always a weapon."

"Stay a moment, Duchesse; would you like me to tell you why I will not buy your letters?"

"Pray tell me?"

"Because the letters you say are Mazarin's are false."

"What an absurdity."

"I have no doubt of it, for it would, to say the least, be very singular, that after you had quarrelled with the Queen through M. Mazarin's means, you should have kept up any intimate acquaintance with the latter."

But the Duchesse had said enough, and advanced towards the door, made a sign to her servant, who resumed his musket, and left the house where such tender friends had not been able to understand each other, only because they had understood each other too well.

Chapter 2

WHEREIN MAY BE SEEN THAT A BARGAIN WHICH CANNOT BE MADE WITH ONE PERSON, CAN BE CARRIED OUT WITH ANOTHER

ARAMIS had been perfectly correct in his supposition; for hardly had she left the house in the Place Baudoyer, than Madame de Chevreuse proceeded homeward. She was, doubtless, afraid of being followed, and by this means thought she might succeed in throwing those who might be following her off their guard; but scarcely had she arrived within the door of the hotel, and hardly had assured herself that no one who could cause her any uneasiness was on her track, when she opened the door of the garden, leading into another street, and hurried towards the Rue Croix des Petits Champs, where M. Colbert resided.

"What is the subject, madame, which procures me the honour of a visit from you?" he inquired.

Madame de Chevreuse sat down in the arm-chair which M. Colbert advanced towards her. "Monsieur Colbert, you are the Intendant of Finances, and are ambitious of becoming the Surintendant?"

"M. Fouquet's fortune, madame, enables him to withstand all attempts. The Surintendant in this age plays the part of the Colossus of Rhodes; the vessels pass beneath him and do not overthrow him."

"Oh, I am perfectly aware of what I am saying," returned Madame de Chevreuse coldly. "I do not live at such a distance from Paris as not to know what takes place there. The King does not like M. Fouquet, and he would willingly sacrifice M. Fouquet if an opportunity were only given him."

"It must be a good one, though."

"Good enough, and one I estimate to be worth five hundred thousand francs."

"In what way?" said Colbert.

"I mean, monsieur, that holding this opportunity in my own hands, I will not allow it to be transferred to yours except for a sum of five hundred thousand francs."

"I understand you perfectly, madame. But since you have fixed a price for the sale, let me now see the value of the articles to be sold."

"Oh, a mere trifle; six letters, as I have already told you, from M. de Mazarin; and the autographs will most assuredly not be regarded as too highly priced, if they establish, in an irrefutable manner, that M. Fouquet has embezzled large sums of money from the treasury, and appropriated them to his own purposes."

"In an irrefutable manner, do you say?" observed Colbert, whose eyes sparkled with delight.

"Perfectly so; would you like to read the letters?"

"With all my heart. Copies of course?"

"Of course, the copies," said the Duchesse, as she drew from her bosom a small packet of papers flattened by her velvet bodice. "Read," she said.

Colbert eagerly snatched the papers and devoured them.

"Excellent!" he said.

"It is clear enough, is it not?"

"Yes, madame, yes; M. Mazarin must have handed the money to M. Fouquet, who must have kept it for his own purposes; but the question is, what money?"

"Exactly,—what money? if we come to terms I will join to these six letters a seventh, which will supply you with the fullest particulars."

Colbert reflected. "And the originals of those letters?"

"A useless question to ask; exactly as if I were to ask you, Monsieur Colbert, whether the money-bags you will give me will be full or empty."

"Very good, madame."

"How much will you offer me?"

"Two hundred thousand francs," said Colbert.

The Duchesse laughed in his face, and then said suddenly, "Wait a moment, I have another arrangement to propose; will you give me three hundred thousand francs?"

"No, no."

"Oh, you can either accept or refuse my terms; besides, that is not all."

"More still! you are becoming too impraticable to deal with, madame."

"Less so than you think, perhaps, for it is not money I am going to ask you for."

"What is it, then?"

"A service. You know that I have always been most affectionately attached to the Queen, and I am desirous of having an interview with Her Majesty."

And rising from her seat with this decisive remark, the old Duchesse plunged M. Colbert into a disagreeable perplexity. To bargain any further was out of the question; and not to bargain was to pay a great deal too dearly for them. "Madame," he said, "I shall have the pleasure of handing you over a hundred thousand crowns; but how shall I get the actual letters themselves?"

"In the simplest manner in the world, my dear Monsieur Colbert—whom will you trust?"

The financier began to laugh silently, so that his large eyebrows went up and down like the wings of a bat upon the deep lines of his yellow forehead. "No one," he said.

"You surely will make an exception in your own favour, Monsieur Colbert?"

"In what way, madame?"

"I mean that if you would take the trouble to accompany me to the place where the letters are, they would be delivered into your own hands, and you would be able to verify and check them."

"I have reflected, madame, and I shall not accompany you."

"Really—and why not?"

"Because I have the most perfect confidence in you."

"You overpower me. But provided I receive the hundred thousand crowns?"

"Here they are, madame," said Colbert, scribbling a few lines on a piece of paper, which he handed to the Duchesse, adding, "You are paid."

"The trait is a fine one, Monsieur Colbert, and I will reward you for it," she said, beginning to laugh.

Madame de Chevreuse's laugh was a very sinister sound; every man who feels youth, faith, love, life itself throbbing in his heart, would prefer tears to such a lamentable laugh. The Duchesse opened the front of her dress and drew forth from her bosom, somewhat less white than it once had been, a small packet of papers, tied with a flamecoloured ribbon, and, still laughing, she said, "There, Monsieur Colbert, are the originals of Cardinal Mazarin's letters; they are now your own property," she added, refastening the body of her dress; "your fortune is secured, and now accompany me to the Queen."

"No, madame; if you are again about to run the chance of Her Majesty's displeasure, and it were known at the Palais Royal that I had been the means of introducng you there, the Queen would never forgive me while she lived. No; there are certain persons at the palace who are devoted to me, who will procure you an admssion without my being compromised."

"Just as you please, provided I enter."

"What do you term those religious women at Bruges who cure disorders?"

"Béguines."

"Good; you are one."

"As you please, but I must soon cease to be one."

"That is your affair."

"Excuse me, but I do not wish to be exposed to a refusal."

"That is again your own affair, madame. I am going to give directions to the head valet of the gentleman in waiting on Her Majesty to allow admission to a Béguine, who brings an effectual remedy for Her Majesty's sufferings. You are the bearer of my letter, you will undertake to be provided with the remedy, and will give every explanation on the subject. I admit a knowledge of a Béguine, but I deny all knowledge of Madame de Chevreuse. Here, madame, then, is your letter of introduction."

Chapter 3

THE SKIN OF THE BEAR

COLBERT handed the Duchesse the letter, and gently drew aside the chair behind which she was standing; Madame de Chevreuse, with a very slight bow, immediately left the room. Colbert, who had recognised Mazarin's handwriting, and had counted the letters, rang to summon his secretary, whom he enjoyed to go in immediate search of M. Vanel, a counsellor of the Parliament. The secretary replied that, according to his usual practice, M. Vanel had just that moment entered the house, in order to render to the Intendant an account of the principal details of the business which had been transacted during the day in the sitting of the Parliament. Colbert approached one of the lamps, read the letters of the deceased Cardinal over again, smiled repeatedly as he recognised the great value of the papers Madame de Chevreuse had just delivered to him, and burying his head in his hands for a few minutes, reflected profoundly. In the meantime, a tall, large-made man entered the room; his spare thin face, steady look, and hooked nose, as he entered Colbert's cabinet, with a modest assurance of manner, revealed a character at once supple and decided,—supple towards the master who could throw him the prey, firm towards the dogs who might possibly be disposed to dispute it with him. M. Vanel carried a voluminous bundle of papers under his arm, and placed it on the desk on which Colbert was leaning both his elbows, as he supported his head.

"Good-day, M. Vanel," said the latter, rousing himself from his meditation.

"Good-day, monseigneur," said Vanel naturally.

"You should say monsieur, and not monseigneur," replied Colbert gently.

"We give the title of monseigneur to ministers," returned Vanel, with extreme self-possession, "and you are a minister."

"Not yet."

Colbert coughed. "Vanel," he said suddenly to his protégé, "you are a hard-working man, I know. You must not grow rusty in your post of counsellor."

"What must I do to avoid it?"

"Purchase a high place. Mean and low ambitions are very difficult to satisfy."

"Small purses are the most difficult to fill, monseigneur."

"Vanel, would you like to be Procureur-Général?" said Colbert suddenly, softening both his look and his voice.

Vanel rose, quite bewildered by this offer which had been so suddenly and unexpectedly made to him. "You are not trifling with me, monseigneur," he said.

"Stay; you say that M. Gourville has spoken to you about M. Fouquet's post."

"Yes; and M. Pélisson also."

"Well, Monsieur Vanel, you will go at once, and find out either M. Gourville or M. Pélisson. Do you know any other friend of M. Fouquet?"

"I know M. de la Fontaine very well."

"La Fontaine, the rhymester?"

"Yes; he used to write verses to my wife, when M. Fouquet was one of our friends."

"Go to him, then, and try to procure an interview with the Surintendant."

"Willingly—but the sum itself?"

"On the day and the hour you arrange to settle the matter, Monsieur Vanel, you shall be supplied with the money; so, do not make yourself uneasy on that account."

"Monseigneur, such munificence! You eclipse kings even—you surpass M. Fouquet himself."

"Stay a moment—do not let us mistake each other. I do not make you a present of fourteen hundred thousand francs, Monsieur Vanel; for I have children to provide for—but I will lend you that sum."

"Ask whatever interest, whatever security you please, monseigneur: I am quite ready. And when all your requisitions are satisfied, I will still repeat, that you surpass kings and M. Fouquet in munificence. What conditions do you impose?"

"The repayment in eight years, and a mortgage upon the appointment itself."

"Certainly. Is that all?"

"Wait a moment. I reserve to myself the right of repurchasing the post from you at one hundred and fifty thousand francs profit for yourself, if, in your mode of filling the office, you do not follow out a line of conduct in conformity with the interests of the King and with my projects."

"Ah! ah!" said Vanel, in a slightly altered tone.

"Is there anything in that which can possibly be objectionable to you, Monsieur Vanel?" said Colbert coldly.

"Oh! no, no," replied Vanel quickly.

"Very good. We will sign an agreement to that effect, whenever you like. And now, go as quickly as you can to M. Fouquet's friends, obtain an interview with the Surintendant; do not be too difficult in making whatever concessions may be required of you; and when once the arrangements are all made——"

"I will press him to sign."

"Be most careful to do nothing of the kind; do not speak of signatures with M. Fouquet, nor of deeds, nor even ask him to pass his word. Understand this, otherwise you will lose everything. All you have to do is to get M. Fouquet to give you his hand on the matter. Go, go."

Chapter 4

AN INTERVIEW WITH THE QUEEN-MOTHER

THE Queen-Mother was in her bedroom at the Palais-Royal with Madame de Motteville and the Senora Molena. A sharp, acute pain seized the Queen, who turned deadly pale, and threw herself back in the chair, with every symptom of a sudden fainting fit. Molena ran to a richly-gilded tortoiseshell cabinet, from which she took a large rock-crystal smelling-bottle, and immediately held it to the Queen's nostrils, who inhaled it wildly for a few minutes, and murmured:

"It will hasten my death—but Heaven's will be done!"

"We must put her to bed," said La Molena.

"Presently, Molena."

"Let us leave the Queen alone," added the Spanish attendant.

Madame de Motteville rose; large and glistening tears were fast rolling down the Queen's pallid face; and Molena, having observed this sign of weakness, fixed her black vigilant eyes upon her.

"Yes, yes," replied the Queen. "Leave us, Motteville; go."

Madame de Motteville bowed in submission, and was about to withdraw, when, suddenly, an old female attendant, dressed as if she had belonged to the Spanish court of the year 1620, opened the doors, and surprised the Queen in her tears. "The remedy!" she cried, delightedly, to the Queen, as she unceremoniously approached the group.

"What remedy?" said Anne of Austria.

"For your Majesty's sufferings," the former replied.

"Who brings it?" asked Madame de Motteville eagerly; "Monsieur Vallot?"

"No; a lady from Flanders."

"From Flanders. Is she Spanish?" inquired the Queen.

"I don't know."

"Go, Molena; go and see!" cried the Queen.

"It is needless," suddenly replied a voice, at once firm and gentle in its tone, which proceeded from the other side of the tapestry hangings; a voice which made the attendants start, and the Queen tremble excessively. At the same moment, a masked female appeared through the hangings, and, before the Queen could speak a syllable, she added, "I am connected with the order of the Béguines of Bruges, and do, indeed, bring with me the remedy which is certain to effect a cure of your Majesty's complaint." No one uttered a sound, and the Béguine did not move a step.

"Speak," said the Queen.

"I will, when we are alone," was the answer.

Anne of Austria looked at her attendants, who immediately withdrew. The Béguine, thereupon, advanced a few steps towards the Queen, and bowed reverently before her. The Queen gazed with increasing mistrust at this woman, who, in her turn, fixed a pair of brilliant eyes upon her, through her mask.

"Your Majesty is not irremediably ill."

Hardly had these words escaped her lips, than the Queen rose up proudly. "Speak," she cried, in a short, imperious tone of voice; "explain yourself briefly, quickly, entirely; or, if not—"

"Nay, do not threaten me, your Majesty," said the Béguine gently; "I came to you full of compassion and respect. I came here on the part of a friend."

"I do not understand you," replied the Queen; setting her teeth hard together in order to conceal her emotion.

"I will make myself understood, then. Your Majesty remembers that the King was born on the 5th of September, 1638, at a quarter past eleven o'clock."

"Yes," stammered out the Queen.

"At half-past twelve," continued the Béguine, "the Dauphin who had been baptized by Monseigneur de Meaux in the King's and in your own presence, was acknowledged as the heir of the crown of France. The King then went to the chapel of the old Château de Saint-Germain, to hear the *Te Deum* chanted."

"Quite true, quite true," murmured the Queen.

"Your Majesty's confinement took place in the presence of Monsieur, His Majesty's late uncle, of the princes, and of the ladies attached to the court. The King's physician, Bouvard, and Honoré, the surgeon, were stationed in the antechamber; your Majesty slept from three o'clock until seven, I believe!"

"Yes, yes; but you tell me no more than every one else knows as well as you and myself."

"I am now, madame, approaching that which very few persons are acquainted with. Very few persons, did I say, alas! I might almost say two only, for formerly there were but five in all, and, for many years past, the secret has been well preserved by the deaths of the principal participators in it. The late King now sleeps with his ancestors. Péronne, the midwife, soon followed him, Laporte is already forgotten."

The Queen opened her lips as though about to reply; she felt beneath her icy hand, with which she kept her face half concealed, the beads of perspiration upon her brow.

"It was eight o'clock," pursued the Béguine; "the King was seated at supper, full of joy and happiness; around him on all sides arose wild cries of delight and drinking of healths; the people cheered beneath the balconies; the Swiss guards, the musketeers, and the royal guards wandered through the city, borne about in triumph by the drunken students. Those boisterous sounds of the general joy disturbed the Dauphin, the future King of France, who was quietly lying in the arms of Madame de Hausac, his nurse, and whose eyes, as he opened them, and stared about, might have observed two crowns at the foot of his cradle. Suddenly, your Majesty uttered a piercing cry, and Dame Péronne immediately flew to your bedside. The doctors were dining in a room at some distance from your chamber; the palace, deserted from the frequency of the irruptions made into it, was without either sentinels or guards. The midwife, having questioned and examined your Majesty, gave a sudden exclamation as if in wild astonishment, and taking you in her arms, bewildered almost out of her senses from sheer distress of mind, despatched Laporte to inform the King that Her Majesty the Queen wished to see him in her room. Laporte, you are aware, madame, was a man of the most admirable calmness and presence of mind. He did not approach the King as if he were the bearer of alarming intelligence and wished to inspire the terror which he himself experienced; besides, it was not a very terrifying intelligence which awaited the King. Therefore, Laporte appeared with a smile upon his lips, and approached the King's chair saying to him,—"Sire, the Queen is very happy, and would be still more so to see your Majesty." On that day Louis XIII would have given his crown away to the veriest beggar for a 'God bless you.' Animated, light-hearted, and full of gaiety, the King rose from the table, and said to those around him, in a tone that Henry IV might have adopted,—'Gentlemen, I am going to see my wife.' He came to your bedside, madame, at the very moment Dame Péronne presented to him a second prince, as beautiful and healthy as the former, and said,—'Sire, Heaven will not allow the kingdom of France to fall into the female line.' The King, yielding to a first impulse, clasped the child in his arms, and cried, 'Oh! Heaven, I thank thee!' "

"Ah! do not believe that, because there could be but one Dauphin in France," exclaimed the Béguine, "or that if the Queen allowed that child to vegetate, banished from his royal parents' presence, she was on that account an unfeeling mother. Oh! no, no; there are those alive who know the floods of bitter tears she shed; there are those who have known and witnessed the passionate kisses she imprinted on that innocent creature in exchange for a life of misery and gloom to which State policy condemned the twin brother of Louis XIV."

"Oh! Heaven!" murmured the Queen feebly.

"It is admitted," continued the Béguine, quickly, "that when the King perceived the effect which would result from the existence of two sons, both equal in age and pretensions, he trembled for the welfare of France, for the tranquillity of the State; and it is equally well known that the Cardinal de Richelieu, by the direction of Louis XIII, thought over the subject with deep attention, and after an hour's meditation in His Majesty's cabinet, he pronounced the following sentence: 'One prince is peace and safety for the state; two competitors are civil war and anarchy.' "

The Queen rose suddenly from her seat, pale as death, and her hands clenched together:—"You know too much," she said, in a hoarse, thick voice, "since you refer to secrets of State. As for the friends from whom you have acquired this secret, they are false and treacherous. You are their accomplice in the crime which is now being committed. Now, throw aside your mask, or I will have you arrested by my captain of the guards. Do not think that this secret terrifies me! You have obtained it, you shall restore it to me. Never shall it leave your bosom, for neither your secret nor your own life belongs to you from this moment."

Anne of Austria, joining gesture to the threat, advanced a couple of steps towards the Béguine. "Learn," said the latter, "to know and value the fidelity, the honour, and secrecy of the friends you have abandoned." And, then, suddenly threw aside her mask.

"Madame de Chevreuse!" exclaimed the Queen.

"With your Majesty, the sole living confidante of this secret."

"Ah!" murmured Anne of Austria; "come and embrace me, Duchesse. Alas! you kill your friend in thus trifling with her terrible distress."

And the Queen, leaning her head upon the shoulder of the old Duchesse, burst into a flood of bitter tears. "How young you are still!" said the latter, in a hollow voice, "you can weep!"

Chapter 5

TWO FRIENDS

Madame de Chevreuse collected herself for a moment, and then murmured, "How far removed kings are from other people."

"What do you mean?"

"I mean that they are so far removed from the vulgar herd that they forget that others stand in need of the bare necessaries of life."

The Queen slightly coloured, for she now began to perceive the drift of her friend's remark. "It was very wrong," she said, "to have neglected you."

"Well, then, your Majesty can confer the greatest, the most ineffable pleasure upon me."

"What is it?" said the Queen, a little distant in her manner, from an uneasiness of feeling produced by this remark. "But do not forget, my good Chevreuse, that I am quite as much under my son's influence as I was formerly under my husband's."

"Will your Majesty do me the honour to pass a few days with me at Dampierre?"

"Is that all?" said the Queen stupefied. "Nothing more than that?"

"Good heavens! can you possibly imagine that in asking you that, I am not asking you the greatest conceivable favour. If that really be the case, you do not know me. Will you accept?"

"Yes, gladly. And I shall be happy," continued the Queen, with some suspicion, "if my presence can in any way be useful to you."

"Useful!" exclaimed the Duchesse, laughing; "oh, no, no, agreeable—delightful, if you like; and you promise me, then?"

"I swear it," said the Queen, whereupon the Duchesse seized her beautiful hand, and covered it with kisses. The Queen could not help murmuring to herself, "She is a good-hearted woman, and very generous too."

"Will your Majesty consent to wait a fortnight before you come?"

"Certainly; but why?"

"Because," said the Duchesse, "knowing me to be in disgrace, no one would lend me the hundred thousand francs which I require to put Dampierre into a state of repair. But when it is known that I require that sum for the purpose of receiving your Majesty at Dampierre properly, all the money in Paris will be at my disposal."

"Ah!" said the Queen, gently nodding her head in sign of intelligence, "a hundred thousand francs! you want a hundred thousand francs to put Dampierre into repair?"

"Quite as much as that."

"And no one will lend you them?"

"No one."

"I will lend them to you, if you like, Duchesse."

"Oh, I hardly dare to accept such a sum."

"You would be wrong if you did not. Besides, a hundred thousand francs is really not much. I know but too well that you never set a right value upon your silence and your secrecy. Push that table a little towards me, Duchesse, and I will write you an order on M. Colbert; no, on M. Fouquet, who is a far more courteous and obliging man."

The Queen wrote and handed the Duchesse the order, and afterwards dismissed her with a warm and cheerful embrace.

Chapter 6

THE CHARACTER OF A NEGOTIATOR

WE NOW return to Saint-Mandé, where the Surintendant was in the habit of receiving his select society of epicureans. For some time past, the host had met with some terrible trials. Every one in the house was aware of and felt the minister's distress. No more magnificent or recklessly improvident *réunions*. Money had been the pretext assigned by Fouquet, and never *was* any pretext, as Gourville said, more fallacious, for there was not the slightest appearance of money.

"Have you found a purchaser for my post of procureur-général?" exclaimed Fouquet.

"I have, monsieur," said Gourville.

Within a quarter of an hour afterwards, M. Vanel was introduced into the Surintendant's cabinet. When Fouquet saw him enter, he called to Pélisson, and whispered a few words in his ear. "Do not lose a word of what I am going to say: let all the silver and gold plate, together with the jewels of every description, be packed up in the carriage. You will take the black horses: the jeweller will accompany you; and you will postpone the supper until Madame de Bellière's arrival."

Pélisson set off, not quite clear as to his friend's meaning or intention, but confident, like every true friend, in the judgment of the man he was blindly obeying. It is that which constitutes the strength of such men; distress only arises in the minds of inferior natures.

Vanel bowed low to the Surintendant, and was about to begin a speech. "Do not trouble yourself, monsieur," said Fouquet politely; "I am told that you wish to purchase a post I hold. How much can you give me for it?"

"It is for you, monsieur, to fix the amount you require. I know that offers of purchase have already been made to you for it."

"Madame Vanel, I have been told, values it at fourteen hundred thousand livres."

"That is all we have."

"Can you give me the money immediately?"

"I have not the money with me," said Vanel, frightened almost by the unpretending simplicity, amounting to greatness, of the man, for he had expected disputes, and difficulties, and opposition of every kind.

"When will you be able to have it?"

"Whenever you please, monseigneur;" for he began to be afraid that Fouquet was trifling with him.

"If it were not for the trouble you would have in returning to Paris I would say at once; but we will arrange that the payment and the signature shall take place at six o'clock to-morrow morning."

Chapter 7

MADAME DE BELLIÈRE'S PLATE AND DIAMONDS

HARDLY had Fouquet dismissed Vanel, than he began to reflect for a few moments:—"A man never can do too much for the woman he has once loved. Marguerite wishes to be the wife of a procureur-général—and why not confer this pleasure upon her? And, now that the most scrupulous and sensitive conscience will be unable to reproach me with anything, let my thoughts be bestowed on her who has shown so much devotion for me. Madame de Bellière ought to be there by this time," he said, as he turned towards the secret door.

After he had locked himself in, he opened the subterranean passage, and rapidly hastened towards the means of communicating between the house at Vincennes and his own residence. He had neglected to apprise his friend of his approach, by ringing the bell, perfectly assured that she would never fail to be exact at the rendezvous; as, indeed, was the case, for she was already waiting. The noise the Surintendant made aroused her; she ran to take from under the door the letter that he had thrust there, and which simply said, "Come, marquise; we are waiting supper for you."

With her heart filled with happiness Madame de Bellière ran to her carriage in the Avenue de Vincennes, and in a few minutes she was holding out her hand to Gourville, who was standing at the entrance, where, in order the better to please his master, he had stationed himself to watch her arrival. She had not observed that Fouquet's black horses had arrived at the same time, smoking and covered with foam, having returned to Saint-Mandé with Pélisson and the very jeweller to whom Madame de Bellière had sold her plate and her jewels. Pélisson introduced the goldsmith into the cabinet, which Fouquet had not yet left. The Surintendant thanked him for having been good enough to regard as a simple deposit in his hands, the valuable property which he had had every right to sell; and he cast his eyes on the total of the account, which amounted to thirteen hundred thousand francs. Then, going for a few moments to his desk, he wrote an order for fourteen hundred thousand francs, payable at sight, at his treasury, before twelve o'clock the next day.

"A hundred thousand francs profit!" cried the goldsmith. "Oh, monseigneur, what generosity!"

"Nay, nay, not so, monsieur," said Fouquet, touching him on the shoulder; "there are certain kindnesses which can never be repaid. The profit is about that which you would have made; but the interest of your money still remains to be arranged." And, saying this, he unfastened from his sleeve, a diamond button, which the goldsmith himself had often valued at three thousand pistols. "Take this," he said to the goldsmith, "in remembrance of me. And farewell; you are an honest man."

"And you, monseigneur," cried the goldsmith, completely overcome, "are the noblest man that ever lived."

Fouquet let the worthy goldsmith pass out of the room by a secret door, and then went to receive Madame de Bellière, who was already surrounded by all the guests. The Marquise was always beautiful, but now her loveliness was more dazzling than ever.

The hours passed away so joyously, that contrary to his usual custom, the Surintendant did not leave the table before the end of the dessert. He smiled upon his friends, delighted as a man is, whose heart becomes intoxicated before his head—and, for the first time, he had just looked at the clock. Suddenly, a carriage rolled into the courtyard, and, strange to say, it was heard high above the noise of the mirth which prevailed. Fouquet listened attentively, and then turned his eyes towards the antechamber. It seemed as if he could hear a step passing across it, and that this step, instead of pressing the ground, weighed heavily upon his heart. "M. d'Herblay, Bishop of Vannes," the usher announced. And Aramis's grave and thoughtful face appeared upon the threshold of the door, between the remains of two garlands, of which the flame of a lamp had just burned the thread that had united them.

Chapter 8

M. DE MAZARIN'S RECEIPT

FOUQUET would have uttered an exclamation of delight on seeing another friend arrive, if the cold air and averted aspect of Aramis had not restored all his reserve. "Are you going to join us at our dessert?" he asked. "And yet you would be frightened, perhaps, at the noise which our wild friends here are making."

"Monseigneur," replied Aramis respectfully, "I will begin by begging you to excuse me for having interrupted this merry meeting; and then, I will beg you to give me, as soon as pleasure shall have finished, a moment's audience on matters of business."

As the word "business" had aroused the attention of some of the epicureans present, Fouquet rose, saying: "Business first of all, Monsieur d'Herblay: we are too happy when matters of business arrive only at the end of a meal."

As he said this, he took the hand of Madame de Bellière, who looked at him with a kind of uneasiness, and then led her to an adjoining *salon*, after having recommended her to the most reasonable of his guests. And then, taking Aramis by the arm, he led him towards his cabinet. As soon as Aramis was there, throwing aside the respectful air he had assumed, he threw himself into a chair, saying: "Guess whom I have seen this evening?"

"Do not keep me in suspense," said Fouquet phlegmatically.

"Well, then, I have seen Madame de Chevreuse."

"Well! what harm can she meditate against me? I am no miser with women who are not prudes. That is a quality that is always prized, even by the woman who no longer dares to provoke love."

"Have you never heard speak of a prosecution being instituted for an embezzlement, or appropriation rather, of public funds?"

"Yes, a hundred, nay, a thousand times. Ever since I have been engaged in public matters I have hardly ever heard anything else but that."

"Very good; but take a particular instance, for the Duchesse asserts that M. de Mazarin alludes to certain particular instances."

"What are they?"

"Something like a sum of thirteen millions of francs, of which it would be very difficult for you to define the precise nature of the employment."

"Thirteen millions!" said the Surintendant, stretching himself in his arm-chair, in order to enable him the more comfortably to look up towards the ceiling. "I remember the story of those thirteen millions, now. Yes, yes, I remember them quite well."

"I am delighted to hear it; tell me about them."

"Well, then, one day Signor Mazarin, Heaven rest his soul! made a profit of thirteen millions upon a concession of lands in the Valtelline; he cancelled them in the registry of receipts, sent them to me, and then made me advance them to him for war expenses."

"Very good, then, there is no doubt of their proper destination."

"No: the Cardinal made me invest them in my own name, and gave me a receipt."

"You have the receipt?"

"Of course," said Fouquet, as he quietly rose from his chair, and went to his large ebony bureau inlaid with mother-of-pearl and gold. And with a confident hand he felt the bundles of papers which were piled up in the open drawer. "I remember the paper as if I saw it; it is thick, somewhat crumpled, with gilt edges; Mazarin had made a blot upon the figure of the date. Ah!" he said, "the paper knows we are talking about it, and that we want it very much, and so it hides itself out of the way."

And as the Surintendant looked into the drawer, Aramis rose from his seat.

"This is very singular," said Fouquet.

"Your memory is treacherous, my dear monseigneur; look in another drawer."

"Quite useless; I have never made a mistake; no one but myself arranges any papers of mine of this nature; no one but myself ever opens this drawer, of which, besides, no one, with my own exception, is aware of the secret."

"What do you conclude, then?" said Aramis, agitated.

"That Mazarin's receipt has been stolen from me; Madame de Chevreuse was right, Chevalier; I have appropriated the public funds; I have robbed the state coffers of thirteen millions of money; I am a thief, Monsieur d'Herblay."

"Oh!" said Aramis, smiling, "not so fast as that."

"And why not? why not so fast? What do you suppose Madame de Chevreuse will have done with those letters, for you refused them, I suppose?"

"Yes; at once. I suppose that she went and sold them to M. Colbert."

"Well?"

"I said I supposed so; I might have said I was sure of it, for I had her followed, and when she left me, she returned to her own house, went out by a back door, and proceeded straight to the Intendant's house."

"Legal proceedings will be instituted then, scandal and dishonour will follow, and all will fall upon me like a thunderbolt, blindly, harshly, pitilessly."

"Those criminals who know how to find a safe asylum are never in danger."

"What! make my escape! Fly!"

"No! I do not mean that; you forget that all such proceedings originate in the Parliament, that they are instituted by the Procureur-Général, and that you are Procureur-Général. You see that unless you wish to condemn yourself——"

"I am Procureur-Général no longer."

Aramis looked as if he had been thunder-stricken; the intelligent and mocking expression of his countenance assumed an aspect of such profound gloom and terror, that it had more effect upon the Surintendant than all the exclamations and speeches in the world. "You had need of money, then?" he said.

"Yes; to discharge a debt of honour." And in a few words, he gave Aramis an account of Madame de Bellière's generosity, and the manner in which he had thought it but right to discharge that act of generosity.

"You shall receive the fourteen hundred thousand francs from me, at a quarter before twelve."

"Stay a moment; it is at six o'clock, this very morning, that I am to sign."

"Oh! I will answer that you do not sign."

"I have given my word, Chevalier."

"If you have given it, you will take it back again, that is all."

"Can I believe what I hear?" cried Fouquet, in a most expressive tone. "Fouquet recall his word, after it has been once pledged?"

"And so you are determined to sign the sale of the very appointment which can alone defend you against all your enemies."

"Yes, I shall sign."

"Whom are you in treaty with? What man is it?"

"I am not aware whether you know the Parliament."

"Most of its members. One of the presidents, perhaps?"

"No; only a counsellor, of the name of Vanel."

Aramis became perfectly purple. "Vanel," he cried, rising abruptly from his seat; "Vanel! the husband of Marguerite Vanel."

"Exactly."

"Of your former mistress?"

"Yes, my dear fellow; she is anxious to be the wife of the Procureur-Général. I certainly owed poor Vanel that slight concession, and I am a gainer by it; since I, at the same time, can confer a pleasure on his wife."

Aramis walked up straight to Fouquet, and took hold of his hand. "Do you know," he said very calmly, "the name of Madame Vanel's new lover?"

"Ah! she has a new lover, then: I was not aware of it; no, I have no idea what his name is."

"His name is M. Jean-Baptiste Colbert; he is Intendant of the Finances; he lives in the Rue Croix-des-Petits-Champs, where Madame de Chevreuse has been this evening, to take him Mazarin's letters, which she wishes to sell."

Fouquet held out his hand to him, and at the very moment a richly-ornamented tortoise-shell clock, supported by golden figures, which was standing on a console table opposite to the fireplace, struck six. The sound of a door being opened in the vestibule was heard, and Gourville came to the door of the cabinet to inquire if Fouquet would receive M. Vanel. Fouquet turned his eyes from the eyes of Aramis, and then desired that M. Vanel should be shown in to him.

Chapter 9

MONSIEUR COLBERT'S ROUGH DRAFT

VANEL, who entered at this stage of the conversation, was nothing less for Aramis and Fouquet than the full stop which completes a phrase. But, for Vanel, Aramis's presence in Fouquet's cabinet had quite another signification: and, therefore, at his first step into the room, he paused as he looked at the delicate yet firm features of the Bishop of Vannes, and his look of astonishment soon became one of scrutinising attention. As for Fouquet, a perfect politician, that is to say, complete master of himself, he had already, by the energy of his own resolute will, contrived to remove from his face all traces of the emotion which Aramis's revelation had occasioned. He was no longer, therefore, a man overwhelmed by misfortune and reduced to resort to expedients; he held his head proudly erect, and indicated by a gesture that Vanel could enter. He was now the first minister of the State, and in his own palace. Aramis knew the Surintendant well; the delicacy of the feelings of his heart and the exalted nature of his mind could not any longer surprise him. He confined himself, then, for the moment—intending to resume later an active part in the conversation—to the performance of the difficult part of a man who looks on and listens, in order to learn and understand. Vanel was visibly overcome, and advanced into the middle of the cabinet, bowing to everything and everybody. "I am come," he said.

"You are exact, Monsieur Vanel," returned Fouquet.

"In matters of business, monseigneur," returned Vanel, "I look upon exactitude as a virtue."

"You would be wrong to exaggerate such notions as those, monsieur," said the Surintendant; "for a man's mind is variable, and full of these very excusable caprices, which are, however, sometimes estimable enough; and a man may have wished for something yesterday of which he repents to-day."

Vanel felt a cold sweat trickle down his face. "Monseigneur!" he muttered.

"Yesterday I wished to sell."

"Monseigneur did more than wish to sell, for you actually sold."

"I know that, and that is the reason why now I entreat you; do you understand me? I entreat you to restore it to me."

"I am overcome, monseigneur, at the honour you do me to consult me upon a matter of business which is already completed; but——"

"Nay, do not say *but*, dear Monsieur Vanel."

"Alas! monseigneur, you see," he said, as he opened a large pocketbook, "I have brought the money with me,—the whole sum, I mean. And here, monseigneur, is the contract of sale which I have just effected of a property belonging to my wife. The order is authentic in every way, the necessary signatures have been attached to it, and it is made payable at sight; it is ready money, in fact, and, in one word, the whole affair is complete."

"Enough!" cried Fouquet. "Where is this deed?"

Vanel tremblingly searched in his pockets, and as he drew out his pocket-book, a paper fell out of it, while Vanel offered the other to Fouquet. Aramis pounced upon the paper which had fallen out, as soon as he recognised the handwriting.

"I beg your pardon," said Vanel, "that is a rough draft of the deed."

"I see that very clearly," retorted Aramis, with a smile far more cutting than a lash of a whip would have been; "and what I admire most is, that this draft is in M. Colbert's handwriting. Look, monseigneur, look."

And he handed the draft to Fouquet, who recognised the truth of the fact; for, covered with erasures, with inserted words, the margins filled with additions, this deed—a living proof of Colbert's plot—had just revealed everything to its unhappy victim. "Well!" murmured Fouquet.

Vanel, completely humiliated, seemed as if he were looking for some deep hole where he could hide himself.

"Well!" said Aramis, "if your name were not Fouquet, and if your enemy's name were not Colbert—if you had not this mean thief before you I should say to you, 'Repudiate it'; such a proof of this absolves you from your word; but these fellows would think you were afraid; they would fear you less than they do; therefore sign the deed at once." And he held out a pen towards him.

Fouquet pressed Aramis's hand; but, instead of the deed which Vanel handed to him, he took the rough draft of it.

"No, not that paper," said Aramis hastily; "this is the one. The other is too precious a document for you to part with."

"No, no!" replied Fouquet; "I will sign under M. Colbert's own handwriting even; and I write, 'The handwriting is approved of' " He then signed, and said, "Here it is, Monsieur Vanel." And the latter seized the paper, laid down his money, and was about to make his escape.

"One moment," said Aramis. "Are you quite sure the exact amount is there? It ought to be counted over, Monsieur Vanel; particularly since M. Colbert makes presents of money to ladies, I see. Ah, that worthy M. Colbert is not so generous as M. Fouquet." And Aramis, spelling every word, every letter of the order, to pay, distilled his wrath and his contempt, drop by drop, upon the miserable wretch, who had to submit to this torture for a quarter of an hour; he was then dismissed not in words, but by a gesture, as one dismisses or discharges a beggar or a menial.

As soon as Vanel had gone, the minister and the prelate, their eyes fixed on each other, remained silent for a few moments.

"Well," said Aramis, the first to break the silence; "first of all, let us talk about business. Did you not some time ago," he continued, as Fouquet looked at him with a bewildered air, "speak to me about an idea you had of giving a fête at Vaux?"

"Oh," said Fouquet, "that was when affairs were flourishing."

"A fête, I believe, to which the King invited himself of his own accord?"

"No, no, my dear prelate; a fête to which M. Colbert advised the King to invite himself."

"From to-morrow," interrupted Aramis quietly, "you will occupy yourself, without the slightest delay, with your fête at Vaux, which must hereafter be spoken of as one of the most magnificent productions of your most prosperous days."

"You are mad, Chevalier d'Herblay."

"I!—you do not think that."

"What do you mean, then? Do you not know that a fête at Vaux, of the very simplest possible character, would cost four or five millions?"

"You shall spend twenty if you require it," said Aramis, in a perfectly calm voice.

"Where shall I get them?" exclaimed Fouquet.

"That is my affair, Monsieur le Surintendant; and do not be uneasy for a moment about it. The money will be placed at once at your disposal, as soon as you shall have arranged the plans of your fête."

"Chevalier! Chevalier!" said Fouquet, giddy with amazement, "whither are you hurrying me?"

"I mean that you will make of me, on that day, a major-domo, a sort of inspector-general, or factotum—something between a captain of the guard and manager or steward. I will look after the people, and will keep the keys of the doors. You will give your orders, of course; but will give them to no one but to me; they will pass through my lips, to reach those for whom they are intended—you understand?"

"No, I am very far from understanding."

"But you agree?"

"Of course, of course, my friend."

Chapter 10

THE VICOMTE DE BRAGELONNE MAKES INQUIRIES

WE WISH our readers now to follow Raoul de Bragelonne's story.

He had arrived from London because he had been told of the existence of a danger; and almost on his arrival, this appearance of danger was manifest. His friend, de Guiche, had written and advised his return to France.

Raoul was now in Madame's presence. Henrietta, more charming than ever, was half lying, half reclining in her armchair, her little feet upon an embroidered velvet cushion; she was playing with a little kitten with long silky fur, which was biting her fingers and hanging by the lace of her collar.

Henrietta rose hurriedly and walked a few paces up and down her room. "What did M. de Guiche tell you?" she said suddenly.

"Nothing, madame."

"Nothing! Did he say nothing? Ah! how well I recognise him in that."

"No doubt he wished to spare me."

"Monsieur de Bragelonne," she said, "that which your friends have refused to do, I will do for you, whom I like and esteem very much. I will be your friend on this occasion. You hold your head high, as a man of honour should do; and I should regret that you should have to bow it down under ridicule, and in a few days, it may be, under contempt."

"Ah!" exclaimed Raoul, perfectly livid. "It is as bad as that, then?"

"If you do not know," said the Princess, "I see that you guess; you were affianced, I believe, to Mademoiselle de la Vallière?"

"Yes, madame."

"By that right, then, you deserve to be warned about her, as some day or another I shall be obliged to dismiss Mademoiselle de la Vallière from my service——"

"Dismiss La Vallière!" cried Bragelonne.

"How deeply you must love her, yet she loves the King."

Henrietta's words seemed to convince Raoul. Dejected, he made his way to his father's lodgings.

Chapter 11

RIVAL POLITICS

On his return from a promenade, the King found M. Fouquet waiting for an audience. M. Colbert had laid in wait for His Majesty in the corridor, and followed him like a jealous and watchful shadow. Fouquet, at the sight of his enemy, remained perfectly unmoved, and during the whole of the scene which followed scrupulously resolved to observe that line of conduct which is so difficult to be carried out by a man of superior mind, who does not even wish to show his contempt, from the fear of doing his adversary too much honour.

"Your Majesty is aware," he said, "that I destine my estate at Vaux to receive the most amiable of princes, the most powerful of monarchs."

"What day have you fixed?"

"Any day your Majesty may find most convenient."

"This is Tuesday; if I give you until next Sunday week, will that be sufficient?"

"The delay which your Majesty deigns to accord me will greatly aid the various works which my architects have in hand for the purpose of adding to the amusement of your Majesty and your friends."

Fouquet, therefore, took leave of Louis XIV, after a few words had been added with regard to the details of certain matters of business. He turned back again immediately, as soon indeed as he had reached the door, and addressing the King, said, "I was forgetting that I had to crave your Majesty's forgiveness."

"In what respect?" said the King graciously.

"For having committed a serious fault without perceiving it."

"What is it?"

"Sire," said Fouquet, with an easy unconcerned air, "since you have had the kindness to forgive me, I am perfectly indifferent about my confession; this morning I sold one of the official appointments I hold."

"Is it really possible," said the King, as soon as Fouquet had disappeared, "that he has sold that office?"

"He must be mad," the King added.

"Yes, sire," said Colbert meaningly.

Colbert had departed only a few minutes when the usher appeared at the door of the cabinet. "What is the matter?" inquired the King, "and why do you presume to come when I have not summoned you?"

"Sire," said the usher, "your Majesty desired me to permit M. le Comte de la Fère to pass freely on any and every occasion, when he might wish to speak to your Majesty."

"Well, monsieur?"

"M. le Comte de la Fère is now waiting to see your Majesty."

Chapter 12

KING AND NOBILITY

A FEW minutes afterwards Athos, in full court dress, and with his breast covered with the orders that he alone had the right to wear at the court of France, presented himself with a grave and solemn air. Louis advanced a step towards the Comte, and, with a smile, held out his hand to him over which Athos bowed with the air of the deepest respect.

"Your Majesty will remember that at the period of the Duke of Buckingham's departure, I had the honour of an interview with you."

"At or about that period, I think, I remember you did; only with regard to the subject of the conversation, I have quite forgotten it."

Athos started, as he replied, "I shall have the honour to remind your Majesty of it. It was with regard to a formal demand I had addressed to you respecting a marriage which M. de Bragelonne wished to contract with Mademoiselle de la Vallière."

"Ah!" thought the King, "we have come to it now. I remember," he said aloud.

"At that period," pursued Athos, "your Majesty was so kind and generous towards M. de Bragelonne and myself, that not a single word which then fell from your lips has escaped my memory; and, when I asked your Majesty to accord me Mademoiselle de la Vallière's hand for M. de Bragelonne, you refused."

"Quite true," said Louis dryly.

"M. de Bragelonne is now so exceedingly unhappy that he cannot any longer defer asking your Majesty for a solution of the matter."

The King turned pale; Athos looked at him with fixed attention.

"And what," said the King, with considerable hesitation, "does M. de Bragelonne request?"

"Precisely the very thing that I came to ask your Majesty for at my last audience, namely, your Majesty's consent to his marriage."

The King pressed his hands impatiently together. "Does your Majesty hesitate?" inquired the Comte, without losing a particle either of his firmness or his politeness.

"I do not hesitate—I refuse," replied the King.

"And may we, therefore, be permitted to ask your Majesty, with the greatest humility, for your reason for this refusal?"

"The reason!—a question to me!" exclaimed the King.

"A demand, sire!"

The King, leaning with both his hands upon the table, said in a deep tone of concentrated passion, "You have lost all recollection of what is usual at court. At court, please to remember, no one ventures to put a question to the King."

"Sire, I am obliged to seek elsewhere for what I thought I should find in your Majesty. Instead of obtaining a reply from you, I am compelled to make one for myself."

The King tore his gloves, which he had been biting for some time. "Mademoiselle de la Vallière does not love M. de Bragelonne," said the King hoarsely.

"Does your Majesty know that to be the case?" remarked Athos with a searching look.

"I do know it."

"Since a very short time, then; for, doubtlessly, had your Majesty known it when I first preferred my request, you would have taken the trouble to inform me of it."

The King during these remarks was walking hurriedly to and fro, his hands thrust into the breast of his coat, his head haughtily raised, his eyes blazing with wrath. "Monsieur," he cried suddenly, "if I acted towards you as the King, you would be already punished; but I am only a man, and I have the right to love in this world every one who loves me,—a happiness which is so rarely found."

"You cannot pretend to such a right as a man any more than as a king, sire; or, if you intended to exercise that right in a loyal manner, you should have told M. de Bragelonne so, and not have exiled him."

"You have forgotten you are speaking to the King, monsieur. It is a crime."

"You have forgotten you are destroying the lives of two men, sire. It is a mortal sin."

"Leave the room."

"Not until I have said this, 'Son of Louis XIII, you begin your reign badly, for you begin it by abduction and disloyalty! My race—myself too—are now freed from all that affection and respect towards you, which I made my son swear to observe in the vaults of Saint-Denis, in the presence of the relics of your noble forefathers. You are now become our enemy, sire, and henceforth we have nothing to do save with Heaven alone, our sole master. Be warned.'"

Thus saying, Athos broke his sword across his knee, slowly placed the two pieces upon the floor, and saluting the King, who was almost choking from rage and shame, he quitted the cabinet. Louis, who sat near the table, completely overwhelmed, was several minutes before he could collect himself; but he suddenly rose and rang the bell violently; "Tell M. d'Artagnan to come here," he said to the terrified ushers.

Chapter 13

AFTER THE STORM

WHEN Athos returned to his lodgings, Raoul, pale and dejected, had not quitted his attitude of despair. At the sound, however, of the opening doors, and of his father's footsteps as he approached him, the young man raised his head. Athos's face was very pale, his head uncovered, and his manner full of seriousness; he gave his cloak and hat to the lackey, dismissed him with a gesture, and sat down near Raoul.

"Well, monsieur," inquired the young man, "are you quite convinced now?"

"I am, Raoul; the King loves Mademoiselle de la Vallière."

"He confesses it, then?" cried Raoul.

"Yes," replied Athos.

"And she?"

"I have not seen her."

"No; but the King spoke to you about her. What did he say?"

"He says that she loves him."

"Oh, you see—you see, monsieur!" said the young man with a gesture of despair.

"Raoul," resumed the Comte, "I told the King, believe me, all that you yourself could possibly have said; and I believe I did so in becoming language, though sufficiently firm."

"And what did you say to him, monsieur?"

"I told him, Raoul, that everything was now at an end between him and ourselves; that you would never serve him again. I told him that I, too, should remain aloof."

At this moment the servant announced M. d'Artagnan. This name sounded very differently to the ears of Athos and of Raoul. The musketeer entered the room with a vague smile upon his lips. Raoul paused. Athos walked towards his friend with an expression of face which did not escape Bragelonne. D'Artagnan answered Athos's look by an imperceptible movement of the eyelid; and then, advancing towards Raoul, whom he took by the hand, he said, addressing both father and son, "Well, you are trying to console this poor boy, it seems."

"And you, kind and good as usual, are come to help me in my difficult task."

As he said this, Athos pressed d'Artagnan's hand between both his own; Raoul fancied he observed in this pressure something beyond the sense his mere words conveyed.

"Yes," replied the musketeer, smoothing his moustache with the hand that Athos had left free, "yes, I have come also."

"You are most welcome, chevalier; not from the consolation you bring with you, but on your own account. I am already consoled," said Raoul; and he attempted to smile, but the effect was far more sad than any tears d'Artagnan had ever seen shed.

"That is well and good then," said d'Artagnan. "Do you know what I would advise you to do?"

"Tell me, monsieur, for the advice is sure to be good as it comes from you."

"Very good, then; I advise you, after your long journey from England, to take a few hours' rest; go and lie down, sleep for a dozen hours, and when you wake up, go and ride one of my horses until you have tired him to death."

And drawing Raoul towards him he embraced him as he would have done his own child. Athos did the like; only it was very visible that the kiss was more affectionate, and the pressure of his lips still warmer with the father than with the friend. The young man again looked at both his companions, endeavouring to penetrate their real meaning, or their real feelings, with the utmost strength of his intelligence; but his look was powerless upon the smiling countenance of the musketeer, or upon the calm and composed features of the Comte de la Fère. "Where are you going, Raoul?" inquired the latter, seeing that Bragelonne was preparing to go out.

"To my own apartments," replied the latter in his soft and sad voice.

Raoul, observing the perfect composure which marked every gesture of his two friends, quitted the Comte's room, carrying away with him nothing but the individual feeling of his own particular distress.

Chapter 14

WHAT RAOUL HAD GUESSED

As soon as Raoul had quitted Athos and d'Artagnan, and as soon as the two exclamations which had followed his departure had escaped their lips, they found themselves face to face alone. Athos immediately resumed the earnest air that he had assumed at d'Artagnan's arrival.

"Well," he said, "what have you come to announce to me, my friend?"

"I?" inquired d'Artagnan.

"Yes; I do not see you in this way without some reason for it," said Athos, smiling.

"The deuce!" said d'Artagnan.

"I will place you at your ease. The King is furious, I suppose?"

"Well, I must say he is not altogether pleased."

"And you have come to arrest me, then?"

"My dear friend, you have hit the very mark."

"Oh! I expected it. I am quite ready to go with you."

"Deuce take it!" said d'Artagnan, "what a hurry you are in."

"I am afraid of delaying you," said Athos, smiling.

"Very well, 'let us go,'" said d'Artagnan quietly.

"As I broke my sword in the King's presence, and threw the pieces at his feet, I presume that will dispense with the necessity of delivering it over to you."

"You are quite right; and, besides that, what the deuce do you suppose I could do with your sword?"

"Am I to walk behind or before you?" inquired Athos, laughing.

"You will walk arm-in-arm with me," replied d'Artagnan, as he took the Comte's arm to descend the staircase; and in this manner they arrived at the landing. Grimaud, whom they had met in the anteroom, looked at them as they went out together in this manner, with some little uneasiness; his experience of affairs was quite sufficient to give him good reason to suspect that there was something wrong.

"Ah! is that you, Grimaud?" said Athos kindly. "We are going——"

"To take a turn in my carriage," interrupted d'Artagnan, with a friendly nod of the head.

Grimaud thanked d'Artagnan by a grimace, which was evidently intended for a smile, and accompanied both the friends to the door. Athos entered first into the carriage, d'Artagnan following him, without saying a word to the coachman. The departure had taken place so quietly, that it excited no disturbance or attention even in the neighbourhood. When the carriage had reached the quays, "You are taking me to the Bastille, I perceive," said Athos.

"I?" said d'Artagnan. "I take you wherever you may choose to go; nowhere else, I can assure you."

"What do you mean?" said the Comte, surprised.

"Why, surely, my dear friend," said d'Artagnan, "you quite understand that I undertook the mission with no other object in view than that
of carrying it out exactly as you liked. You surely did not expect that I
was going to get you thrown into prison like that, brutally, and without
any reflection. If I had not anticipated that, I should have let the captain
of the guards undertake it."

"And so——?" said Athos.

"And so, I repeat again, we will go wherever you may choose."

"My dear friend," said Athos, embracing d'Artagnan, "how like you
that is."

"Well, it seems simple enough to me. The coachman will take you to the
barrier of the Cours-la-Reine; you will find a horse there which I have
ordered to be kept ready for you; with that horse you will be able to do
three posts without stopping; and I, on my side, will take care not to return
to the King, to tell him that you have gone away, until the very moment
it will be impossible to overtake you. In the meantime you will have
reached Havre, and from Havre across to England, where you will find
the charming residence of which M. Monk made me a present, without
speaking of the hospitality which King Charles will not fail to show you.
Well, what do you think of this project?"

Athos shook his head, and then said, smiling as he did so, "No, no; take
me to the Bastille."

"You are an obstinate-headed fellow, dear Athos," returned d'Artagnan; "reflect for a few moments."

"My dear friend," replied Athos, with perfect calmness. "I should like
to persuade you of one thing; namely, that I wish to be arrested; that I
desire above all things that my arrest should take place."

D'Artagnan made a slight movement of his shoulders.

"Nay; I wish it, I repeat, more than anything; if you were to let me
escape, it would only be to return of my own accord, and constitute
myself a prisoner. I wish to prove to this young man, who is dazzled by
the power and splendour of his crown, that he can be regarded as the first
and chiefest among men only on the condition of his proving himself to
be the most generous and the wisest among them. He may punish me,
imprison or torture me, it matters not. He abuses his opportunities, and
I wish him to learn the bitterness of remorse, while Heaven teaches him
what a chastisement is."

"Well, well," replied d'Artagnan, "I know, only too well, that when
you have once said 'no,' you mean 'no.' I do not insist any longer; you
wish to go to the Bastille?"

"I do wish to go there."

"Let us go then! To the Bastille!" cried d'Artagnan to the coachman.

Chapter 15

THREE GUESTS ASTONISHED TO FIND THEMSELVES AT SUPPER TOGETHER

THE carriage arrived at the outside gate of the Bastille. A soldier on guard stopped it, but d'Artagnan had only to utter a single word to procure admittance, and the carriage passed on without further difficulty. Whilst they were proceeding along the covered way which led to the courtyard of the governor's residence, d'Artagnan, whose lynx eye saw everything, even through the walls, suddenly cried out, "What is that out yonder?"

"Well, a carriage; very likely conveying a prisoner like myself."

At that very moment a second sentinel stopped d'Artagnan, and while the formalities were being gone through, Athos could see at a hundred paces from him the man whom his friend had pointed out to him. He was, in fact, getting out of the carriage at the door of the governor's house. "Well," inquired d'Artagnan, "do you see him?"

"Yes; he is a man in a grey suit."

"Athos, I will wager anything it is he."

"He—who?"

"Aramis."

"Aramis arrested? Impossible!"

"I do not say he is arrested, since we see him alone in his carriage."

"Well, then, what is he doing here?"

"Oh! he knows Baisemeaux, the governor," replied the musketeer slyly; "so we have arrived just in time."

"What for?"

"In order to see what we can see."

The carriage stopped where the one we have just now pointed out had stopped; namely, at the door of the governor's house. In a few minutes they were in the governor's dining-room, and the first face which attracted d'Artagnan's observation was that of Aramis, who was seated side by side with Baisemeaux, and awaited the announcement of a good meal, whose odour impregnated the whole apartment. If d'Artagnan pretended surprise, Aramis did not pretend at all; he started when he saw his two friends, and his emotion was very apparent. Athos and d'Artagnan however, complimented him as usual, and Baisemeaux, amazed, completely stupefied by the presence of his three guests, began to perform a few evolutions around them all. "By what lucky accident——"

"We were just going to ask you," retorted d'Artagnan.

"Are we going to give ourselves up as prisoners?" cried Aramis, with an affectation of hilarity.

"Ah! ah!" said d'Artagnan; "it is true the walls smell deucedly like a prison. Monsieur de Baisemeaux, you know you invited me to sup with you the other day."

"I!" cried Baisemeaux.

"Yes, of course you did, although you now seem so struck with amazement. Don't you remember it?"

Baisemeaux turned pale and then red, looked at Aramis, who looked at him, and finished by stammering out, "Certainly—I am delighted—but upon my honour—I have not the slightest—Ah! I have such a wretched memory. I beg you a thousand pardons. But now, once for all, my dear M. d'Artagnan, be sure that at this present time, as at any other, whether invited or not, you are perfectly at home here, you and M. d'Herblay, your friend," he said, turning towards Aramis; "and this gentleman too," he added, bowing to Athos.

"Well, I thought it would be sure to turn out so," replied d'Artagnan, "and that is the reason I came. Having nothing to do this evening at the Palais-Royal, I wish to judge for myself what your ordinary style of living was like; and as I was coming along, I met the Comte de la Fère."

"The Comte is welcome, I am sure."

"And he will sup with you two, I suppose, whilst I, unfortunate dog that I am, must run off on a matter of duty. Oh! what happy beings you are, compared to myself," he added, sighing as loud as Porthos might have done.

"You will be sure to return, though?" said Athos, with an expression of doubt.

"Most certainly," he said, pressing his friend's hand confidently; and he added in a low voice, "Wait for me, Athos; be cheerful and lively as possible, and above all, don't allude even to business affairs, for Heaven's sake."

Chapter 16

WHAT TOOK PLACE AT THE LOUVRE DURING THE SUPPER AT THE BASTILLE

THE King rose when the curtain before the door was raised. His first idea was that a letter from Louise had arrived; but, instead of a letter of love, he only saw his captain of musketeers standing upright and perfectly silent in the doorway. "M. d'Artagnan," he said, "ah! Well, monsieur? Is it done?"

"I have come to get myself arrested too."

"To get yourself arrested,—you!"

"Of course. My friend will get wearied to death in the Bastille by himself; and I have come to propose to your Majesty to permit me to bear him company; if your Majesty will but give the word, I will arrest myself; I shall not need the captain of the guard for that, I assure you."

The King darted towards the table and seized hold of a pen to write the order for d'Artagnan's imprisonment. "Pay attention, monsieur, that this is for ever," cried the King in a tone of stern menace.

"I can quite believe that," returned the musketeer, "for when you have done such an act as that, you will never be able to look me in the face again."

"Monsieur," said the King, "do you think you can excuse your friend by exceeding him in insolence?"

"Oh, sire! I should go much further than he did," said d'Artagnan, "and it would be your own fault. I should tell you what he, a man full of the finest sense of delicacy, did not tell you; I should say—'Sire, you have sacrificed his son, and he defended his son—you sacrificed himself; he addressed you in the name of honour, of religion, of virtue—you repulsed, drove him away, imprisoned him.' I should be harder than he was, for I should say to you—'Sire, it is for you to choose. Do you wish to have friends or lackeys—soldiers or slaves—great men or mere puppets? Do you wish men to serve you, or to bend and crouch before you? Do you wish men to love you, or to be afraid of you? If you prefer baseness, intrigue, cowardice, say so at once, sire, and we will leave you,—we who are the only individuals who are left, nay, I will say more, the only models of the valour of former times; we who have done our duty, and have exceeded, perhaps, in courage and in merit, the men already great for posterity. Choose, sire! and that too without delay. Whatever remains to you of great nobles, guard it with a jealous eye; you will never be deficient in courtiers. Delay not—and send me to the Bastille with my friend; for, if you have not known how to listen to the Comte de la Fère, whose voice is the sweetest and noblest when honour is his theme; if you do not know how to listen to d'Artagnan, the frankest and honestest voice of sincerity, you are a bad King, and to-morrow will be a poor King. And learn from me, sire, that bad kings are hated by their people, and poor kings are driven ignominiously away.' That is what I had to say to you, sire; you were wrong to have driven me to do it."

D'Artagnan had said all he had to say. Comprehending the King's anger, he drew his sword, and, approaching Louis XIV respectfully, he placed it on the table. But the King, with a furious gesture, thrust aside the sword, which fell to the ground and rolled to d'Artagnan's feet. Notwithstanding the perfect mastery which d'Artagnan exercised over himself, he, too, in his turn, became pale, and, trembling with indignation, said—"A king may disgrace a soldier,—he may exile him, and may even condemn him to death; but were he a hundred times a king he has no right to insult him by casting a dishonour upon his sword! Sire, a King of France has never repulsed with contempt the sword of a man such as I am! Stained with disgrace as this sword now is, it has henceforth no other sheath than either your heart or my own! I choose my own, sire; and you have to thank Heaven and my own patience that I do so." Then snatching up his sword, he cried, "My blood be upon your head!" and with a rapid gesture, he placed the hilt upon the floor and directed the point of the blade towards his breast. The King, however, with a movement far more rapid than that of d'Artagnan, threw his right arm round the musketeer's neck, and with his left hand seized hold of the blade by the middle, and returned it silently to the scabbard. D'Artagnan, upright, pale, and still trembling, let the King do all to the very end. Louis, overcome, and softened by gentler feelings, returned to the table, took a pen in his hand, wrote a few lines, signed them, and then held it out to d'Artagnan.

"What is this paper, sire?" inquired the captain.

"An order for M. d'Artagnan to set the Comte de la Fère at liberty immediately."

D'Artagnan seized the King's hand, and imprinted a kiss upon it; he then folded the order, placed it in his belt, and quitted the room.

Chapter 17

POLITICAL RIVALS

D'ARTAGNAN had promised M. de Baisemeaux to return in time for dessert, and he kept his word. They had just reached the finer and more delicate class of wines and liqueurs with which the governor's cellar had the reputation of being most admirably stocked, when the spurs of the captain resounded in the corridor, and he himself appeared at the threshold. Athos and Aramis had played a close game; neither of the two had been able to gain the slightest advantage over the other. They had supped, talked a good deal about the Bastille, of the last journey to Fontainebleau, of the intended fête that M. Fouquet was about to give at Vaux; they had generalised on every possible subject; and no one, excepting Baisemeaux, had, in the slightest degree, alluded to private matters. D'Artagnan arrived in the very midst of the conversation, still pale and much disturbed by his interview with the King. Baisemeaux hastened to give him a chair; d'Artagnan accepted a glass of wine, and set it down empty. Athos and Aramis both remarked his emotion; as for Baisemeaux, he saw nothing more than the captain of the King's musketeers, to whom he endeavoured to show every possible attention. But, although Aramis had remarked his emotion, he had not been able to guess the cause of it. Athos alone believed he had detected it. For him, d'Artagnan's return, and particularly the manner in which he, usually so impassible, seemed overcome, signified, "I have just asked the King something which the King has refused me." Thoroughly convinced that his conjecture was correct, Athos smiled, rose from the table, and made a sign to d'Artagnan, as if to remind him that they had something else to do than to sup together. D'Artagnan immediately understood him, and replied by another sign. Aramis and Baisemeaux watched this silent dialogue, and looked inquiringly at each other. Athos felt that he was called upon to give an explanation of what was passing.

"The truth is, my friends," said the Comte de la Fère, with a smile, "that you, Aramis, have been supping with a state criminal, and you, Monsieur de Baisemeaux, with your prisoner."

"So that," said Baisemeaux, trembling at having supped so familiarly with a man who had fallen into disgrace with the King; "so that, Monsieur le Comte——"

"So that, my dear governor," said Athos, "my friend d'Artagnan will communicate to you the contents of the paper which I perceive just peeping out of his belt, and which assuredly can be nothing else than the order for my incarceration."

Baisemeaux held out his hand with his accustomed eagerness. D'Artagnan drew two papers from his belt, and presented one of them to the governor, who unfolded it, and then read, in a low tone of voice, looking at Athos over the paper, as he did so, and pausing from time to time; " 'Order to detain in my château of the Bastille, Monsieur le Comte de la Fère.' Oh! monsieur! this is indeed a very melancholy honour for me."

"You will have a patient prisoner, monsieur," said Athos, in his calm, soft voice.

"A prisoner, too, who will not remain a month with you, my dear governor," said Aramis; while Baisemeaux, still holding the order in his hand, transcribed it upon the prison registry.

"Not a day, or rather not even a night," said d'Artagnan, displaying the second order of the King, "for now, dear M. de Baisemeaux, you will have the goodness to transcribe also this order for setting the Comte immediately at liberty."

"Ah!" said Aramis, "it is a labour that you have deprived me of, d'Artagnan;" and he pressed the musketeer's hand in a significant manner, at the same moment as that of Athos.

"Well, then I think," resumed d'Artagnan, "that the Comte cannot do better than return to his own château. However, my dear Athos, you have only to speak, to tell me what you want. If any particular place of residence is more agreeable to you than another, I am influential enough, perhaps, to obtain it for you."

"No, thank you," said Athos; "nothing can be more agreeable to me, my dear friend, than to return to my solitude beneath my noble trees, on the banks of the Loire." And then, turning to d'Artagnan, he said, "Let us go, my dear friend. Shall I have that greatest of all pleasures for me—that of having you as my companion?"

"To the city gate only," replied d'Artagnan, "after which I will tell you what I told the King. I am on duty."

"And you, my dear Aramis," said Athos, smiling; "will you accompany me? La Fère is on the road to Vannes."

"Thank you, my dear friend," said Aramis, "but I have an appointment in Paris this evening, and I cannot leave without very serious interests suffering by my absence."

Whilst the *dénouement* of the scene of the Palais-Royal was taking place at the Bastille, let us relate what was going on at the lodgings of Athos and Bragelonne. Grimaud, as we have seen, had accompanied his master to Paris; and, as we have said, he was present when Athos went out; he had observed d'Artagnan gnaw the corners of his moustaches; he had seen his master get into the carriage; he had narrowly examined both their countenances, and he had known them both for a sufficiently long period to read and understand, through the mask of their impassibility, that something serious was the matter.

The first step he took was to search in his master's coat for M. d'Artagnan's letter; he found the letter still there, with contained the following:

MY DEAR FRIEND,—Raoul has been to ask me for some particulars about the conduct of Mademoiselle de la Vallière, during our young friend's residence in London. I am a poor captain of musketeers, and am sickened to death every day by hearing all the scandal of the barracks and bedside conversations. If I had told Raoul all I believe I know, the poor fellow would have died from it; but I am in the King's service, and cannot relate all I hear about the King's affairs. If your heart tells you to do it, set off at once; the matter concerns you more than myself, and almost as much as Raoul.

Grimaud tore, not a handful, but a finger-and-thumbful of hair out of his head; he would have done more if his head of hair had been in more flourishing circumstances.

"Yes," he said, "that is the key of the whole enigma. The young girl has been playing her pranks; what people say about her and the King is true, then; our young master has been deceived; he ought to know it. Monsieur le Comte has been to see the King, and has told him a piece of his mind; and then the King sent M. d'Artagnan to arrange the affair. Ah! gracious goodness!" continued Grimaud, "Monsieur le Comte, I now remember, returned without his sword."

This discovery made the perspiration break out all over poor Grimaud's face. He did not waste any more time in useless conjecture, but clapped his hat on his head, and ran to Raoul's lodgings.

Raoul, after Louise had left him, had mastered his grief, if not his affection; and, compelled to look forward on that perilous road on which madness and rebellion were hurrying him, he had seen, from the very first glance, his father exposed to the royal obstinacy; since Athos had himself been the first to oppose any resistance to the royal will. At this moment, from a very natural sympathy of feeling, the unhappy young man remembered the mysterious signs which Athos had made, and the unexpected visit of d'Artagnan; the result of the conflict between a sovereign and a subject revealed itself to his terrified vision. As d'Artagnan was on duty, that is, fixed to his post without possibility of leaving it, it was certainly not likely that he had come to pay Athos a visit merely for the pleasure of seeing him. He must have come to say something to him. This something, in such painful conjectures, was either a misfortune or a danger. Raoul trembled at having been so selfish as to have forgotten his father for his affection; at having, in a word, passed his time in idle dreams, or in an indulgence of despair, at a time when a necessity existed for repelling the imminent attack directed against Athos. The very idea nearly drove him wild; he buckled on his sword and ran towards his father's lodging. On his way there he encountered Grimaud, who, having set off from the opposite pole, was running with equal eagerness in search of the truth.

Chapter 18

IN WHICH PORTHOS IS CONVINCED WITHOUT HAVING UNDERSTOOD ANYTHING

THE good and worthy Porthos, faithful to all the laws of ancient chivalry, had determined to wait for M. de Saint-Aignan until sunset; and, as Saint-Aignan did not come, as Raoul had forgotten to communicate with his second, and as he found that waiting so long was very wearisome, Porthos had desired one of the gatekeepers to fetch him a few bottles of good wine and a good joint of meat,—so that he at least might pass away the time with a glass of wine and a mouthful of something to eat. He had just finished when Raoul arrived, escorted by Grimaud, both riding at full speed.

"Raoul," cried Porthos, surprised. "You have killed him?"

"Who?"

"Saint-Aignan; or if that is not the case, what is the matter?"

"The matter is that Monsieur le Comte de la Fère has by this time been arrested."

"Do you know," said Raoul, advancing nearer to Porthos, "that the arrest was made by order of the King?"

Porthos looked at the young man, as if to say, "What does that matter to me?" This dumb language seemed so eloquent of meaning to Raoul, that he did not ask another question. He mounted his horse again; and Porthos, assisted by Grimaud, had already done the same.

"Let us arrange our plan of action," said Raoul.

"Yes," returned Porthos, "that is the best thing we can do."

Raoul sighed deeply, and then paused suddenly.

"What is the matter?" asked Porthos; "are you faint?"

"No, only I feel how utterly helpless our position is. Can we three pretend to go and take the Bastille?"

"Well, if d'Artagnan were only here," replied Porthos, "I don't know about that."

Raoul could not resist a feeling of admiration at the sight of such a perfect confidence, heroic in its simplicity. These were truly the celebrated men who, by three or four, attacked armies, and assaulted castles! Those men who had terrified death itself, and who survived the wrecks of an age, and were still stronger than the most robust of the young.

"Monsieur," said he to Porthos, "you have just given me an idea; we absolutely must see M. d'Artagnan."

"Undoubtedly."

"He ought by this time to have returned home, after having taken my father to the Bastille. Let us go to his house."

"First inquire at the Bastille," said Grimaud, who was in the habit of speaking little, but that to the purpose.

Accordingly, they hastened towards the fortress, when one of those chances which Heaven bestows on men of strong will, caused Grimaud suddenly to perceive the carriage, which was entering by the great gate of the drawbridge. This was at the moment that d'Artagnan was, as we have seen, returning from his visit to the King. In vain was it that Raoul urged on his horse in order to join the carriage, and to see whom it contained. The horses had already gained the other side of the great gate, which again closed, while one of the sentries struck the nose of Raoul's horse with his musket; Raoul turned about, only too happy to find he had ascertained something respecting the carriage which had contained his father.

"We have him," said Grimaud.

"If we wait a little it is certain he will leave; don't you think so, my friend?"

"Unless, indeed, d'Artagnan also be a prisoner," replied Porthos, "in which case everything is lost."

Raoul returned no answer, for any hypothesis was admissible. He instructed Grimaud to lead the horses to the little street Jean-Beausire, so as to give rise to less suspicion, and himself, with his piercing gaze, watched for the exit either of d'Artagnan or the carriage. Nor had he decided wrongly; for twenty minutes had not elapsed before the gate reopened and the carriage reappeared. A dazzling of the eyes prevented Raoul from distinguishing what figures occupied the interior. Grimaud averred that he had seen two persons, and that one of them was his master. Porthos kept looking at Raoul and Grimaud by turns, in the hope of understanding their idea.

"It is clear," said Grimaud, "that if the Comte is in the carriage, either he is set at liberty or they are taking him to another prison."

"We shall soon see that by the road he takes," answered Porthos.

"If he is set at liberty," said Grimaud, "they will conduct him home."

"True," rejoined Porthos.

"The carriage does not take that way," cried Raoul; and indeed the horses were just disappearing down the faubourg St. Antoine.

"Let us hasten," said Porthos; "we will attack the carriage on the road and tell Athos to flee."

"Rebellion," murmured Raoul.

Porthos darted a second glance at Raoul, quite worthy of the first. Raoul replied only by spurring the flanks of his steed. In a few moments the three cavaliers had overtaken the carriage, and followed it so closely that their horses' breath moistened the back of it. D'Artagnan, whose senses were ever on the alert, heard the trot of the horses, at the moment when Raoul was telling Porthos to pass the chariot so as to see who was the person accompanying Athos. Porthos complied, but could not see anything, for the blinds were lowered. Rage and impatience were gaining mastery over Raoul. He had just noticed the mystery preserved by Athos's companion, and determined on proceeding to extremities. On his part d'Artagnan had perfectly recognised Porthos, and Raoul also, from under the blinds, and had communicated to the Comte the result of his observation. They were desirous only of seeing whether Raoul and Porthos would push the affair to the uttermost. And this they speedily did, for Raoul presenting his pistol threw himself on the leader, commanding the coachman to stop. Porthos seized the coachman and dragged him from his seat. Grimaud already had hold of the carriage door. Raoul threw open his arms, exclaiming, "M. le Comte! M. le Comte!"

"Ah! is it you, Raoul," said Athos, intoxicated with joy.

"Not bad, indeed!" added d'Artagnan, with a burst of laughter, and they both embraced the young man and Porthos who had taken possession of them.

"Come, my son," added the Comte, gently passing his arm round Raoul's neck to draw him into the carriage, and again embracing him. "Grimaud," continued the Comte, "you will return quietly to Paris with your horse and M. de Vallon's, for Raoul and I will mount here and give up the carriage to these two gentlemen to return to Paris in; and then, as soon as you arrive, you will take my clothes and letters and forward the whole to me at home."

"But," observed Raoul, who was anxious to make the Comte converse, "when you return to Paris, there will not be a single thing there for you— which will be very inconvenient."

"I think it will be a very long time, Raoul, ere I return to Paris. The last sojourn we have made there has not been of a nature to encourage me to repeat it."

Raoul hung his head and said not a word more. Athos descended from the carriage and mounted the horse which had brought Porthos, and which seemed no little pleased at the exchange. Then they embraced, clasped each other's hands, interchanged a thousand pledges of eternal friendship. Porthos promised to spend a month with Athos at the first opportunity. D'Artagnan engaged to take advantage of his first leave of absence; and then having embraced Raoul for the last time: "To you, my boy," said he, "I will write." Coming from d'Artagnan, who he knew wrote but very seldom, these words expressed everything. Raoul was moved even to tears. He tore himself away from the musketeer and departed.

D'Artagnan rejoined Porthos in the carriage: "Well," said he, "my dear friend, what a day we have had!"

Chapter 19

M. DE BAISEMEAUX'S "SOCIETY"

THE reader has not forgotten that, on quitting the Bastille, d'Artagnan and the Comte de la Fère had left Aramis in close confabulation with Baisemeaux.

"Tell me, my dear M. Baisemeaux," said he, "have you never any other diversions at the Bastille than those at which I assisted during the two or three visits I have had the honour to pay you?"

"Visits are not frequent at the Bastille."

"What, are visits rare, then?"

"Very much so."

"Even on the part of your society?"

"What do you term by my society—the prisoners?"

"Oh, no!—your prisoners, indeed! I know well it is you who visit them, and not they you. By your society I mean, my dear de Baisemeaux, the society of which you are a member."

"Allow me," said Baisemeaux, "I should not like to say absolutely."

"There is an engagement entered into by all the governors and captains of fortresses affiliated to the order." Baisemeaux grew pale.

"Now the engagement," continued Aramis firmly, "is of this nature."

Baisemeaux rose, manifesting unspeakable emotion. "Go on, dear M. d'Herblay; go on," said he.

Aramis then spoke, or rather recited the following paragraph in the same tone as if he had been reading it from a book. "The aforesaid captain or governor of a fortress shall allow to enter, when need shall arise, and on demand of the prisoner, a confessor affiliated to the order." He stopped, Baisemeaux was quite distressing to look at, being so wretchedly pale and trembling. "Is not that the text of the agreement?" quietly asked Aramis.

But, gentle as the words were, they had the same effect on the unhappy governor as a clap of thunder. Baisemeaux became livid, and it seemed to him as if Aramis's beaming eyes were two forks of flame, piercing to the very bottom of his soul. "The confessor!" murmured he; "you, monseigneur, the confessor to the order!"

"Yes, I; but we have nothing to unravel together, seeing that you are not one of the affiliated."

"Monseigneur, I do not say that I have nothing to do with the society."

"Ah, ah!"

"But," replied the unhappy man, "having no notice, I was far from expecting."

"Does not the Gospel say, 'Watch, for the moment is known only of God.' Do not the rules of the order say, 'Watch, for that which I will you ought always to will also.' And on what pretext is it that you did not expect the confessor, M. de Baisemeaux?"

"Because, monseigneur, there is at present in the Bastille, no prisoner ill."

"M. de Baisemeaux," said Aramis, turning round in his chair, "here is your servant, who wishes to speak with you;" and, at this moment, de Baisemeaux's servant appeared at the threshold of the door.

"What is it?" asked Baisemeaux sharply.

"Monsieur," said the man, "they are bringing you the doctor's return." Aramis looked at Baisemeaux with a calm and confident eye.

"Well," said he, "let the messenger enter."

The messenger entered, saluted, and handed in the report. Baisemeaux ran his eye over it, and raising his head said, in surprise, "No. 12 is ill."

"How was it then," said Aramis carelessly, "that you told me everybody was well in your hotel, M. de Baisemeaux?" And he emptied his glass without removing his eyes from Baisemeaux.

The governor then made a sign to the messenger, and when he had quitted the room said, still trembling, "I think there is in the article, 'on the prisoner's demand.'"

"Yes, it is so;" answered Aramis. "But see what it is they want with you now."

At that moment, a sergeant put his head in at the door. "What do you want now?" cried Baisemeaux. "Can you not leave me in peace, for ten minutes?"

"Monsieur," said the sergeant, "the sick man, No. 12, has commissioned the turnkey to request you to send him a confessor."

Baisemeaux very nearly sank on the floor; but Aramis disdained to reassure him, just as he had disdained to terrify him. "What must I answer?" inquired Baisemeaux.

"Just what you please," replied Aramis, compressing his lips; "that is your business. *I* am not governor of the Bastille."

"Tell the prisoner," cried Baisemeaux quickly—"tell the prisoner that his request is granted." The sergeant left the room. "O monseigneur, monseigneur," murmured Baisemeaux, "how could I have suspected!—how could I have forseen this!"

Chapter 20

THE PRISONER

ON A bed of green serge, similar in all respects to the other beds in the Bastille, save that it was newer, and under curtains half-drawn, reposed a young man. According to custom, the prisoner was without a light. At the hour of curfew, he was bound to extinguish his lamp, and we perceive how much he was favoured in being allowed to keep it burning even till then. Near the bed a large leathern armchair, with twisted legs, sustained his clothes. A little table—without pens, books, paper or ink—stood neglected in sadness near the window; while several plates, still unemptied, showed that the prisoner had scarcely touched his recent repast. Aramis saw that the young man was stretched upon his bed, his face half-concealed by his arms. The arrival of a visitor did not cause any change of position, either he was waiting in expectation, or was asleep. Aramis lighted the candle from the lantern, pushed back the armchair, and approached the bed with an evident mixture of interest and respect. The young man raised his head. "What is it?" said he.

"Have you not desired a confessor," replied Aramis.

"Yes."

"Because you are ill?"

"Yes."

"Very ill?"

The young man gave Aramis a piercing glance, and answered, "I thank you." After a moment's silence, "I have seen you before," he continued. Aramis bowed.

Doubtless, the scrutiny the prisoner had just made of the cold, crafty, and imperious character stamped upon the features of the Bishop of Vannes, was little reassuring to one in his situation, for he added, "I am better."

"And then?" said Aramis.

"Why, then—being better, I have no longer the same need of a confessor, I think."

"Not even of the haircloth, which the note you found in your bread informed you of?"

The young man started; but before he had either assented or denied, Aramis continued. "Not even of the ecclesiastic from whom you were to hear an important revelation?"

"If it be so," said the young man, sinking again on his pillow; "it is different, I listen."

"Well, then, try to understand me." The prisoner looked fixedly at Aramis. "Sometimes it seems to me," said the latter, "that I have before me the man whom I seek, and then——"

"And then your man disappears,—is it not so?" said the prisoner, smiling. "So much the better."

Aramis rose. "Certainly," said he; "I have nothing further to say to a man who mistrusts me as you do."

"And I, monsieur," said the prisoner, in the same tone, "have nothing to say to a man who will not understand that a prisoner ought to be mistrustful of everybody."

"Even of his old friends?" said Aramis. "Oh! monseigneur, you are *too* prudent!"

"Of my old friends?—you one of my old friends,—you?"

"Do you no longer remember," said Aramis, "that you once saw, in the village where your early years were spent——"

"Do you know the name of the village?" asked the prisoner.

"Noisy-le-Sec, monseigneur," answered Aramis firmly.

"Who *are* you?"

"Do you remember, fifteen or eighteen years ago, seeing at Noisy-le-Sec a cavalier accompanied by a lady in black silk, with flame-coloured ribands in her hair?"

"Yes," said the young man; "I once asked the name of this cavalier, and they told me he called himself the Abbé d'Herblay. I was astonished that the Abbé had so warlike an air, and they replied that there was nothing singular in that, seeing that he was one of Louis XIII's musketeers."

"Well," said Aramis, "that musketeer and abbé, afterwards Bishop of Vannes, is your confessor now."

"I know it; I recognised you."

"Then, monseigneur, if you know that, I must further add a fact of which you are ignorant—that if the King were to know this evening of the presence of this musketeer, this abbé, this bishop, this confessor, *here*—he, who has risked everything to visit you, would tomorrow see glitter the executioner's axe at the bottom of a dungeon more gloomy and more obscure than yours."

While hearing these words, delivered with emphasis, the young man had raised himself on his couch, and gazed more and more eagerly at Aramis.

The result of his scrutiny was that he appeared to derive some confidence from it. "Yes," he murmured, "I remember perfectly. The woman of whom you speak came once with you, and twice afterwards with another." He hesitated.

"With another woman, who came to see you every month,—is it not so, monseigneur?"

"Yes."

"Do you know who this lady was?"

The light seemed ready to flash from the prisoner's eyes. "I am aware that she was one of the ladies of the court," he said.

"You remember that lady well, do you not?"

"Oh, my recollection can hardly be very confused on this head," said the young prisoner. "I saw that lady once with a gentleman about forty-five years old. I saw her once with you, and with the lady dressed in black. I have seen her twice since with the same person. These four people, with my master, and old Perronnette, my jailer, and the governor of the prison, are the only persons with whom I have ever spoken, and, indeed, almost the only persons I have ever seen."

"Then you were in prison?"

"If I am a prisoner here, there I was comparatively free, although in a very narrow sense—a house which I never quitted, a garden surrounded with walls I could not clear, these constituted my residence; but you know it, as you have been there. In a word, being accustomed to live within these bounds, I never cared to leave them. And so you will understand, monsieur, that not having seen anything of the world, I have nothing left to care for; and therefore, if you relate anything, you will be obliged to explain everything to me."

"And I will do so," said Aramis bowing, "for it is my duty, monseigneur."

"Well, then, begin by telling me who was my tutor."

"A worthy and, above all, an honourable gentleman, monseigneur; fit guide both for body and soul. Had you ever any reason to complain of him?"

"Oh, no; quite the contrary. But this gentleman of yours often used to tell me that my father and mother were dead. Did he deceive me, or did he speak the truth?"

"He was compelled to comply with the orders given him."

"Then he lied?"

"In one respect. Your father is dead."

"And my mother?"

"She is dead for you."

"But then she lives for others, does she not?"

"Yes."

"And I—and I, then" (the young man looked sharply at Aramis) "am compelled to live in the obscurity of a prison?"

"Alas! I fear so."

"And that, because my presence in the world would lead to the revelation of a great secret?"

"Certainly, a very great secret."

"My enemy must indeed be powerful, to be able to shut up in the Bastille a child such as I then was."

"He is."

"More powerful than my mother, then?"

"And why do you ask that?"

"Because my mother would have taken my part."

Aramis hesitated. "Yes, monseigneur; more powerful than your mother."

"Seeing, then, that my nurse and preceptor were carried off, and that I, also, was separated from them—either they were, or I am, very dangerous to my enemy?"

"Yes; a peril from which he freed himself, by causing the nurse and preceptor to disappear," answered Aramis quietly.

"Disappear!" cried the prisoner—"but how did they disappear?"

"In the surest possible way," answered Aramis;—"they are dead."

The young man turned visibly pale, and passed his hand tremblingly over his face.

"From poison?" he asked.

"From poison."

"Oh, you tell me nothing I am not aware of," said the prisoner, knitting his brows.

"Listen, then; I will in a few words tell you what has passed in France during the last twenty-three or twenty-four years, that is, from the probable date of your birth; in a word, from the time that interests you."

"Say on." And the young man resumed his serious and attentive attitude.

"Do you know who was the son of Henry IV?"

"At least I know who his successor was."

"How?"

"By means of a coin dated 1610, which bears the effigy of Henry IV; and another of 1612, bearing that of Louis XIII. So I presumed that, there being only two years between the two dates, Louis was Henry's successor."

"Then," said Aramis, "you know that the last reigning monarch was Louis XIII?"

"I do," answered the youth, slightly reddening.

"Well, he was a prince full of noble ideas and great projects, always, alas! deferred by the troubles of the times and the struggles that his minister Richelieu had to maintain against the great nobles of France. The King himself was of a feeble character; and died young and unhappy."

"I know it."

"He had been long anxious about having an heir; a care which weighs heavily on princes, who desire to leave behind them more than one pledge that their thoughts and works will be continued."

"Did the King, then, die childless?" asked the prisoner, smiling.

"No, but he was long without one, and for a long while thought he should be the last of his race. This idea had reduced him to the depths of despair, when suddenly, his wife, Anne of Austria——"

The prisoner trembled.

"Did you know," said Aramis, "that Louis XIII's wife was called Anne of Austria?"

"Continue," said the young man, without replying to the question.

"When suddenly," resumed Aramis, "the Queen announced an interesting event. There was great joy at the intelligence, and all prayed for her happy delivery. On the 5th of September, 1638, she gave birth to a son."

Here Aramis looked at his companion, and thought he observed him turning pale. "You are about to hear," said Aramis, "an account which few could now give; for it refers to a secret which they think buried with the dead or entombed in the abyss of the confessional."

"And you will tell me this secret?" broke in the youth.

"Oh!" said Aramis with unmistakable emphasis, "I do not know that I ought to risk this secret by entrusting it to one who has no desire to quit the Bastille."

"I hear you, monsieur."

"The Queen, then, gave birth to a son. But while the court was rejoicing over the event, when the King had shown the new-born child to the nobility and people and was sitting gaily down to table to celebrate the event, the Queen, who was alone in her room, was again taken ill, and gave birth to a second son."

"Oh!" said the prisoner, betraying a better acquaintance with the affair than he had owned to, "I thought that Monsieur was only born a——"

Aramis raised his finger: "Let me continue," he said.

The prisoner sighed impatiently, and paused.

"Yes," said Aramis, "the Queen had a second son, whom dame Perronnette, the midwife, received in her arms."

"Dame Perronnette!" murmured the young man.

"They ran at once to the banqueting-room, and whispered to the King what had happened; he rose and quitted the table. But this time it was no longer happiness that his face expressed, but something akin to terror. The birth of twins changed into bitterness the joy to which that of an only son had given rise, seeing that in France (a fact you are assuredly ignorant of) it is the oldest of the King's sons who succeeds his father."

"I know it."

"And that the doctors and jurists assert that there is ground for doubting whether he who first makes his appearance is the elder by the law of Heaven and of nature."

The prisoner uttered a smothered cry, and became whiter than the coverlet under which he hid himself.

"Now you understand," pursued Aramis, "that the King, who, with so much pleasure, saw himself repeated in one, was in despair about two; fearing that the second might dispute the first's claim to seniority, which had been recognised only two hours before; and so this second son, relying on party interests and caprices, might one day sow discord and engender civil war in the kingdom; by these means destroying the very dynasty he should have strengthened."

"Oh, I understand!—I understand!" murmured the young man.

"Well," continued Aramis; "this is what they relate, what they declare; this is why one of the Queen's two sons, shamefully parted from his brother, shamefully sequestered, is buried in the profoundest obscurity; this is why that second son has disappeared, and so completely, that not a soul in France, save his mother, is aware of his existence."

"Yes! his mother who has cast him off!" cried the prisoner in a tone of despair.

"Except, also," Aramis went on, "the lady in the black dress; and finally, excepting——"

"Excepting yourself—Is it not? You, who come and relate all this; you, who arouse in my soul curiosity, hatred, ambition, and, perhaps, even the thirst of vengeance; except you, monsieur, who if you are the man whom expect, whom the note I have received applies to; whom, in short, Heaven ought to send me, must possess about you——"

"What?" asked Aramis.

"A portrait of the King, Louis XIV, who at this moment reigns upon the throne of France."

"Here is the portrait," replied the Bishop, handing the prisoner a miniature in enamel, on which Louis was depicted, life-like, with a handsome, lofty mien. The prisoner eagerly seized the portrait, and gazed at it with devouring eyes.

"And now, monseigneur," said Aramis, "here is a mirror.".Aramis left the prisoner time to recover his ideas.

"So high!—so high!" murmured the young man, eagerly comparing the likeness of Louis with his own countenance reflected in the glass.

"What do you think of it?" at length said Aramis.

"I think that I am lost," replied the captive; "the King will never set me free."

"Monseigneur," answered Aramis, with a respect he had not yet manifested, "the King, mark me, will, if you desire it, be he who, quitting his dungeon, shall maintain himself upon the throne, on which his friends will place him."

"Tempt me not, monsieur," broke in the prisoner bitterly.

"But I, monseigneur, wish you to be a king for the good of humanity."

"Ah!" said the Prince, with fresh distrust inspired by the word; "ah! with what then has humanity to reproach my brother?"

"I forgot to say, monseigneur, that if you would allow me to guide you, and if you consent to become the most powerful monarch on earth, you will have promoted the interests of all the friends whom I devote to the success of your cause, and these friends are numerous."

"Numerous?"

"Less numerous than powerful, monseigneur."

"Explain yourself."

"It is impossible; I will explain, I swear before Heaven, on that day that I see you sitting on the throne of France."

"But my brother?"

"You shall decree his fate. Do you pity him?"

"Him, who leaves me to perish in a dungeon? No, I pity him not."

"So much the better."

"And now, are you aware of one thing, monsieur?"

"Tell me, my Prince."

"It is that I will hear nothing further from you till I am clear of the Bastille."

"I was going to say to your Highness that I should only have the pleasure of seeing you once again."

"And when?"

"The day when my Prince leaves these gloomy walls."

"Heavens! how will you give me notice of it?"

"By myself coming to fetch you."

"Yourself?"

"My Prince, do not leave this chamber save with me, or if in my absence you are compelled to do so, remember that I am not concerned in it."

"And so I am not to speak a word of this to any one whatever, save to you."

"Save only to me." The Prince offered his hand to Aramis, who sank upon his knee and kissed it. "It is the first act of homage paid to our future King," said he. "When I see you again, I shall say, 'Goodday, sire.'"

"Till then," said the young man, pressing his wan and wasted fingers over his heart,—"till then, no more dreams, no more strain upon my life—it would break! Oh, monsieur, how small is my prison—how low the window—how narrow are the doors! To think that so much pride, splendour, and happiness, should be able to enter in and remain here!"

"Your Royal Highness makes me proud," said Aramis, "since you infer it is I who brought all this." And he rapped immediately on the door. The jailer came to open it with Baisemeaux, who, devoured by fear and uneasiness, was beginning, in spite of himself, to listen at the door. Happily, neither of the speakers had forgotten to smother his voice, even in the most passionate outbreaks.

"What a confessor!" said the governor, forcing a laugh; "who would believe that a mere recluse, a man almost dead, could have committed crimes so numerous, and so long to tell of?"

Aramis made no reply. He was eager to leave the Bastille, where the secret which overwhelmed him seemed to double the weight of the walls. As soon as they reached Baisemeaux's quarters, "Let us proceed to business, my dear governor," said Aramis.

"Alas!" replied Baisemeaux.

"You have to ask me for my receipt for one hundred and fifty thousand livres," said the Bishop.

"And to pay over the first third of the sum," added the poor governor, with a sigh, taking three steps towards his iron strong-box.

"Here is the receipt," said Aramis.

"And here is the money," returned Baisemeaux, with a threefold sigh.

"The order instructed me only to give a receipt; it said nothing about receiving the money," rejoined Aramis.

"Adieu, Monsieur le Gouverneur!"

And he departed, leaving Baisemeaux almost more than stifled with joy and surprise at this regal present so liberally bestowed by the confessor extraordinary to the Bastille.

Chapter 21

WHO MESSIRE JEAN PERCERIN WAS

SINCE the departure of Athos for Blois, Porthos and d'Artagnan were seldom together. One was occupied with harassing duties for the King; the other had been making many purchases of furniture, which he intended to forward to his estate, and by aid of which he hoped to establish in his various residences something of that court luxury which he had witnessed in all its dazzling brightness in His Majesty's society. D'Artagnan, ever faithful, one morning during an interval of service thought about Porthos, and being uneasy at not having heard anything of him for a fortnight, directed his steps towards his hotel, and pounced upon him just as he was getting up. The worthy Baron had a pensive—nay, more than pensive—a melancholy air.

"But you seem in the dumps here?" exclaimed d'Artagnan.

Porthos replied by a look expressive of dejection. "Well, then, tell me all about it, Porthos, my friend, unless it is a secret."

"The fact is, I have received an invitation for the fête at Vaux," said Porthos, with a lugubrious expression.

"Well! do you complain of that? The King has caused a hundred mortal heartburnings among the courtiers by refusing invitations. And so, my dear friend, you are really going to Vaux?"

"Indeed I am!"

"You will see a magnificent sight."

"Alas! I doubt it, though."

"But what is it then?"

"'Tis that I have no clothes!"

D'Artagnan stood petrified. "No clothes, Porthos, no clothes!" he cried, "when I see at least fifty suits on the floor."

"Fifty, truly; but not one which fits me!"

"I understand your difficulty. You have how many new suits? nine? thirty-six? and yet not one to wear. Well, you must have a thirty-seventh made, and give the thirty-six to Mouston."

"Ah, monsieur!" said Mouston, with a gratified air. "The truth is that monsieur has always been very generous to me."

"Do you mean to think that I hadn't that idea, or that I was deterred by the expense? But it wants only two days to the fête; I received the invitation yesterday; made Mouston post hither with my wardrobe, and only this morning discovered my misfortune; and from now till the day after to-morrow there isn't a single fashionable tailor who will undertake to make me a suit."

"That is to say, one covered all over with gold, isn't it?"

"I wish it so! all over!"

"Oh, we shall manage it. You won't leave for three days. The invitations are for Wednesday, and this is only Sunday morning."

"'Tis true; but Aramis has strongly advised me to be at Vaux twenty-four hours beforehand."

"How, Aramis?"

"Yes, it was Aramis who brought me the invitation."

"Ah! to be sure, I see. You are invited on the part of M. Fouquet."

"By no means! by the King, dear friend. The letter bears the following as large as life: 'M. de Baron du Vallon is informed that the King has condescended to place him on the invitation list——"

"Very good; but you leave with M. Fouquet?"

"And when I think," cried Porthos, stamping on the floor, "when I think I shall have no clothes, I am ready to burst with rage! I should like to strangle somebody or destroy something."

"Neither strangle anybody nor destroy anything, Porthos; I will manage it all; put on one of your thirty-six suits and come with me to a tailor."

"Pooh! my agent has seen them all this morning."

"Even M. Percerin?"

"Who is M. Percerin?"

"Only the King's tailor!"

"Oh, ah, yes," said Porthos, who wished to appear to know the King's tailor, but now heard his name mentioned for the first time;—"to M. Percerin's, by Jove! I thought he would be too much engaged."

"Doubtless he will be; but be at ease, Porthos; he will do for me what he won't do for another. Only you must allow yourself to be measured."

"Ah!" said Porthos, with a sigh, "'tis vexatious, but what would you have me do?"

"Do? as the others do; as the King does."

"What! do they measure the King too? does *he* put up with it?"

"The King is a beau, my good friend, and so are you, too, whatever you may say about it."

Porthos smiled triumphantly. "Let us go to the King's tailor," he said; "and since he measures the King, I think, by my faith, I may well allow him to measure me."

The King's tailor, Messire Jean Percerin, occupied a rather large house in the Rue St. Honoré, near the Rue de l'Arbre Sec. He was a man of great taste in elegant stuffs, embroideries, and velvet, being hereditary tailor to the King. The preferment of his house reached as far back as the time of Charles IX; from whose reign dated, as we know, fancies in *bravery* difficult enough to gratify.

It was to the house of this great lord of tailors that d'Artagnan took the despairing Porthos.

They both alighted and made their way on foot towards the establishment. D'Artagnan, pushing on Porthos, succeeded in gaining the counter, behind which the journeymen tailors were doing their best to answer queries. The poor fellows had enough to do, and did their best, to reply to the demands of the customers in the absence of their master, leaving off drawing a stitch to turn a sentence; and when wounded pride, or disappointed expectation, brought down upon them too cutting rebukes, he who was attacked made a dive and disappeared under the counter. The line of discontented lords formed a very remarkable picture. Our captain of musketeers, a man of sure and rapid observation, took it all in at a glance; but having run over the groups, his eye rested on a man in front of him.

"Well my dear Monsieur Molière, but you will go and tell M. Percerin I am here."

"I!" exlaimed Molière, in the tone of a courageous dog, from which you snatch the bone it has legitimately gained; "I disturb myself! Ah! Monsieur d'Artagnan, how hard you are upon me!"

Chapter 22

THE PATTERNS

DURING all this time the crowd was slowly rolling away, leaving at every angle of the counter either a murmur or a menace, as the waves leave foam or scattered seaweed on the sands, when they retire with the ebbing tide. In about ten minutes Molière reappeared, making another sign to d'Artagnan from under the hangings. The latter hurried after him, with Porthos in the rear, and after threading a labyrinth of corridors, introduced him to M. Percerin's room. The old man, with his sleeves turned up, was gathering up in folds a piece of gold-flowered brocade, so as the better to exhibit its lustre. Perceiving d'Artagnan, he put the silk aside, and came to meet him, by no means radiant with joy, and by no means courteous, but take it altogether, in a tolerably civil manner.

"The captain of the musketeers will excuse me, I am sure, for I am engaged."

"Eh! yes, on the King's costumes; I know that, my dear Monsieur Percerin. You are making three, they tell me."

"Five, my dear monsieur, five."

"Three or five, 'tis all the same to me, my dear monsieur; and I know that you will make them most exquisitely."

"Yes, I know. Once made, they will be the most beautiful in the world, I do not deny it; but that they may be the most beautiful in the world, they must first be made; and to do this, captain, I am pressed for time."

"My dear Percerin," said d'Artagnan, "you will make a dress for the Baron. 'Tis I who ask you."

"To you I will not say nay, captain."

"But that it not all; you will make it for him at once."

"'Tis impossible before eight days."

"By no means, dear Monsieur Percerin, above all if *I* ask you," said a mild voice at the door, a silvery voice which made d'Artagnan prick up his ears. It was the voice of Aramis.

"Monsieur d'Herblay!" cried the tailor.

"Aramis," murmured d'Artagnan.

"Ah! our Bishop," said Porthos.

"Good morning, d'Artagnan; good morning, Porthos; good morning, my dear friends," said Aramis. "Come, come, M. Percerin, make the Baron's dress; and I will answer for it you will gratify M. Fouquet." And he accompanied the words with a sign, which seemed to say, "Agree, and dismiss them."

It appeared that Aramis had over Master Percerin an influence superior even to d'Artagnan's, for the tailor bowed in assent, and turning round upon Porthos, "Go and get measured on the other side," said he rudely.

Porthos coloured in a formidable manner. D'Artagnan saw the storm coming, and, addressing Molière, said to him in an undertone, "You see before you, my dear monsieur, a man who considers himself disgraced if you measure the flesh and bones that Heaven has given him; study this type for me, Master Aristophanes, and profit by it."

Molière had no need of encouragement, and his gaze dwelt upon the Baron Porthos. "Monsieur," he said, "if you will come with me, I will make them take your measure without the measurer touching you."

"But how in the world can it be done?" asked Porthos, delighted.

"Monsieur," said Molière, bowing, "if you will deign to follow me, you will see."

Aramis observed this scene with all his eyes. Perhaps he fancied from d'Artagnan's liveliness that he would leave with Porthos, so as not to lose the conclusion of a scene so well begun. But, clear-sighted as he was, Aramis deceived himself. Porthos and Molière left together alone. D'Artagnan remained with Percerin. Why? From curiosity, doubtless; probably to enjoy a little longer the society of his good friend Aramis. As Molière and Porthos disappeared, d'Artagnan drew near the Bishop of Vannes, a proceeding which appeared particularly to disconcert him.

"A dress for you also, is it not, my friend?"

Aramis smiled. "No," said he.

"Ah! you had something particular to say to M. Percerin? Why did you not tell me so at once?"

"Something particular, certainly," repeated Aramis, "but not for you, d'Artagnan. But, at the same time, I hope you will believe that I can never have anything so particular to say that a friend like you may not hear it."

"Oh, no, no! I am going," said d'Artagnan, imparting to his voice an evident tone of curiosity; for Aramis's annoyance, well dissembled as it was, had not a whit escaped him; and he knew that, in that impenetrable mind, everything, even the most apparently trivial, was designed to some end; an unknown one; but one which, from the knowledge he had of his friend's character, the musketeer felt must be important.

On his part, Aramis saw that d'Artagnan, was not without suspicion, and pressed him. "Stay, by all means," he said, "this is what it is." Then turning towards the tailor, "My dear Percerin," said he, "I am even very happy that you are here, d'Artagnan."

"Oh, indeed," exclaimed the Gascon, for the third time, even less deceived this time than before.

Percerin never moved. Aramis roused him violently by snatching from his hands the stuff upon which he was engaged. "My dear Percerin," said he, "I have near at hand, M. Lebrun, one of M. Fouquet's painters."

"Ah, very good," thought d'Artagnan; "but why 'Lebrun'?"

"Come in, M. Lebrun, come in," said Aramis, opening a side-door with his right hand, and holding d'Artagnan with his left.

"I' faith I am quite in the dark," quoth Percerin.

Aramis took an "opportunity," as is said in theatrical matters.—"My dear M. Percerin," Aramis continued, "you are making fine dresses for the King, are you not? One in brocade, one in hunting-cloth, one in velvet, one in satin, and one in Florentine stuffs?"

"Yes; but how—do you know all that, monseigneur?" said Percerin, astounded.

"It is all very simple, my dear monsieur; there will be a hunt, a banquet, concert, promenade, and reception. These five kinds of dress are required by etiquette."

"You know everything, monseigneur!"

"And a great many more things, too," murmured d'Artagnan.

"But," cried the tailor, in triumph, "what you do not know, monseigneur—prince of the church though you are—what nobody will know—what only the King, Mademoiselle de la Vallière, and myself do know, is the colour of the materials, and the nature of the ornaments, and the cut, the *ensemble*, the finish of it all!"

"Well," said Aramis, "that is precisely what I have come to ask you, dear Percerin."

Percerin made a bound backwards, which d'Artagnan,—calmest and most appreciative of men—did not consider overdone; so many strange and startling aspects wore the proposal which Aramis had just hazarded. "The King's dresses! Give the King's dresses to any mortal whatever! Oh! for once, monseigneur, your grace is mad!" cried the poor tailor in extremity.

"Help me now, d'Artagnan," said Aramis, more and more calm and smiling. "Help me now to persuade monsieur, for *you* understand, do you not?"

"Eh! eh!—not exactly, I declare."

"What! you do not understand that M. Fouquet wishes to afford the King the surprise of finding his portrait on his arrival at Vaux; and that the portrait, which will be a striking resemblance, ought to be dressed exactly as the King will be on the day it is shown?"

"Oh! yes, yes;" said the musketeer, nearly convinced, so plausible was this reasoning. "Yes, my dear Aramis, you are right; it is a happy idea. I will wager it is one of your own, Aramis."

"Well, I don't know," replied the Bishop; "either mine, or M. Fouquet's." Then scanning Percerin, after noticing d'Artagnan's hesitation, "Well, monsieur Percerin," he asked, "what do you say to this?"

"I say that——"

"That you are doubtless free to refuse. I know well—and I by no means count upon compelling you, my dear monsieur. I will say more; I even understand all the delicacy you feel in taking up with M. Fouquet's idea; you dread appearing to flatter the King. A noble spirit, M. Percerin, a noble spirit!" The tailor stammered. "It would, indeed, be a very pretty compliment to pay the young prince," continued Aramis; "but as the Surintendant told me, 'If Percerin refuse, tell him that it will not at all lower him in my opinion, and I shall always esteem him, only——' "

"Only?" repeated Percerin, rather troubled.

"Only," continued Aramis, " 'I shall be compelled to say to the King.'—you understand my dear Monsieur Percerin, that these are M. Fouquet's words—'I shall be constrained to say to the King, "Sire, I had intended to present your Majesty with your portrait, but owing to a feeling of delicacy, slightly exaggerated perhaps, although creditable, M. Percerin opposed the project." ' "

"Opposed!" cried the poor tailor, terrified at the responsibility which would weigh upon him; "I to oppose the desire, the will of M. Fouquet when he is seeking to please the King! Oh, what a hateful word you have uttered, monseigneur. Oppose! Oh, 'tis not I who said it. Heaven have mercy on me. I call the captain of the musketeers to witness it! Is it not true, Monsieur d'Artagnan, that I have opposed nothing?"

D'Artagnan made a sign indicating that he wished to remain neutral. He felt that there was an intrigue at the bottom of it, whether comedy or tragedy; he was at his wit's end at not being able to fathom it, but in the meantime wished to keep clear.

But already Percerin, goaded by the idea that the King should be told he had stood in the way of a pleasant surprise, had offered Lebrun a chair, and proceeded to bring from a wardrobe four magnificent dresses, the fifth being still in the workmen's hands, and these masterpieces he successively fitted upon four lay figures, which, imported into France in the time of Concini, had been given to Percerin II by Marshal d'Onore, after the discomfiture of the Italian tailors, ruined in their competition. The painter set to work to draw and then to paint the dresses. But Aramis, who was closely watching all the phases of his toil, suddenly stopped him.

"An idea, M. Lebrun, an idea! If we had a pattern of the materials, for example, and with time, and a better light—"

"Oh, then," cried Lebrun, "I would answer for the effect."

"Good!" said d'Artagnan, "this ought to be the knotty point of the whole thing; they want a pattern of each of the materials. *Mordieux*! will this Percerin give it now?"

Percerin, beaten in his last retreat, and duped, moreover, by the feigned good-nature of Aramis, cut out five patterns and handed them to the Bishop of Vannes.

Lebrun packed up, Percerin put back the dresses into the closet, Aramis put his hand on his pocket to assure himself the patterns were secure,—and they all left the study.

Chapter 23

ANOTHER SUPPER AT THE BASTILLE

THE Bishop of Vannes, much annoyed at having met d'Artagnan at M. Percerin's, returned at Saint Mandé in no very good humour.

He went to exchange a parting word with the Surintendant. "Oh, everyone is laughing!" said Fouquet with a sigh.

"And do not you laugh, monseigneur?"

Fouquet grasped his hand. "And where are you going?" he said.

"I am off to Paris, when you shall have given me a certain letter."

"For whom?"

"M. de Lyonne."

"And what do you want with Lyonne?"

"I wish to make him sign a *lettre de cachet*."

"*Lettre de cachet!* Do you desire to put somebody in the Bastille?"

"On the contrary—to let somebody out."

"And who?"

"A poor devil—a youth, a lad who has been bastilled these ten years, for two Latin verses he made against the Jesuits."

"And his name is——?"

"Seldon."

"Yes.—But it is too bad. You knew this, and never told me!"

"'Twas only yesterday his mother applied to me, monseigneur."

"And the woman is poor."

"In the deepest misery."

"Oh! Heaven!" said Fouquet, "you sometimes bear with such unjustice on earth, that I understand why there are wretches who doubt in your existence. Stay, M. d'Herblay." And Fouquet, taking a pen, wrote a few rapid lines to his colleague Lyonne. Aramis took the letter and made ready to go.

"Wait," said Fouquet. He opened his drawer, and took out ten government notes which were there, each for a thousand francs. "Stay," he said; "set the son at liberty, and give this to the mother; but, above all, tell her not——"

"What, monseigneur?"

"That she is ten thousand livres richer than I. She would say, I am but a poor surintendant! Go! and I hope that God will bless those who are mindful of His poor!"

"So also do I hope," replied Aramis, kissing Fouquet's hand.

And he went out quickly, carrying off the letter for Lyonne and the notes for Seldon's mother.

Seven o'clock sounded from the great clock of the Bastille, that famous clock, which like all the accessories of the state prison, the very use of which is a torture, recalled to the prisoners' minds the destination of every hour of their punishment. The timepiece of the Bastille, adorned with figures, like most of the clocks of the period, represented St. Peter in bonds. It was the supper hour of the unfortunate captives.

Baisemeaux, seated at table, was rubbing his hands and looking at the Bishop of Vannes, who, booted like a cavalier, dressed in grey, and sword at side, kept talking of his hunger and testifying the liveliest impatience. M. de Baisemeaux de Montlezun was not accustomed to the unbending movements of his greatness, my Lord of Vannes, and this evening, Aramis becoming quite sprightly, volunteered confidence on confidence.

"Bravo!" said Baisemeaux, and he poured out a great glass of wine and drank it off at a draught, trembling with joy at the idea of being, by hook or by crook, in the secret of some high archiepiscopal misdemeanour. While he was drinking he did not see with what attention Aramis was noting the sounds in the great court. A courier came in about eight o'clock as François brought in the fifth bottle, and, although the courier made a great noise, Baisemeaux heard nothing.

François re-entered; Baisemeaux took from his hands the courier's order. He slowly undid it, and as slowly read it. Aramis pretended to be drinking, so as to be able to watch his host through the glass. Then, Baisemeaux having read it: "What was I just saying?" he exclaimed.

"What is it?" asked the Bishop.

"An order of release! There, now; excellent news indeed to disturb us!"

"Excellent news for him whom it concerns, you will at least agree, my dear governor!"

Baisemeaux leaned back to ring for François, and by a very natural motion turned round towards the door. The order had remained on the table; Aramis seized the opportunity when Baisemeaux was not looking to change the paper for another, folded in the same manner, and which he took from his pocket. "François," said the governor, "let the major come up here with the turnkeys of the Bertaudière." François bowed and quitted the room, leaving the two companions alone.

Chapter 24

THE GENERAL OF THE ORDER

"FRANCOIS, tell the major to go and open the cell of M. Seldon, No. 3, Bertaudière."

"Seldon!" exclaimed Aramis, very naturally. "You said Seldon, I think?"

"I said Seldon, of course. 'Tis the name of the man they set free."

"Oh! you meant to say Marchiali?" said Aramis.

"Marchiali? Oh, yes, indeed. No, no, Seldon."

"I think you are making a mistake, Monsieur Baisemeaux."

"I have read the order."

"And I also."

"And I saw 'Seldon' in letters as large as that," and Baisemeaux held up his finger.

"And I read 'Marchiali' in characters as large as this," said Aramis, also holding up two fingers.

"To the proof; let us throw a light on the matter," said Baisemeaux, confident he was right. "There is the paper, you have only to read it."

"I read, 'Marchiali,'" returned Aramis, spreading out the paper. "Look."

Baisemeaux looked, and his arms dropped suddenly.

"Monseigneur," he said, "this Marchiali is the very same prisoner whom the other day a priest, confessor of *our order,* came to visit in so imperious and no secret a manner."

Aramis made no reply, but recommenced eating and drinking. As for Baisemeaux, no longer touching anything that was on the table, he again took up the order and examined it in every way. This investigation, under ordinary circumstances, would have made the ears of the impatient Aramis burn with anger; but the Bishop of Vannes did not become incensed for so little, above all, when he had murmured to himself that to do so was dangerous. "Are you going to release Marchiali?" he said. "What mellow and fragrant sherry this is, my dear governor."

"Monseigneur," replied Baisemeaux, "I shall release the prisoner Marchiali when I have summoned the courier who brought the order, and above all, when, by interrogating him, I have satisfied myself."

"The order is sealed, and the courier is ignorant of the contents. What do you want to satisfy yourself about?"

"Be it so, monseigneur; but I shall send to the ministry, and M. de Lyonne will either confirm or withdraw the order."

"What is the good of all that?" asked Aramis coldly.

"What good?"

"Yes; what is your object, I ask."

"The object of never deceiving oneself, monseigneur, nor being wanting in the respect which a subaltern owes to his superior officers, nor infringing the duties of that service which one has voluntarily accepted."

"Well, Monsieur de Baisemeaux," said Aramis, bending an eagle glance on the governor, "I adopt so frankly your doubts, and your mode of clearing them up, that I will take a pen, if you will give me one."

Baisemeaux gave him a pen.

"And a sheet of white paper," added Aramis.

Baisemeaux handed some paper.

"Now, I—I, also—I, here present—incontestably, I—am going to write an order to which I am certain you will give credence, incredulous as you are!"

Aramis took a pen and wrote. Baisemeaux, in terror read over his shoulder.

"A.M.D.G." wrote the Bishop; and he drew a cross under these four letters, which signify *ad majorem, Dei gloriam,* "to the greater glory of God"; and thus he continued, "It is our pleasure that the order brought to M. de Baisemeaux de Montlezun, governor, for the King, of the castle of the Bastille, be held good and effectual, and be immediately carried into operation.

"(Signed) D'Herblay,
"General of the Order, by the grace of God."

Baisemeaux was so profoundly astonished, that his features remained contracted, his lips parted, and his eyes fixed. He did not move an inch, nor articulate a sound. Nothing could be heard in that large chamber but the buzzing of a little moth, which was fluttering about the candles. Aramis, without even deigning to look at the man whom he had reduced to so miserable a condition, drew from his pocket a small case of black wax; he sealed the letter, and stamped it with a seal suspended at his breast, beneath his doublet, and when the operation was concluded, presented—still in silence—the missive to M. de Baisemeaux. The latter, whose hands trembled in a manner to excite pity, turned a dull and meaningless gaze upon the letter. A last gleam of feeling played over his features, and he fell, as if thunderstruck, on a chair.

"Come, come," said Aramis, after a long silence, during which the governor of the Bastille had slowly recovered his senses, "do not lead me to believe, dear Baisemeaux, that the presence of the General of the Order is as terrible as His, and that men die merely from having seen Him. Take courage; rouse yourself; give me your hand, and obey."

Baisemeaux obeyed. He summoned his lieutenant, and gave him an order, which the latter passed on, without disturbing himself about it, to the next whom it concerned.

Half an hour aferwards they heard a gate shut in the court; it was the door to the dungeon, which had just rendered up its prey to the free air. Aramis blew out all the candles which lighted the room but one, which he left burning behind the door. This flickering glare prevented the sight from resting steadily on any object. It multiplied tenfold the changing forms and shadows of the place, by its wavering uncertainty. Steps drew near.

"Go and meet your men," said Aramis to Baisemeaux.

The governor obeyed. The sergeant and turnkeys disappeared. Baisemeaux re-entered, followed by a prisoner. Aramis had placed himself in the shade; he saw without being seen. Baisemeaux, in an agitated tone of voice, made the young man acquainted with the order which set him at liberty. The prisoner listened without making a single gesture, or saying a word.

"You will swear ('tis the regulation that requires it)" added the governor, "never to reveal anything that you have seen or heard in the Bastille."

The prisoner perceived a crucifix; he stretched out his hands, and swore with his lips. "And now, monsieur, you are free; whither do you intend going?"

The prisoner turned his head, as if looking behind him for some protection, on which he ought to rely. Then was it that Aramis came out of the shade: "I am here," he said, "to render the gentleman whatever service he may please to ask."

The prisoner slightly reddened, and without hesitation passed his arm through that of Aramis. "God have you in his holy keeping," he said, in a voice the firmness of which made the governor tremble as much as the form of the blessing astonished him.

Aramis, on shaking hands with Baisemeaux, said to him: "Does my order trouble you? Do you fear their finding it here, should they come to search?"

"I desire to keep it, monseigneur," said Baisemeaux. "If they found it here it would be a certain indication I should be lost, and in that case you would be a powerful and a last auxiliary for me."

"Being your accomplice, you mean?" answered Aramis, shrugging his shoulders. "Adieu, Baisemeaux," said he.

The horses were in waiting, making the carriage shake again with their impatience. Baisemeaux accompanied the Bishop to the bottom of the steps. Aramis caused his companion to mount before him, then followed, and without giving the driver any further order, "Go on," said he. The carriage rattled over the pavement of the courtyard. An officer with a torch went before the horses, and gave orders at every post to let them pass. During the time taken in opening all the barriers, Aramis barely breathed, and you might have heard his "sealed heart knock against his ribs." The prisoner, buried in a corner of the carriage, made no more sign of life than his companion. At length a jolt more severe than the others announced to them that they had cleared the last watercourse. Behind the carriage closed the last gate, that in the Rue St. Antoine. No more walls either on the right or left; heaven everywhere, liberty everywhere, and life everywhere. The horses, kept in check by a vigorous hand, went quietly as far as the middle of the faubourg. There they began to trot. Little by little, whether they warmed over it, or whether they were urged, they gained in swiftness, and once past Bercy, the carriage seemed to fly, so great was the ardour of the coursers. These horses ran thus as far as Villeneuve St. George's, where relays were waiting. Then four instead of two whirled the carriage away in the direction of Melun, and pulled up for a moment in the middle of the forest of Senart. No doubt, the order had been given the postilion beforehand, for Aramis had no occasion even to make a sign.

"What is the matter?" asked the prisoner, as if waking from a long dream.

"The matter is, monseigneur," said Aramis, "that before going further, it is necessary your Royal Highness and I should converse."

"I will wait an opportunity, monsieur," answered the young Prince.

"We could not have a better, monseigneur; we are in the middle of a forest, and no one can hear us."

"The postilion?"

"The postilion of this relay is deaf and dumb. monseigneur."

"I am at your service, M. d'Herblay."

"Is it your pleasure to remain in the carriage?"

"Yes, we are comfortably seated, and I like this carriage, for it has restored me to liberty."

"Wait, monseigneur; there is yet a precaution to be taken."

"What?"

"We are here on the highway; cavaliers or carriages travelling like ourselves might pass, and seeing us stopping deem us in some difficulty. Let us avoid offers of assistance which would embarrass us."

"Give the postilion orders to conceal the carriage in one of the side avenues."

"'Tis exactly what I wished to do, monseigneur."

Aramis made a sign to the deaf and dumb driver of the carriage, whom he touched on the arm. The latter dismounted, took the leaders by the bridle, and led them over the velvet sward and the mossy grass of a winding alley, at the bottom of which, on this moonless night the deep shades formed a curtain blacker than ink. This done, the man lay down on a slope near his horses, who, on either side, kept nibbling the young oak shoots.

"I am listening," said the young Prince to Aramis; "but what are you doing there?"

"I am disarming myself of my pistols, of which we have no further need, monseigneur."

Chapter 25

CROWN AND TIARA

Black was the darkness which fell wide and dense from the summits of the intertwining trees. The carriage, covered in by this vast roof, would not have received a particle of light, nor even if a ray could have struggled through the wreaths of mist which were rising in the avenue of the wood.

"Monseigneur," resumed Aramis, "you know the history of the government which to-day controls France. The King issued from an infancy imprisoned like yours, obscure as yours, and confined as yours; only, instead of ending, like yourself, this slavery in a prison—this obscurity in solitude —these straitened circumstances in concealment, he was fain to bear all these miseries, humiliations, and distresses, in full daylight, under the pitiless sun of royalty; or an elevation so flooded with light, where every stain appears a miserable blemish and every glory a stain. The King has suffered; it rankles in his mind; and he will avenge himself. He will be a bad king. I say not that he will pour out blood, like Louis XI or Charles IX, for he has no mortal injuries to avenge; but he will devour the means and substance of his people; for he has himself undergone wrongs in his own interest and money. In the first place, then, I quite acquit my conscience when I consider openly the merits and faults of this Prince; and if I condemn him, my conscience absolves me."

Aramis paused. It was not to listen if the silence of the forest remained undisturbed, but it was to gather up his thoughts from the very bottom of his soul—to leave the thoughts he had uttered sufficient time to eat deeply into the mind of his companion.

"You are the son of King Louis XIII, brother of Louis XIV, natural and legitimate heir to the throne of France. In keeping you near him, as Monsieur has been kept—Monsieur, your younger brother—the King reserved to himself the right of being legitimate sovereign. The doctors only could dispute his legitimacy. But the doctors always prefer the King who is to the king who is not. Providence has willed that you should be persecuted; and this persecution to-day consecrates you King of France. You had then a right to reign, seeing that it is disputed, you had a right to be proclaimed, seeing that you have been concealed; and you possess royal blood, since no one has dared to shed yours, as your servants' has been shed. Now see, then, what this Providence, which you have so often accused of having in every way thwarted you, has done for you. It has given you the features, figure, age, and voice of your brother; and the very causes of your persecution are about to become those of your triumphant restoration. To-morrow, after to-morrow—from the very first, regal phantom, living shade of Louis XIV, you will sit upon his throne, whence the will of Heaven, confided in execution to the arm of man, will have hurled him, without hope of return."

"A King, ignorant and embarassed as I shall be, will, as a matter of course, require a first minister of state."

"Your Majesty will require a friend."

"I have only one, and that is yourself."

"You will have many others by-and-by, but none so devoted, none so zealous for your glory."

"You will be my first minister of state."

"Not immediately, monseigneur; for that would give rise to too much suspicion and astonishment."

"You shall be nominated before two months are past, Monsieur d'Herblay. But that is a matter of very trifling moment; you would not offend me if you were to ask more than that, and you would cause me serious regret if you were to limit yourself to that."

"In that case I have something still further to hope for, monseigneur."

"Speak! speak!"

"You will not be a King such as your father was; delicate in health, slow in judgment, whom all things wearied; you will be a king governing by your brain and by your sword; you will have in the government of the state no more than you could manage unaided; I should only interfere with you. Besides, our friendship ought never to be, I do not say impaired, but in any way affected, by a secret thought. I shall have given you the throne of France, you will confer on me the throne of St. Peter. Whenever your loyal, firm, and mailed hand shall have joined in ties of intimate association the hand of a pope such as I shall be, neither Charles the Fifth, who owned two-thirds of the habitable globe, nor Charlemagne, who possessed it entirely, will be able to reach to half your stature. I have no alliances, I have no predilections; I will not throw you into persecutions of heretics, nor will I cast you into the troubled waters of family dissension. I will simply say to you: The whole universe is our own; for me the minds

of men, for you their bodies. And as I shall be the first to die, you will
have my inheritance. What do you say of my plan, monseigneur?"

"I say that you render me happy and proud, for no other reason than
that of having comprehended you thoroughly. Monsieur d'Herblay, you
shall be Cardinal, and when Cardinal, my Prime Minister; and then you
shall point out to me the neccessary steps to be taken to secure your elec-
tion as Pope, and I will take them. You can ask what guarantees from me
you please."

"It is useless. I shall never act except in such a manner that you are
the gainer; I shall never ascend the ladder of fortune, fame, or position,
until I shall have first seen you placed upon the round of the ladder
immediately above me; I shall always hold myself sufficiently aloof from
you to escape incurring your jealousy, sufficiently near to sustain your
personal advantage and to watch over your friendship."

"And so—my brother—will disappear?"

"Simply. We will remove him from his bed by means of a plank which
yields to the pressure of the finger. Having retired to rest as a crowned
sovereign, he will awaken in captivity. Alone you will rule from that
moment, and you will have no interest dearer and better than that of
keeping me near you."

"I believe it. There is my hand on it, Monsieur d'Herblay."

"Allow me to kneel before you, sire, most respectfully. We will embrace
each other on the day we shall both have on our temples, you the crown,
and I the tiara."

"Still embrace me this very day also, and be, for and towards me, more
than great, more than skilful, more than sublime in genius; be kind and
indulgent—be my father."

Aramis was almost overcome as he listened to his voice; he fancied he
detected in his own heart an emotion hitherto unknown to him; but this
impression was speedily removed. "His father!" he thought; "yes, his Holy
Father."

And they resumed their places in the carriage, which sped rapidly along
the road leading to Vaux-le-Vicomte.

Chapter 26

THE CHÂTEAU DE VAUX-LE-VICOMTE

THE château of Vaux-le-Vicomte, situated about a league from Melun,
had been built by Fouquet in 1655, at a time when there was a scarcity of
money in France; Mazarin had taken all that there was, and Fouquet
expended the remainder. However, as certain men have fertile faults and
useful vices, Fouquet, in scattering broadcast millions of money in the
construction of this palace, had found a means of gathering, as the result
of his generous profusion, three illustrious men together: Levan, the

architect of the building; Lenôtre, the designer of the gardens; and Lebrun, the decorator of the apartments. If the Château de Vaux possessed a single fault with which it could be reproached, it was its grand, portentous character.

With a perfect reliance that Aramis had made arrangements fairly to distribute the vast number of guests throughout the palace, and that he had not omitted to attend to any of the internal regulations for their comfort, Fouquet devoted his entire attention to the *ensemble* alone; in one direction Gourville showed him the preparations which had been made for the fireworks; in another, Molière led him over the theatre; at last, after he had visited the chapel, the *salons*, and the galleries, and was again going downstairs, exhausted with fatigue, Fouquet saw Aramis on the staircase. The prelate beckoned to him. The Surintendant joined his friend, and, with him, paused before a large picture scarcely finished. Applying himself heart and soul to his work, the painter, Lebrun, covered with perspiration, stained with paints, pale from fatigue and inspiration of genius, was putting the last finishing touches with his rapid brush. It was the portrait of the King, whom they were expecting, dressed in the court-suit which Percerin had condescended to show beforehand to the Bishop of Vannes.

In the direction of Melun, in the still empty, open plain, the sentinels of Vaux had perceived the advancing procession of the King and the Queens. Her Majesty was entering into Melun, with her long train of carriages and cavaliers.

"In an hour——" said Aramis to Fouquet.

"In an hour!" replied the latter, sighing.

"And the people who ask one another what is the good of these royal fêtes!" continued the Bishop of Vannes, laughing, with his false smile.

"Where are you going?" returned Fouquet, with a gloomy look.

"To my own apartment, in order to change my costume, monseigneur."

"Whereabouts are you lodging, d'Herblay?"

"In the blue room on the second story."

"The room immediately over the King's room?"

"Precisely."

"You will be subject to very great restraint there. What an idea to condemn yourself to a room where you cannot stir or move about."

"During the night, monseigneur, I sleep or read in my bed."

"And your servants?"

"I have only one person with me. I find my reader quite sufficient. Adieu, monseigneur; do not over-fatigue yourself; keep yourself fresh for the arrival of the King."

"We shall see you by-and-by, I suppose, and shall see our friend du Vallon also?"

"He is lodging next to me, and is at this moment dressing."

And Fouquet, bowing, with a smile, passed on like a commander-in-chief who pays the different outposts a visit after the enemy has been signalled in sight.

Chapter 27

NECTAR AND AMBROSIA

M. FOUQUET held the stirrup of the King, who, having dismounted, bowed most graciously, and more graciously still held out his hand to him, which Fouquet, in spite of a slight resistance on the King's part, carried respectfully to his lips. The King wished to wait in the first courtyard for the arrival of the carriages, nor had he long to wait, for the roads had been put into excellent order by the Surintendant, and a stone would hardly have been found of the size of an egg the whole way from Melun to Vaux; so that the carriages, rolling along as though on a carpet, brought the ladies to Vaux, without jolting or fatigue, by eight o'clock. They were received by Madame Fouquet, and at the moment they made their appearance, a light as bright as day burst forth from all the trees, and vases, and marble statues. This species of enchantment lasted until their Majesties had retired into the palace.

As for the King, his eyes filled with tears; he dared not look at the Queen. Anne of Austria, whose pride, as it ever had been, was superior to that of any creature breathing, overwhelmed her host by the contempt with which she treated everything handed to her. The young Queen, kind-hearted by nature and curious by disposition, praised Fouquet, ate with an exceedingly good appetite, and asked the names of the different fruits which were placed upon the table.

The King had expressly declared that so long as he remained under M. Fouquet's roof he did not wish his own different repasts to be served in accordance with the usual etiquette, and that he would, consequently, dine with the rest of the society; but, by the thoughtful attention of the Surintendant, the King's dinner was served up separately, if one may so express it, in the middle of the general table; the dinner, wonderful in every respect, from the dishes of which it was composed, comprised everything the King liked, and which he generally preferred to anything else.

As soon, however, as his hunger was appeased, the King became dull and gloomy again; the more so in proportion to the satisfaction he fancied he had manifested, and particularly on account of the deferential manner which his courtiers had shown towards Fouquet. D'Artagnan, who ate a good deal and drank but little, without allowing it to be noticed, did not lose a single opportunity, but made a great number of observations which he turned to good profit.

When the supper was finished, the King expressed a wish not to lose the promenade. The park was illuminated; the moon, too, as if she had placed herself at the orders of the lord of Vaux, silvered the trees and lakes with her bright phosphoric light. The air was soft and balmy; the gravelled walks through the thickly set avenues yielded luxuriously to the feet. The fête was complete in every respect, for the King, having met La Vallière in one of the winding paths of the wood, was able to press her by the hand and say, "I love you," without anyone overhearing him, except d'Artagnan, who followed him, and M. Fouquet who preceded him.

The night of magical enchantments stole on. The King having requested to be shown his room, there was immediately a movement in every direction. The Queens passed to their own apartments, accompanied by the music of theorbos and lutes; the King found his musketeers awaiting him on the grand flight of steps, for M. Fouquet had brought them on from Melun, and had invited them to supper. D'Artagnan's suspicions at once disappeared. He was weary, he had supped well, and wished, for once in his life, thoroughly to enjoy a fête given by a man who was in every sense of the word a king. "M. Fouquet," he said, "is the man for me."

The King was conducted with the greatest ceremony to the chamber of Morpheus, of which we owe some slight description to our readers. It was the handsomest and the largest in the palace. Lebrun had painted on the vaulted ceiling the happy, as well as disagreeable dreams with which Morpheus affects kings as well as other men. Everything that sleep gives birth to that is lovely, its perfumes, its flowers, and nectar, the wild voluptuousness or deep repose of the senses, had the painter enriched with his frescoes. It was a composition as soft and pleasing in one part as dark and gloomy and terrible in another. The poisoned chalice, the glittering dagger suspended over the head of the sleeper; wizards and phantoms with hideous masks, those half-dim shadows more terrific than the brightness of flame or the blackness of night; these, and such as these, he had made the companions of his more pleasing pictures. No sooner had the King entered the room than a cold shiver seemed to pass through him, and on Fouquet asking him the cause of it, the King replied, as pale as death,—

"I am sleepy, that is all."

"Does your Majesty wish for your attendants at once."

"No; I have to talk with a few persons first," said the King. "Will you have the goodness to tell M. Colbert I wish to see him." Fouquet bowed and left the room.

Chapter 28

A GASCON, AND A GASCON AND A HALF

D'ARTAGNAN had determined to lose no time, and in fact he never was in the habit of doing so. After having inquired for Aramis, he had looked for him in every direction until he had succeeded in finding him. Besides, no sooner had the King entered into Vaux, than Aramis had retired to his own room, meditating doubtlessly some new piece of gallant attention for His Majesty's amusement. D'Artagnan desired the servants to announce him, and found on the second story (in a beautiful room called the Blue Room, on account of the colour of its hangings) the Bishop of Vannes in company with Porthos and several of the modern epicureans. Aramis came forward to embrace his friend, and offered him the best seat. As it was after awhile generally remarked among those present that the musketeer was reserved, and wished for an opportunity for conversing secretly with Aramis, the epicureans took their leave. Porthos, however, did not stir; for true it is that having dined exceedingly well, he was fast asleep in his armchair; and the freedom of conversation therefore was not interrupted by a third person. Porthos had a deep, harmonious snore, and people might talk in the midst of its loud bass without fear of disturbing him. D'Artagnan felt that he was called upon to open the conversation.

"Do you know what idea occurred to me this evening, Aramis?"

"No; tell me what it was, for I should never be able to guess it, you have so many."

"Well, the idea occurred to me that the true King of France is not Louis XIV."

"What!" said Aramis involuntarily, looking the musketeer full in the eyes.

"No, it is Monsieur Fouquet."

Aramis breathed again, and smiled. "Ah! you are like all the rest, jealous," he said. "I would wager that it was M. Colbert who turned that pretty phrase. He comes of a mean race, does Colbert."

"Quite true."

"When I think, too," added the Bishop, "that that fellow will be your minister within four months, and that you will serve him as blindly as you did Richelieu or Mazarin——"

"And as you serve M. Fouquet," said d'Artagnan.

"With this difference, though, that M. Fouquet is not M. Colbert."

"True, true," said d'Artagnan, as he pretended to become sad and full of reflection; and then, a moment after, he added, "Why do you tell me that M. Colbert will be minister in four months?"

"Because M. Fouquet will have ceased to be so," replied Aramis.

"He will be ruined, you mean?" said d'Artagnan.

"Completely so."

"Why does he give these fêtes, then?" said the musketeer, in a tone so full of thoughtful consideration, and so well assumed, that the Bishop was for a moment deceived by it. "Why did you not dissuade him from it?"

The latter part of the phrase was just a little too much, and Aramis's former suspicions were again aroused. "It is done with the object of humouring the King."

"By ruining himself?"

"Yes, by ruining himself for the King."

"A singular calculation that."

"Necessity."

"I don't see that, dear Aramis."

"Do you not? Have you not remarked M. Colbert's daily increasing antagonism, and that he is doing his utmost to drive the King to get rid of the Surintendant?"

"One must be blind not to see it."

"And that a cabal is formed against M. Fouquet?"

"That is well known."

"What likelihood is there that the King would join a party formed against a man who will have spent everything he had to please him?"

"True, true," said d'Artagnan slowly, hardly convinced, yet curious to broach another phase of the conversation. "There are follies and follies," he resumed, "and I do not like those you are committing."

"What do you allude to?"

D'Artagnan went up to his friend, took hold of both his hands, and looking him full in the eyes, said, "Aramis, do you still care for me a very little?"

"What a question to ask!"

"Very good. One favour then. Why did you take some patterns of the King's costumes at Percerin's?"

"Come with me and ask poor Lebrun, who has been working upon them for the last two days and two nights."

"No, no; that would be too trifling a matter for you to take in hand, and it was not on that account you asked Percerin for those patterns of the King's costumes. Oh! Aramis, we are not enemies, remember, but brothers. Tell me what you wish to undertake, and upon the word of a d'Artagnan, if I cannot help you, I will swear to remain neuter."

"I am undertaking nothing," said Aramis.

"Aramis, a voice speaks within me, and seems to enlighten my darkness; it is a voice which has never yet deceived me. It is the King you are conspiring against."

"You to suspect me of wishing to assassinate the King!"

"Who spoke of that at all?" said the musketeer.

"Well, let us understand each other. I do not see what any one can do to a legitimate King as ours is, if he does not assassinate him." D'Artagnan did not say a word. "Besides, you have your guards and your musketeers here," said the Bishop.

"True."

"You are not in M. Fouquet's house, but in your own."

"True; but in spite of that, Aramis, grant me, for pity's sake, but one single word of a true friend."

"A friend's word is the truth itself. If I think of touching, even with my finger, the son of Anne of Austria, the true King of this realm of France—if I have not the firm intention of prostrating myself before his throne—if in every idea I may entertain to-morrow here at Vaux will not be the most glorious day my King ever enjoyed—may Heaven's lightning blast me where I stand!" The earnestness of his words, the studied slowness with which he pronounced them, the solemnity of his oath, gave the musketeer the most complete satisfaction. He took hold of both Aramis's hands, and shook them cordially. Aramis had endured reproaches without turning pale, and had blushed as he listened to words of praise. D'Artagnan, deceived, did him honour; but d'Artagnan, trustful and reliant, made him feel ashamed. "Are you going away?" he said as he embraced him, in order to conceal the flush on his face.

"Yes; my duty summons me. I have to get the watchword. It seems I am to be lodged in the King's ante-room. Where does Porthos sleep?"

"Take him away with you, if you like, for he snores like a park of artillery."

"Ah! he does not stay with you, then?" said d'Artagnan.

"Not the least in the world. He has his room to himself, but I don't know where!"

"Very good!" said the musketeer, from whom this separation of the two associates removed his last suspicion, and he touched Porthos lightly on the shoulder. The latter replied by a terrible yawn." Come," said d'Artagnan.

"What, d'Artagnan, my dear fellow, is that you? What a lucky chance! Oh, yes—true; I had forgotten; I am at the fêtes at Vaux."

"Hush!" said Aramis. "You are walking so heavily, you will make the flooring give way."

"True," said the musketeer; "this room is above the dome, I think."

"And I did not choose it for a fencing-room, I assure you," added the Bishop. "The ceiling of the King's room has all the sweetness and calm delights of sleep. Do not forget, therefore, that my flooring is merely the covering of his ceiling. Good-night, my friends, and in ten minutes I shall be fast asleep." And Aramis accompanied them to the door, laughing quietly all the while. As soon as they were outside, he bolted the door hurriedly; closed up the chinks of the windows, and then called out, "Monseigneur!—monseigneur!" Philippe made his appearance from the alcove, as he pushed aside a sliding panel placed behind the bed.

"You will go and take up your post at our place of observation, and watch the moment of the King's retiring to rest, so as to learn how that ceremony is performed."

"Very good. Where shall I place myself?"

"Sit down on this folding-chair. I am going to push aside a portion of the flooring; you will look through the opening, which answers to one of the false windows made in the dome of the King's apartment. Can you see?"

"Yes," said Philippe, starting as at the sight of an enemy, "I see the King!"

"What is he doing?"

"He seems to wish some man to sit down close to him."

"M. Fouquet?"

"No, no; wait a moment—"

"Look at the notes and portraits, my Prince."

"The man whom the King wishes to sit down in his presence is M. Colbert."

We have seen that Louis XIV had sent for Colbert and that Colbert had arrived. The conversation began between them by the King according to him one of the highest favours that he had ever done; it was true the King was alone with his subject. "Colbert," said he, "sit down."

The intendant, overcome with delight, for he feared he should be dismissed, refused the unprecedented honour.

"Does he accept?" said Aramis.

"No, he remains standing."

"Let us listen then." And the future King and the future Pope listened eagerly to the simple mortals whom they held under their feet, ready to crush them if they had liked.

"Colbert," said the King, "you have annoyed me exceedingly today."

"I know it, sire."

"Very good; I like that answer. Yes, you knew it, and there was courage in having done it."

"I ran the risk of displeasing your Majesty, but I risked also concealing what were your true interests from you."

"What! you were afraid of something on my account?"

"I was, sire, even if it were of nothing more than an indigestion," said Colbert; "for people do not give their sovereigns such banquets as the one of to-day, except it be to stifle them under the weight of good living." Colbert waited the effect which this coarse jest would produce upon the King; and Louis XIV, who was the vainest and most fastidiously delicate man in his kingdom, forgave Colbert the joke.

"The truth is," he said, "that M. Fouquet has given me too good a meal. Tell me, Colbert, where does he get all the money required for this enormous expenditure,—can you tell?"

"Yes, I do know, sire."

"Ah!" murmured Aramis, in the Prince's ear, who, close beside him, listened without losing a syllable, "since you are placed here, monseigneur, in order to learn your vocation of a king, listen to a piece of infamy of a nature truly royal. You are about to be a witness of one of those scenes which the foul fiend alone can conceive and execute. Listen attentively; you will find your advantage in it."

The Prince redoubled his attention, and saw Louis XIV take from Colbert's hand a letter which the latter held out to him.

"The late Cardinal's handwriting," said the King.

"Your Majesty has an excellent memory," replied Colbert, bowing; "it is an immense advantage for a King who is destined for hard work to recognise handwritings at the first glance."

"I see that it refers to money which had been given to M. Fouquet."

"Thirteen millions. A tolerably good sum."

"Yes. Well, and these thirteen millions are wanting to balance the total of the accounts. That is what I do not very well understand. How is this deficit possible?"

"Possible, I do not say; but there is no doubt about the fact that it really is so."

"Well, and consequently——"

"Well, sire, in that case, inasmuch as M. Fouquet has not yet given back the thirteen millions, he must have appropriated them to his own purposes; and with those thirteen millions one could incur four times and a little more as much expense, and make four times as great a display, as your Majesty was able to do at Fontainebleau, where we only spent three millions altogether, if you remember."

"Are you aware what is the natural consequence of all this, Monsieur Colbert?" said the King, after a few minutes' reflection.

"No, sire, I do not know."

"Well, then, the fact of the appropriation of the thirteen millions, if it can be proved——"

"But it is so already."

"I mean, if it were to be declared and certified, Monsieur Colbert."

"I think it will be to-morrow, if your Majesty——"

"Were we not under M. Fouquet's roof, you were going to say, perhaps," replied the King, with something of nobleness in his manner.

"The King is in his own palace wherever he may be, and especially in houses which his own money has paid for."

Louis XIV at last raised his eyes, and finding Colbert attentively waiting for his next remark, said, hastily changing the conversation, "Monsieur Colbert, I perceive it is getting very late, and I shall now retire to bed. By to-morrow morning I shall have made up my mind."

"Very good sire," returned Colbert, greatly incensed, although he restrained himself in the presence of the King.

The King made a gesture of adieu, and Colbert withdrew with a respectful bow. "My attendants," cried the King; and, as they entered the apartment, Philippe was about to quit his post of observation.

"A moment longer," said Aramis to him, with his accustomed gentleness of manner; "what has just now taken place is only a detail, and to-morrow we shall have no occasion to think anything more about it; but the ceremony of the King's retiring to rest, the etiquette observed in addressing the King, that indeed is of the greatest importance. Learn, sire, and study well how you ought to go to bed of a night. Look! look!"

Chapter 29

COLBERT

HISTORY will tell us, or rather history has told us, of the various events of the following day, of the splendid fêtes given by the Surintendant to his sovereign. There was nothing but amusement and delight allowed to prevail throughout the whole of the following day; there was a promenade, a banquet, a comedy to be acted.

The evening came. The King had expressed a wish not to walk in the park until after cards in the evening. In the interval between supper and the promenade, cards and dice were introduced. The King won a thousand pistoles, and, having won them, put them in his pocket, and then rose, saying, "And now, gentlemen, to the park." He found the ladies of the court already there. The King, we have before observed, had won a thousand pistoles and had put them in his pocket; but M. Fouquet had somehow contrived to lose ten thousand, so that among the courtiers there was still left a hundred and ninety thousand francs profit to divide, a circumstance which made the countenances of the courtiers and the officers of the King's household the most joyous countenances in the world. It was not the same, however, with the King's face; for, notwithstanding his success at play, to which he was by no means insensible, there still remained a slight shade of coldness. Colbert was waiting for or upon him at the corner of one of the avenues; he was most probably waiting there in consequence of a rendezvous which had been given him by the King, as Louis XIV, who had avoided him, or who had seemed to avoid him, suddenly made him a sign, and they then struck into the depths of the park together. But La Vallière, too, had observed the King's gloomy aspect and kindling glances; she had remarked this; and, as nothing which lay hidden or smouldering in his heart was impenetrable to her affection, she understood that this repressed wrath menaced some one; she prepared to withstand the current of his vengeance and intercede like an angel of mercy. Overcome by sadness, nervously agitated, deeply distressed at having been so long separated from her lover, disturbed at the sight of that emotion which she had divined, she accordingly presented herself to the King with an embarrassed aspect, which, in his then disposition of mind, the King interpreted unfavourably. Then as they were alone, or nearly alone, inasmuch as Colbert, as soon as he perceived the young girl approaching, had stopped and drawn back a dozen paces—the King advanced towards La Vallière and took her by the hand: "Mademoiselle," he said to her, "should I be guilty of an indiscretion if I were to inquire if you are indisposed? for you seem to breathe as if you were oppressed by some secret cause of uneasiness, and your eyes are filled with tears."

"Oh! sire, if I be indeed so, and if my eyes are indeed full of tears, I am sorrowful only at the sadness which seems to oppress your Majesty."

"My sadness? You are mistaken, mademoiselle; no, it is not sadness I experience."

"What is it then, sire?"

"Humiliation."

"Humiliation? oh! sire, what a word for you to use."

"I mean, mademoiselle, that whatever I may happen to be, no one else ought to be the master. Well, then, look around you on every side, and judge whether I am not eclipsed—I, the King of France—before the king of these wide domains. Oh!" he continued, clenching his hands and teeth, "when I think that this king——"

"Well, sire?" said Louise terrified.

"—That this king is a faithless, unworthy servant, who becomes proud and self-sufficient with property which belongs to me, and which he has stolen. And, therefore, am I about to change this impudent minister's fête into a sorrow and mourning, of which the nymph of Vaux, as the poets say, shall not soon lose the remembrance."

"Oh! your Majesty——"

"Well, mademoiselle, are you about to take M. Fouquet's part?" said Louis impatiently.

"No, sire; I will only ask whether you are well informed. Your Majesty has more than once learned the value of accusations made at the court."

Louis XIV made a sign for Colbert to approach. "Speak, Monsieur Colbert," said the young Prince, "for I almost believe that Mademoiselle de la Vallière has need of your assurance before she can put any faith in the King's word. Tell mademoiselle what M. Fouquet has done; and you, mademoiselle, will perhaps have the kindness to listen. It will not be long."

"Speak, monsieur," said La Vallière to Colbert, who had advanced; "speak, since the King wishes me to listen to you. Tell me, what is the crime with which M. Fouquet is charged?"

"Oh! not very heinous, mademoiselle," he returned; "a simple abuse of confidence."

"Speak, speak, Colbert; and when you shall have related it, leave us, and go and inform M. d'Artagnan that I have certain orders to give him."

"M. d'Artagnan, sire!" exclaimed La Vallière; "but why send for M. d'Artagnan? I entreat you to tell me?"

"*Pardieu!* in order to arrest this haughty, arrogant Titan, who, true to his menace, threatens to scale my heaven."

"Sire, you would be dishonouring yourself, if you were to give such an order."

"Dishonour myself!" murmured the King, turning pale with anger. "In plain truth, mademoiselle, you show a strange persistence in what you say."

"If I do so, sire, my only motive is that of serving your Majesty," replied the noble-hearted girl; "for that I would risk, I would sacrifice my very life, without the slightest reserve."

Colbert seemed inclined to grumble and complain. La Vallière, that timid, gentle lamb, turned round upon him, and with a glance like lightning, imposed silence upon him. "Monsieur," she said, "when the King acts well, whether, in doing so, he does either myself or those who belong to me, an injury, I have nothing to say; but were the King to confer a benefit either upon me or mine, and if he acted badly, I should tell him so."

"But it appears to me, mademoiselle," Colbert ventured to say, "that I too love the King."

"Yes, monsieur, we both love him, but each in a different manner," replied La Vallière, with such an accent that the heart of the young King was powerfully affected by it. "I love him so deeply, that the whole world is aware of it; so purely, that the King himself does not doubt my affection. He is my king and my master; I am the humblest of his servants. But he who touches his honour touches my life. Therefore, I repeat, that they dishonour the King who advise him to arrest M. Fouquet under his own roof."

La Vallière paused and was silent. In spite of himself, the King could not but admire her; he was overpowered by the passionate energy of her voice; by the nobleness of the cause she advocated. Colbert yielded, overcome by the inequality of the struggle. At last, the King breathed again more freely, shook his head, and held out his hand to La Vallière. "Mademoiselle," he said gently, "why do you decide against me? Do you know what this wretched fellow will do, if I give him time to breathe again?"

"Is he not a prey which will always be within your grasp?"

"And if he escapes, and takes to flight?" exclaimed Colbert.

"Well, monsieur, it will always remain on record, to the King's eternal honour, that he allowed M. Fouquet to flee; and the more guilty he may have been, the greater will the King's honour and glory appear, when compared with such misery and such shame."

Louis kissed La Vallière's hand, as he knelt before her.

"I am lost," thought Colbert; then suddenly his face brightened up again. "Oh! no, no, not yet," he said to himself.

And while the King, protected from observation by the thick covert of an enormous lime, pressed La Vallière to his breast, with all the ardour of ineffable affection, Colbert tranquilly looked among the papers in his pocket-book, and drew out of it a paper folded in the form of a letter, slightly yellow, perhaps, but which must have been very precious, since the Intendant smiled as he looked at it; he then bent a look full of hatred upon the charming group which the young girl and the King formed together—a group which was revealed for a moment, as the light of the approaching torches shone upon it. Louis noticed the light reflected upon La Vallière's white dress. "Leave me, Louise," he said, "for some one is coming."

"Mademoiselle, mademoiselle, some one is coming," cried Colbert, to expedite the young girl's departure.

Louise disappeared rapidly among the trees; and then, as the King, who had been on his knees before the young girl, was rising from his humble posture, Colbert exclaimed, "Ah! Mademoiselle de la Vallière has let something fall."

"What is it?" inquired the King.

"A paper—a letter—something white; look there, sire."

The King stooped down immediately, and picked up the letter, crumpling it in his hand as he did so; and at the same moment the torches arrived, inundating the darkness of the scene with a flood of light as bright as day.

Chapter 30

JEALOUSY

THE TORCHES we have just referred to, the eager attention which every one displayed, and the new ovation paid to the King by Fouquet, arrived in time to suspend the effect of a resolution which La Vallière had already considerably shaken in Louis XIV's heart. He looked at Fouquet with a feeling almost of gratitude for having given La Vallière an opportunity of showing herself so generously disposed, so powerful in the influence she exercised over his heart. The moment of the last and greatest display had arrived. Hardly had Fouquet conducted the King towards the château, than a mass of fire burst from the dome of Vaux, with a prodigious uproar, pouring a flood of dazzling light on every side, and illumining the remotest corners of the gardens. The fireworks began. Colbert, at twenty paces from the King, who was surrounded and fêted by the owner of Vaux, seemed, by the obstinate persistence of his gloomy thoughts, to do his utmost to recall Louis's attention, which the magnificence of the spectacle was already, in his opinion, too easily diverting. Suddenly, just as Louis was on the point of holding it out to Fouquet, he perceived in his hand the paper, which, as he believed, La Vallière had dropped at his feet as she hurried away. The still stronger magnet of love drew the Prince's attention towards the souvenir of his idol; and, by the brilliant light, which increased momentarily in beauty, and drew from the neighbouring villages loud exclamations of admiration, the King read the letter which he supposed was a loving and tender epistle which La Vallière had destined for him. But as he read it, a death-like pallor stole over his face, and an expression of deep-seated wrath, illumined by the many-coloured fires which rose brightly and soaringly around the scene, produced a terrible spectacle, which every one would have shuddered at, could they only have read into his heart, which was torn by the most stormy and most bitter passions. There was no truce for him now, influenced as he was by jealousy and mad passion. From the very moment when the dark truth was revealed to him, every gentler feeling seemed to disappear; pity, kindness of consideration, the religion of hospitality, all were forgotten. In the bitter pang which wrung his heart, he, too weak to hide his feelings, was almost on the point of uttering a cry of alarm, and calling his guards to gather round him. This letter which Colbert had thrown down at the King's feet was the same that had disappeared long ago at Fontainebleau, after the one attempt which Fouquet had made upon La Vallière's heart. Fouquet saw the King's pallor, and was far from guessing the evil; Colbert saw the King's anger, and rejoiced inwardly at the approach of the storm. Fouquet's voice drew the Prince from his wrathful reverie.

"What is the matter, sire?" inquired the Surintendant, with an expression of graceful interest.

Louis made a violent effort over himself, as he replied, "Nothing."

"I am afraid your Majesty is suffering."

"I am suffering, and have already told you so, monsieur; but it is nothing."

And the King, without waiting for the termination of the fireworks, turned towards the château. Fouquet accompanied him, and the whole court followed after them, leaving the remains of the fireworks burning for their own amusement. The Surintendant endeavoured again to question Louis XIV, but could not succeed in obtaining a reply. He imagined there had been some misunderstanding between Louis and La Vallière in the park, which had resulted in a slight quarrel; and that the King, who was not ordinarily sulky by disposition, but completely absorbed by his passion for La Vallière, had taken a dislike to every one because his mistress had shown herself offended with him. This idea was sufficient to console him; he had even a friendly and kindly smile for the young King, when the latter wished him good night. This, however, was not all the King had to submit to; he was obliged to undergo the usual ceremony, which on that evening was marked by the closest adherence to the strictest etiquette. The next day was the one fixed for the departure; it was but proper that the guests should thank their host, and should show him a little attention in return for the expenditure of his twelve millions. The only remark, approaching to amiability, which the King could find to say to M. Fouquet, as he took leave of him, was in these words, "Monsieur Fouquet, you shall hear from me. Be good enough to desire M. d'Artagnan to come here."

And the blood of Louis XIII, who had so profoundly dissimulated his feelings, boiled in his veins; and he was perfectly ready to get M. Fouquet's throat cut, with the same readiness, indeed, as his predecessor had caused the assassination of Maréchal d'Ancre; and so he disguised the terrible resolution he had formed, beneath one of those royal smiles, which are the lightning flashes indicating *coups d'état*. Fouquet took the King's hand and kissed it; Louis shuddered throughout his whole frame, but allowed M. Fouquet to touch his hand with his lips. Five minutes afterwards, d'Artagnan to whom the royal order had been communicated, entered Louis XIV's apartment. Aramis and Philippe were in theirs, still eagerly attentive, and still listening with all their ears. The King did not even give the captain of the musketeers time to approach his arm-chair, but ran forward to meet him. "Take care," he exclaimed, "that no one enters here."

"Very good, sire," replied the captain, whose glance had for a long time past analysed the ravages on the King's countenance. He gave the necessary orders at the door; but, returning to the King, he said, "Is there something fresh the matter, your majesty?"

"How many men have you here?" inquired the King, without making any other reply to the question addressed to him.

"What for, sire?"

"How many men have you, I say?" repeated the King, stamping upon the ground with his foot.

"I have the musketeers."

"Well; and what others?"

"Twenty guards and thirteen Swiss."

"How many men will be required to——"

"To do what, sire?" replied the musketeer, opening his large, calm eyes.

"To arrest M. Fouquet."

D'Artagnan fell back a step. "To arrest M. Fouquet!" he burst forth.

"Stay," said the King; "do not make his arrest a public affair."

"That will be more difficult."

"Take care of M. Fouqet, until I shall have made up mind by to-morrow morning."

"That shall be done, sire."

"And return, when I rise in the morning, for further orders; and now leave me to myself."

D'Artagnan quitted the room. The King closed the door with his own hands, and began to walk up and down his apartment at a furious pace.

Chapter 31

HIGH TREASON

THE ungovernable fury which took possession of the King at the sight and at the perusal of Fouquet's letter to La Vallière by degrees subsided into a feeling of pain and extreme weariness. Morpheus, the tutelary deity of the apartment, towards whom Louis raised his eyes, wearied by his anger and reddened by his tears, showered down upon him the sleep-inducing poppies with which his hands were filled; so that the King gently closed his eyes and fell asleep. Then it seemed to him, as it often happens in that first sleep, so light and gentle, which raises the body above the couch, the soul above the earth—it seemed to him, we say, as if the god Morpheus, painted on the ceiling, looked at him with eyes resembling human eyes; that something shone brightly, and moved to and fro in the dome above the sleeper; that the crowd of terrible dreams which thronged together in his brain, and which we interrupted for a moment, half revealed a human face, with a hand resting against the mouth, and in an attitude of deep and absorbed meditation. And strange enough, too, this man bore so wonderful a resemblance to the King himself that Louis fancied he was looking at his own face reflected in a mirror; with the exception, however, that the face was saddened by a feeling of the profoundest pity. Then it seemed to him as if the dome gradually retired, escaping from his gaze, and that the figures and attributes painted by Lebrun became darker and darker as the distance became more and more remote. A gentle, easy movement, as regular as that by which a vessel plunges beneath the waves, had succeeded to the immovableness of the bed. Doubtless the King was dreaming, and in this dream the crown of gold, which fastened the cur-

tains together, seemed to recede from his vision, just as the dome, to which
it remained suspended, had done, so that the winged genius which, with
both its hands, supported the crown, seemed, though vainly so, to call upon
the King, who was fast disappearing from it. The bed still sank. Louis,
with his eyes open, could not resist the deception of this cruel hallucina-
tion. At last, as the light of the royal chamber faded away into darkness
and gloom, something cold, gloomy, and inexplicable in its nature seemed
to infect the air. No paintings, nor gold, nor velvet hangings, were visible
any longer, nothing but walls of a dull grey colour, which the increasing
gloom made darker every moment. And yet the bed still continued to descend, and after a minute, which seemed in its duration almost an age to
the King, it reached a stratum of air, black and still as death, and then it
stopped. The King could no longer see the light in his room, except as
from the bottom of a well we can see the light of day. "I am under the
influence of a terrible dream," he thought. "It is time to awaken from it.
Come! let me wake up."

But when he said, "Come, come! wake up," he perceived that not
only was he already awake, but still more, that he had his eyes open
also; he then looked all round him. On his right hand and on his left two
armed men stood silently, each wrapped in a huge cloak and the face
covered with a mask; one of them held a small lamp in his hand, whose
glimmering light revealed the saddest picture a King could look upon.
Louis could not help saying to himself that his dream still lasted, and that
all he had to do to cause it to disappear was to move his arms or to say
something aloud; he darted from his bed, and found himself upon the
damp, moist ground. Then, addressing himself to the man who held the
lamp in his hand, he said,—

"What is this, monsieur, and what is the meaning of this jest?"

"It is no jest," replied in a deep voice the masked figure that held the
lantern.

"Do you belong to M. Fouquet?" inquired the King, greatly astonished
at his situation.

"It matters very little to whom we belong," said the phantom; "we are
your masters now; that is sufficient."

The King, more impatient than intimidated, turned to the other masked
figure. "If this is a comedy," he said, "you will tell M. Fouquet that I find
it unseemly and improper, and that I desire it should cease."

The second masked person to whom the King had addressed himself
was a man of huge stature and vast circumference. He held himself erect
and motionless as a block of marble. "Well," added the King, stamping his
foot, "you do not answer!"

"We do not answer you, my good monsieur," said the giant in a
stentorian voice, "because there is nothing to answer."

"At least tell me what you want?" exclaimed Louis, folding his arms
with a passionate gesture.

"You will know by-and-by," replied the man who held the lamp.

"In the meantime tell me where I am?"

"Look."

Louis looked all around him; but, by the light of the lamp which the masked figure raised for the purpose, he could perceive nothing but the damp walls which glistened here and there with the slimy traces of the snail. "Oh! oh! a dungeon," said the King.

"No, a subterranean passage."

"Which leads——"

"Will you be good enough to follow us?"

He shook his head, and said: "It seems I have fallen into the hands of a couple of assassins. Move on, then."

"Come," replied the figure with the lamp, with a kind of respect in his manner, and leading his prisoner towards a carriage which seemed to be waiting.

"Get in," said the same man, opening the carriage door, and letting down the step. The carriage set off immediately at a quick trot, turned into the road to Paris, and in the forest of Sénart found a relay of horses fastened to trees in the same manner as the first horses had been, and without a postilion. The man on the box changed the horses, and continued to follow the road towards Paris with the same rapidity, and entered the city about three o'clock in the morning. The carriage proceeded along the Faubourg Sainte-Antoine, and, after having called out to the sentinel, "by the King's order," the driver conducted the horses into the circular enclosure of the Bastille, looking out upon the courtyard, called La Cour du Gouvernement. There the horses drew up, reeking with sweat, at the flight of steps, and a sergeant of the guard ran forward. "Go and wake the governor," said the coachman, in a voice of thunder.

With the exception of this voice, which might have been heard at the entrance of the Faubourg Saint-Antoine, everything remained as calm in the carriage as in the prison. Ten minutes afterwards, M. de Baisemeaux appeared in his dressing-gown on the threshold of the door. "What is the matter now?" he asked, "and whom have you brought me there?"

The man with the lantern opened the carriage door, and said two or three words to the one who acted as driver, who immediately got down from his seat, took up a short musket which he kept under his feet, and place its muzzle on the prisoner's chest.

"And fire at once if he speaks!" added aloud the man who alighted from the carriage.

"Very good!" replied his companion, without any other remark.

With this recommendation, the person who had accompanied the King in the carriage ascended the flight of steps, at the top of which the governor was awaiting him. "Monsieur d'Herblay!" said the latter.

"Hush!" said Aramis. "Let us go into your room."

"Good Heavens! what brings you here at this hour?"

"A mistake, my dear Monsieur de Baisemeaux," Aramis replied quietly. "It appears that you were quite right the other day."

"What about?" inquired the governor.

"About the order of release, my dear friend."

"Tell me what you mean, monsieur—no, monseigneur," said the governor, almost suffocated by surprise and terror.

"It is a very simple affair; you remember, dear M. de. Baisemeaux, that an order of release was sent to you."

"Yes, for Marchiali."

"Very good! we both thought that it was for Marchiali."

"Certainly; you will recollect, however, that I would not believe it, but that you compelled me."

"Oh! Baisemeaux, my good fellow, what a word to make use of!—strongly recommended, that was all."

"Strongly recommended, yes; strongly recommended to give him up to you: and that you carried him off with you in your carriage."

"Well, my dear Monsieur de Baisemeaux, it was a mistake; it was discovered at the ministry, so that I now bring you an order from the King to set at liberty—Seldon, that poor Scotch fellow, you know."

"Seldon! are you sure this time?"

"Well, read it yourself," added Aramis, handing him the order.

"Why," said Baisemeaux, "this order is the very same that has already passed through my hands."

"Indeed!"

"It is the very one I assured you I saw the other evening. *Parbleu!* I recognise it by the blot of ink."

"I do not know whether it is that or not; but all I know is, that I bring it for you."

"But, then, about the other?"

"What other?"

"Marchiali?"

"I have got him here with me."

"But that is not enough for me. I require a new order to take him back again."

"Don't talk such nonsense, my dear Baisemeaux; you talk like a child! Where is the order you received respecting Marchiali?"

Baisemeaux ran to his iron chest and took it out. Aramis seized hold of it, coolly tore it in four pieces, held them to the lamp, and burnt them. "Good Heavens! what are you doing?" exclaimed Baisemeaux, in an extremity of terror.

"Look at your position a little quietly, my dear governor," said Aramis, with his imperturbable self-possession, "and you will see how very simple the whole affair is. You no longer possess any order justifying Marchiali's release."

Baisemeaux clasped his hands together. "But why, at all events, after having taken Marchiali away from me, do you bring him back again?" cried the unhappy governor, in a paroxysm of terror and completely dumbfounded.

"For a friend such as you are," said Aramis,—"for so devoted a servant,
I have no secret;" and he put his mouth close to Baisemeaux's ear, as he
said in a low tone of voice, "you know the resemblance between that
unfortunate fellow, and——"

"And the King?—yes!"

"Very good; the very first use that Marchiali made of his liberty was
to persist——Can you guess what?"

"How is it likely I should guess?"

"To persist in saying that he was the King of France; to dress himself
up in clothes like those of the King; and then pretend to assume that he
was the King himself."

"Gracious Heavens!"

"That is the reason why I have brought him back again, my dear friend.
He is mad, and lets every one see how mad he is."

"What is to be done then?"

"That is very simple; let no one hold any communication with him.
You understand, that when his peculiar style of madness came to the
King's ears, the King, who had pitied his terrible affliction, and saw how
his kindness of heart had been repaid by such black ingratitude, became
perfectly furious; so that, now—and remember this very distinctly, dear
Monsieur de Baisemeaux, for it concerns you most closely—so that there
is now, I repeat, sentence of death pronounced against all those who may
allow him to communicate with any one else but me, or the King himself.
You understand, Baisemeaux, sentence of death!"

"You need not ask me whether I understand."

"And now let us go down and conduct this poor devil back to his
dungeon again, unless you prefer he should come up here."

"What would be the good of that?"

"It would be better, perhaps, to enter his name in the prison-book at
once."

"Of course; certainly; not a doubt of it."

"In that case have him up."

Baisemeaux ordered the drums to be beaten, and the bells to be rung,
as a warning to every one to retire, in order to avoid meeting a prisoner,
about whom it was desired to observe a certain mystery. Then, when the
passages were free, he went to take the prisoner from the carriage, at
whose breast, Porthos, faithful to the directions which had been given
him, still kept his musket levelled. "Ah! is that you, miserable wretch?"
cried the governor, as soon as he perceived the King. "Very good, very
good." And immediately, making the King get out of the carriage, he led
him, still accompanied by Porthos, who had not taken off his mask, and
Aramis, who again resumed his, up the stairs, to the second Bertaudière,
and opened the door of the room in which Philippe for six long years had
bemoaned his existence. The King entered into the cell without pro-
nouncing a single word; he was pale and haggard. Baisemeaux shut the
door upon him, turned the key twice in the lock, and then returned to

Aramis. "It is quite true," he said in a low tone, "that he has a rather strong resemblance to the King; but still, less so than you said."

"So that," said Aramis, "you would not have been deceived by the substitution of the one for the other?"

"What a question!"

"You are a most valuable fellow, Baisemeaux," said Aramis; "and now, set Seldon free."

"Oh, yes. I was going to forget that. I will go and give orders at once."

"A man is light and easy enough, when he has faithfully served his King; and, in serving him, saved his country," said Porthos. "The horses will be as light as if they had nothing at all behind them. So let us be off." And the carriage, lightened of a prisoner, who might well be—as he in fact was—very heavy for Aramis, passed across the drawbridge of the Bastille, which was raised again immediately behind it.

Chapter 32

THE SHADOW OF M. FOUQUET

D'ARTAGNAN, drawing by a gesture peculiar to himself his shoulderbelt over his shoulder, went straight off to M. Fouquet, who, after he had taken leave of his guests, was preparing to retire for the night and to sleep tranquilly after the triumphs of the day. The air was still perfumed or infected, whichever way it may be considered, with the odour of the fireworks. Fouquet, almost entirely alone, was being assisted by his *valet-de-chambre* to undress, when M. d'Artagnan appeared at the entrance of the room. D'Artagnan had never been able to succeed in making himself common at the court; and notwithstanding he was seen everywhere and on all occasions, he never failed to produce an effect wherever and whenever he made his appearance. Such is the happy privilege of certain natures, which in that respect resemble either thunder or lightning; every one recognises them; but their appearance never fails to arouse surprise and astonishment, and whenever they occur the impression is always left that the last was the loudest or brightest and most violent. "What! M. d'Artagnan?" said Fouquet, who had already taken his right arm out of the sleeve of his doublet.

"At your service," replied the musketeer.

"Come in, my dear M. d'Artagnan."

"Is that your bed, there?"

"Yes; but why do you ask? Are you not satisfied with your own?"

"May I speak frankly to you?"

"Most assuredly."

"Well, then, I am not."

Fouquet started, and then replied, "Will you take my room, Monsieur d'Artagnan?"

"What! deprive you of it, monseigneur? Never!"

"What am I to do then?"

"Allow me to share yours with you."

"That is quite sufficient, Monsieur d'Artagnan," returned Fouquet, in a cold tone of voice. "It is not idly that you have acquired your reputation as a man of intelligence and full of resources; but with me that is quite superfluous. Let us two come to the point. Grant me a service. Why do you arrest me? What have I done?"

"Oh! I know nothing about what you may have done; but I do not arrest you—this evening, at least!"

"This evening!" said Fouquet, turning pale, "but to-morrow?"

"It is not to-morrow just yet, monseigneur. Who can ever answer for the morrow? If you are satisfied with what I have done, and have somewhat recovered from the shock which I prepared you for as much as I possibly could, let us allow the few hours that remain to pass away undisturbed. You are harassed, and require to arrange your thoughts; I beg you, therefore, to go to sleep, or pretend to go to sleep, either on your bed, or in your bed. I shall sleep in this arm-chair; and when I fall asleep my rest is so sound that a cannon would not wake me."

Fouquet smiled. "I except, however," continued the musketeer, "the case of a door being opened, whether a secret door, or any other; or the case of any one going out of or coming into the room. For anything like that, my ear is as quick and sensitive as possible. Any creaking noise makes me start. It arises, I suppose, from a natural antipathy to anything of the kind. Move about as much as you like; walk up and down in any part of the room; write, efface, destroy, burn—nothing like that will prevent me from going to sleep, or even prevent me from snoring; but do not touch either the key or the handle of the door! for I should start up in a moment, and that would shake my nerves terribly."

"Monsieur d'Artagnan," said Fouquet, "you are certainly the most witty and the most courteous man I ever met with; and you will leave me only one regret; that of having made your acquaintance so late."

D'Artagnan drew a deep sigh, which seemed to say, "Alas! you have perhaps made it too soon." He then settled himself in his arm-chair, while Fouquet, half lying on his bed, and leaning on his arm, was meditating upon his adventure. In this way, both of them, leaving the candles burning, awaited the first dawn of day; and when Fouquet happened to sigh too loudly, d'Artagnan only snored the louder. Not a single visit, not even from Aramis, disturbed their quietude; not a sound, even, was heard throughout the vast palace. Outside, however, the guards of honour on duty, and the patrols of the musketeers, paced up and down; and the sound of their feet could be heard on the gravel walks. It seemed to act as an additional soporific for the sleepers; while the murmuring of the wind through the trees, and the unceasing music of the fountains, whose waters fell tumbling into the basins, still went on uninterruptedly, without being disturbed at the slight noises and matters of trifling moment which constitute the life and death of human nature.

Chapter 33

THE MORNING

THE young Prince descended from Aramis's room, in the same way the King had descended from the apartment dedicated to Morpheus. The dome gradually and slowly sank down under Aramis's pressure, and Philippe stood beside the royal bed, which had ascended again after having deposited its prisoner in the secret depths of the subterranean passage. Alone, in the presence of all the luxury which surrounded him; alone, in the presence of his power; alone, with the part he was about to be forced to act, Philippe for the first time felt his heart, and mind, and soul expand beneath the influence of a thousand varied emotions, which are the vital throbs of a king's heart.

"I am now face to face with my destiny," said Philippe, with his eyes on fire, and his face lividly white. "Is it likely to be more terrifying than my captivity has been sad and gloomy? When I am compelled to follow out, at every moment, the sovereign power and authority I have usurped, shall I never cease to listen to the scruples of my heart?"

With these words, Philippe, notwithstanding an instinctive repugnance of feeling, and in spite of the shudder of terror, which mastered his will, threw himself on the royal bed, and forced his muscles to press the still warm place where Louis XIV had lain, while he buried his burning face in the handkerchief still moistened by his brother's tears. With his head thrown back and buried in the soft down of his pillow, Philippe perceived above him the crown of France, suspended, as we have stated, by angels with outspread golden wings.

Silence, the mortal enemy of restless hearts, the mortal enemy of ambitious minds, shrouded in the thickness of its gloom during the remainder of the night the future King of France, who lay there sheltered beneath his stolen crown. Towards the morning a shadow, rather than a body, glided into the royal chamber. Philippe expected his approach, and neither expressed nor exhibited any surprise.

"Well, M. d'Herblay?" he said.

"Well, sire, all is done."

"Did the governor of the Bastille suspect anything?"

"Nothing."

"And M. du Vallon?" asked Philippe, in order to change the conversation.

"He will be presented to you to-day, and confidentially will congratulate you on the danger which that conspirator has made you run."

"What is to be done with him?"

"With M. du Vallon?"

"Yes; confer a dukedom on him, I suppose."

At this moment, and in the middle of this idle conversation, under the light tone of which the two conspirators concealed their joy and pride at their mutual success, Aramis heard something which made him prick up his ears.

"What is that?" said Philippe.

"The dawn, sire."

"Well?"

"Well, before you retired to bed last night, you probably decided to do something this morning at the break of day."

"Yes, I told my captain of the musketeers," replied the young man hurriedly, "that I should expect him."

"If you told him that, he will certainly be here, for he is a most punctual man."

"Come, let us begin the attack," said the young King, resolutely.

"Be cautious, for Heaven's sake; to begin the attack, and with d'Artagnan, would be madness. D'Artagnan knows nothing, he has seen nothing; he is a hundred miles from suspecting our mystery in the slightest degree; but if he comes into this room the first this morning, he will be sure to detect something which has taken place, and which he would think his business to occupy himself about.

"Before we allow d'Artagnan to penetrate into this room, we must air the room thoroughly, or introduce so many people into it, that the keenest scent in the whole kingdom may be deceived by the traces of twenty different persons."

"But how can I send him away, since I have given him a rendezvous?" observed the Prince, impatient to measure swords with so redoubtable an antagonist.

"I will take care of that," replied the Bishop, "and in order to begin, I am going to strike a blow which will completely stupefy our man."

"He too is striking a blow, for I hear him at the door," added the Prince, hurriedly.

And, in fact, a knock at the door was heard at that moment. Aramis was not mistaken; for it was indeed d'Artagnan who adopted that mode of announcing himself.

We have seen how he passed the night in philosophising with M. Fouquet, but the musketeer was very wearied, even of feigning to fall asleep, and as soon as the dawn illumined with its pale blue light the sumptuous cornices of the Surintendant's room, d'Artagnan rose from his arm-chair, arranged his sword, brushed his coat and hat with his sleeve like a private soldier getting ready for inspection.

"Are you going out?" said Fouquet.

"Yes, monseigneur. Are you?"

"No, I shall remain."

"You give me your word?"

"Certainly."

"Very good. Besides, my only reason for going out is to try to get that reply—you know what I mean?"

And with these words, pronounced with the most affectionate graciousness of manner, the captain took leave of Fouquet in order to wait upon the King. He was on the point of leaving the room, when Fouquet said to him, "One last mark of your kindness."

"What is it, monseigneur?"

"M. d'Herblay; let me see Monsieur d'Herblay."

"I am going to try to get him to come to you."

D'Artagnan did not think himself so good a prophet. It was written that the day would pass away and realise all the predictions that had been made in the morning. He had accordingly knocked, as we have seen, at the King's door. The door opened. The captain thought that it was the King who had just opened it himself; and this supposition was not altogether inadmissable, considering the state of agitation in which he had left Louis XIV the previous evening; but instead of his royal master, whom he was on the point of saluting with the greatest respect, he perceived the long, calm features of Aramis. So extreme was his surprise, that he could hardly refrain from uttering a loud exclamation. "Aramis!" he said.

"Good morning, dear d'Artagnan," replied the prelate coldly.

"You here," stammered the musketeer.

"His Majesty desires you to report that he is still sleeping, after having been greatly fatigued during the whole night."

"Ah!" said d'Artagnan, who could not understand how the Bishop of Vannes, who had been so indifferent a favourite the previous evening, had become in half a dozen hours the largest mushroom of fortune which had ever sprung up in a sovereign's bedroom.

"And then," continued the Bishop, "as an answer to what you were coming to ask the King, my dear d'Artagnan, here is an order of His Majesty, which you will be good enough to attend to forthwith, for it concerns M. Fouquet."

D'Artagnan took the order which was held out to him.

"To be set at liberty!" he murmured. "Ah!" and he uttered a second "Ah!" still more full of intelligence than the former; for this order explained Aramis's presence with the King, and that Aramis, in order to have obtained Fouquet's pardon, must have made considerable progress in the royal favour, and that this favour explained, in its tenor, the hardly conceivable assurance with which M. d'Herblay issued the orders in the King's name. For d'Artagnan it was quite sufficient to have understood something in order to understand everything. He bowed and withdrew a couple of steps, as if he were about to leave.

"I am going with you," said the Bishop.

"Where to?"

"To M. Fouquet; I wish to be a witness of his delight."

"Ah! Aramis, how you puzzled me just now!" said d'Artagnan again.

"And you understand now, I suppose?"

"Of course I understand," he said aloud; but then added in a low tone to himself, almost hissing the words through his teeth, "No, no, I do not understand yet. But it is all the same, for here is the order for it." And then he added, "I will lead the way, monseigneur," and he conducted Aramis to Fouquet's apartments.

Chapter 34

THE KING'S FRIEND

FOUQUET was waiting with anxiety. When he saw d'Artagnan return, and when he perceived the Bishop of Vannes behind him, he could hardly restrain from his delight; it was fully equal to his previous uneasiness. The mere sight of Aramis was a complete compensation to the Surintendant for the unhappiness he had undergone in being arrested. The prelate was silent and grave; d'Artagnan completely bewildered by such an accumulation of events.

"Well, captain; so you have brought M. d'Herblay to me."

"And something better still, monseigneur."

"What is that?"

"Liberty."

"I am free!"

"Oh! yes, you can thank the Bishop of Vannes," pursued d'Artagnan, "for it is indeed to him that you owe the change that has taken place in the King."

D'Artagnan fancied he perceived that these two men had something to say to each other; he, therefore, bowed to Fouquet, and then to Aramis,—to the latter with a slight admixture of ironical respect,—and disappeared.

No sooner had he left, than Fouquet, whose impatience had hardly been able to wait for that moment, darted towards the door to close it, and then returning to the Bishop, he said, "My dear d'Herblay, I think it now high time you should explain to me what has passed, for, in plain and honest truth, I do not understand anything."

"Do you remember," said the Bishop, casting down his eyes, "the birth of Louis XIV?"

"As it were yesterday."

"Have you heard anything particular respecting his birth?"

"Nothing."

"That is where my secret begins." Aramis thereupon related the facts regarding the birth of Philippe and the incidents that took place during the previous night that ended in the substitution of the watchers and the imprisonment of Louis in the Bastille.

Fouquet uttered a thick, smothered cry, as if he had been struck by some invisible blow, and clasping his head between his clenched hands, he murmured: "You did that?"

"Cleverly enough, too; what do you think of it?"

"You dethroned the King? imprisoned him, too?"

"Yes, that has been done."

"And such an action has been committed here at Vaux?"

"Yes, here, at Vaux, in the Chamber of Morpheus. It would almost seem that it had been built in anticipation of such an act."

"And at what time did it occur?"

"Last night, between twelve and one o'clock."

Fouquet made a movement as if he were on the point of springing upon Aramis; he restrained himself. "At Vaux! under my roof!" he said, in a half-strangled voice.

"I believe so! for it is still your house, and is likely to continue so, since M. Colbert cannot rob you of it now."

"It was under my roof, then, monsieur, that you committed this crime?"

"This crime!" said Aramis stupefied.

"This abominable crime!" pursued Fouquet, becoming more and more excited; "this crime more execrable than an assassination! this crime which dishonours my name for ever, and entails upon me the horror of posterity!"

"You are not in your senses, monsieur," replied Aramis, in an irresolute tone of voice; "you are speaking too loudly; take care!"

"I will call out so loudly that the whole world shall hear me."

"Monsieur Fouquet, take care."

Fouquet turned round towards the prelate, whom he looked at full in the face. "You have dishonoured me," he said, "in committing so foul an act of treason, so heinous a crime upon my guest, upon one who was peacefully reposing beneath my roof. Oh! woe, woe, is me!"

"Woe to the man, rather, who beneath your roof meditated the ruin of your fortune, your life. Do you forget that?"

"He was my guest, my sovereign."

Aramis rose, his eyes literally bloodshot, his mouth trembling convulsively. "Have I a man out of his senses to deal with," he said.

"A man who would sooner, oh! far sooner, die; who would kill you, even, rather than allow you to complete his dishonour."

Aramis raised his head gently, and a glimmer of hope might be seen once more to animate his eyes. "Reflect, monseigneur," he said, "upon everything we have to expect. As the matter now stands, the King is still alive, and his imprisonment saves your life."

"Yes," replied Fouquet, "you may have been acting on my behalf, but I will not, do not accept your services. But first of all, I do not wish your ruin. You will leave this house."

Aramis stifled the exclamation which almost escaped his broken heart.

"I am hospitable towards all who are dwellers beneath my roof," continued Fouquet, with an air of inexpressible majesty; "you will not be more fatally lost, than he whose ruin you have consummated."

"You will be so," said Aramis, in a hoarse, prophetic voice; "you will be so, believe me."

"I accept the augury, Monsieur d'Herblay; but nothing shall prevent me, nothing shall stop me. You will leave Vaux—you must leave France; I give you four hours to place yourself out of the King's reach."

"Four hours?" said Aramis scornfully and incredulously.

"Upon the word of Fouquet, no one shall follow you before the expiration of that time. You will therefore have four hour's advance of those whom the King may wish to despatch after you."

"Four hours!" repeated Aramis, in a thick, smothered voice.

"It is more than you will need to get on board a vessel and flee to Belle-Isle, which I give you as a place of refuge."

"Ah!" murmured Aramis.

"Belle-Isle is as much mine for you, as Vaux is mine for the King. Go, d'Herblay, go! as long as I live, not a hair of your head shall be injured."

"Thank you," said Aramis, with a cold irony of manner.

"Go at once then, and give me your hand, before we both hasten away; you to save your life, I to save my honour."

Aramis withdrew from his breast the hand he had concealed there; it was stained with blood. He had dug his nails into his flesh, as if in punishment for having nursed so many projects, more vain, insensate, and fleeting than the life of man himself. Fouquet was horror-stricken, and then his heart smote him with pity. He threw open his arms as if to embrace him.

"I had no arms," murmured Aramis, as wild and terrible in his wrath as the shade of Dido. And then, without touching Fouquet's hand, he turned his head aside, and stepped back a pace or two. His last word was an imprecation, his last gesture a curse, which his blood-stained hand seemed to invoke, as it sprinkled on Fouquet's face a few drops of blood which flowed from his breast. And both of them darted out of the room by the secret staircase which led down to the inner courtyard. Fouquet ordered his best horses, while Aramis paused at the foot of the staircase which led to Porthos's apartment. He reflected profoundly and for some time, while Fouquet's carriage left the stonepaved courtyard at full gallop.

And Aramis, apprehensive of meeting any one to whom his hurried movements might appear suspicious, ascended the staircase without being perceived. Porthos, so recently returned from Paris, was already in a profound sleep; his huge body forgot its fatigue, as his mind forgot its thoughts. Aramis entered, light as a shadow, and placed his nervous grasp on the giant's shoulder. "Come, Porthos," he cried, "come."

Porthos obeyed, rose from his bed, opened his eyes, even before his intelligence seemed to be aroused.

"We are going off," said Aramis.

"Ah!" returned Porthos.

"We shall go mounted, and faster than we have ever gone in our lives."

"Ah!" repeated Porthos.

"Dress yourself, my friend."

And he helped the giant to dress himself, and thrust his gold and diamonds into his pocket. Whilst he was thus engaged, a slight noise attracted his attention, and on looking up he saw d'Artagnan watching them through the half-open door. Aramis started.

"Have you seen M. Fouquet," said Aramis to d'Artagnan.

"Yes, this very minute, in a carriage."

"What did he say to you?"

" 'Adieu'; nothing more."

"Was that all?"

"What else do you think he could say? Am I worth anything now, since you have all got into such high favour?"

"Listen," said Aramis, embracing the musketeer; "your good times are returning again. You will have no occasion to be jealous of any one."

"Ah! bah!"

"I predict that something will happen to you to-day which will increase your importance more than ever."

The two fugitives mounted their horses beneath the captain of the musketeer's eyes, who held Porthos's stirrup for him, and gazed after them until they were out of sight.

"On any other occasion," thought the Gascon, "I should say that those gentlemen are making their escape; but in these days politics seem so changed that that is what is termed going on a mission. I have no objection; let me attend to my own affairs, that is quite enough;" and he philosophically entered his apartments.

Chapter 35

SHOWING HOW THE COUNTERSIGN WAS RESPECTED AT THE BASTILLE

Fouquet tore along as fast as his horses could drag him. On his way he trembled with horror at the idea of what had just been revealed to him.

"What must have been," he thought, "the youth of those extraordinary men, who, even as age is stealing fast upon them, still are able to conceive such plans, and can carry them out without flinching?"

At one moment he could not resist the idea that all that Aramis had just been recounting to him was nothing more than a dream, and whether the fable itself was not the snare; so that when Fouquet arrived at the Bastille he might possibly find an order of arrest, which would send him to join the dethroned King. Strongly impressed with this idea, he gave certain sealed orders on his route, while fresh horses were being harnessed to his carriage. These orders were addressed to M. d'Artagnan and to certain others whose fidelity to the King was far above suspicion.

"In this way," said Fouquet to himself, "prisoner or not, I shall have performed the duty which I owe to my honour. The orders will not reach them until after my return, if I should return free, and consequently they will not have been unsealed. I shall take them back again. If I am delayed, it will be because some misfortune will have befallen me; and in that case assistance will be sent for me as well as for the King."

Prepared in this manner, the Surintendant arrived at the Bastille; he had travelled at the rate of five leagues and a half the hour.

Baisemeaux recognised Fouquet immediately. The latter followed the governor to his official residence. Baisemeaux was already trembling with shame and uneasiness. Aramis's early visit, from that moment, seemed to possess consequences which a functionary such as he (Baisemeaux) was, was perfectly justified in apprehending. It was quite another thing, however, when Fouquet, in a sharp tone of voice, and with an imperious look, said, "You have seen M. d'Herblay this morning?"

"Yes, monseigneur."

"And are you not horrified at the crime of which you have made yourself an accomplice?"

"Well," thought Baisemeaux, "good so far;" and then he added, aloud, "But what crime, monseigneur, do you allude to?"

"That for which you can be quartered alive, monsieur,—do not forget that! But this is not a time to show anger. Conduct me immediately to the prisoner."

"To Marchiali?"

"Who is Marchiali?"

"The prisoner who was brought back this morning by M. d'Herblay."

"He is called Marchiali?" said the Surintendant, his conviction somewhat shaken by Baisemeaux's cool manner.

"Yes, Marchiali. If monseigneur has come here to remove him, so much the better, for I was going to write about him."

"What has he done, then?"

"Ever since this morning he has annoyed me extremely. He has had such terrible fits of passion, as almost to make me believe that he would bring the Bastille itself down about our ears."

"I will soon relieve you of his presence," said Fouquet.

"Ah! so much the better."

"Conduct me to his prison."

"Come with me to the keep, monseigneur, you shall see Marchiali."

Fouquet darted out of the room, followed by Baisemeaux as he wiped the perspiration from his face. "What a terrible morning!" he said; "what a disgrace!"

"Walk faster," replied Fouquet.

Baisemeaux bowed his head, took the keys, and unaccompanied, except by the minister, ascended the staircase. The higher they advanced up the spiral staircase, certain smothered murmurs became distinct cries and fearful imprecations. "What is that?" asked Fouquet.

"That is your Marchiali," said the governor; "that is the way these madmen call out."

"Give me the keys at once!" cried Fouquet, tearing them from his hand. "Which is the key of the door I am to open?"

"That one."

A fearful cry, followed by a violent blow against the door, made the whole staircase resound with the echo. "Leave this place," said Fouquet to Baisemeaux, in a threatening voice.

"I ask nothing better," murmured the latter, "there will be a couple of madmen face to face, and the one will kill the other, I am sure."

"Go!" repeated Fouquet. "If you place your foot in this staircase before I call you, remember that you shall take the place of the meanest prisoner in the Bastille."

"This job will kill me, I am sure it will," muttered Baisemeaux, as he withdrew with tottering steps.

The prisoner's cries became more and more terrible. When Fouquet had satisfied himself that Baisemeaux had reached the bottom of the staircase, he inserted the key in the first lock. It was then that he heard the hoarse, choking voice of the King, crying out, in a frenzy of rage, "Help! help! I am the King." The key of the second door was not the same as the first, and Fouquet was obliged to look for it on the bunch. The King, however, furious, and almost mad with rage and passion, shouted at the top of his voice, "It was M. Fouquet who brought me here. Help me against M. Fouquet! I am the King! Help the King against M. Fouquet!"

These cries tore the minister's heart with mingled emotions. They were followed by a shower of terrible blows levelled against the door with a part of the broken chair with which the King had armed himself. Fouquet at last succeeded in finding the key. The King was almost exhausted; he could hardly articulate distinctly as he shouted, "Death to Fouquet! death to the traitor Fouquet!" The door flew open.

Chapter 36

THE KING'S GRATITUDE

THE TWO men were on the point of darting towards each other when they suddenly and abruptly stopped, as a mutual recognition took place, and each uttered a cry of horror.

"Have you come to assassinate me, monsieur?" said the King, when he recognised Fouquet.

"Sire," said Fouquet, in a voice trembling with emotion, "do you not recognise the most faithful of your friends?"

"A friend—you!" repeated Louis, gnashing his teeth in a manner which betrayed his hate and desire for speedy vengeance.

"The most respectful of your servants," added Fouquet, throwing himself on his knees.

Louis recalled to himself by the change of situation, looked at himself, and ashamed of the disordered state of his apparel, ashamed of his conduct, and ashamed of the air of pity and protection that was shown towards him, drew back. Fouquet did not understand this movement; he did not perceive that the King's feeling of pride would never forgive him for having been a witness of such an exhibition of weakness.

"Come, sire," he said, "you are free."

"Free?" repeated the King. "Oh! you set me at liberty, then, after having dared to lift up your hand against me."

"You do not believe that!" exclaimed Fouquet indignantly; "you cannot believe me to be guilty of such an act."

And rapidly, warmly even, he related the whole particulars of the intrigue, the details of which are already known to the reader. While the recital continued, Louis suffered the most horrible anguish of mind; and when it was finished, the magnitude of the danger he had run struck him far more than the importance of the secret relative to his twin brother.

"But where are these persons, then?" murmured the King.

"Your Majesty will put these men to death!" cried Fouquet.

"To the very meanest of them."

"Sire," said the Surintendant with firmness, as he raised his head proudly, "your Majesty will take the life, if you please, of your brother Philippe of France; that concerns you alone, and you will doubtless consult the Queen-Mother upon the subject. Whatever she may command will be perfectly correct. I do not wish to mix myself up in it, not even for the honour of your crown, but I have a favour to ask of you, and I beg to submit it to you."

"Speak," said the King, in no little degree agitated by his minister's last words. "What do you require?"

"The pardon of M. d'Herblay and M. du Vallon."

"Never, as long as I live," replied the inflexible King. "Do me the kindness not to speak of it again."

"Your Majesty shall be obeyed."

"And you will bear me no ill will for it?"

"Oh! no, sire; for I anticipated it as being most likely."

"You had 'anticipated' that I should refuse to forgive those gentlemen?"

"Certainly; and all my measures were taken in consequence."

"What do you mean to say?" cried the King, surprised.

"M. d'Herblay came, as may be said, to deliver himself into my hands. M. d'Herblay left to me the happiness of saving my King and my country. I could not condemn M. d'Herblay to death; nor could I, on the other hand, expose him to your Majesty's most justifiable wrath; it would have been just the same as if I had killed him myself."

"Well; and what have you done?"

"Sire, I gave M. d'Herblay the best horses in my stables, and four hours' start over all those your Majesty might, probably, despatch after him."

The King became perfectly livid; a lightning flash seemed to dart from his eyes. Fouquet felt that he was lost, but he was not one to shrink when the voice of honour spoke loudly within him. He bore the King's wrathful gaze; the latter swallowed his rage, and after a few moments' silence, said, "Are you going to return to Vaux?"

"I am at your Majesty's orders," replied Fouquet, with a low bow; "but I think that your Majesty can hardly dispense with changing your clothes previous to appearing before your court."

"We shall pass by the Louvre," said the King. "Come." And they left the prison, passing before Baisemeaux, who looked completely bewildered as he saw Marchiali once more leave; and, in his helplessness, tore out the few remaining hairs he had left. It was perfectly true, however, that Fouquet wrote and gave him an authority for the prisoner's release, and that the King wrote beneath it, "Seen and approved, Louis"; a piece of madness that Baisemeaux, incapable of putting two ideas together, acknowledged, by giving himself a terrible blow with his fist on his jaws.

Chapter 37

THE FALSE KING

IN THE meantime, usurped royalty was playing out its part bravely at Vaux. Philippe gave orders for a full reception at his *petit lever*. He determined to give this order notwithstanding the absence of M. d'Herblay, who did not return, and our readers know for what reason. But the Prince, not believing that absence could be prolonged, wished, as all rash spirits do, to try his valour and his fortune when far from all protection and all counsel. Philippe opened his folding doors, and several persons entered silently. His own memory and the notes of Aramis announced everybody to him, first of all Anne of Austria, to whom Monsieur gave his hand, and then Madame with M. de Saint-Aignan. He smiled at seeing these countenances, but trembled on recognising his mother. That figure so noble, so imposing, ravaged by pain, pleaded in his heart the cause of that famous Queen who had immolated a child to reasons of State. He found his mother still handsome. He knew that Louis XIV loved her, and he promised himself to love her likewise, and not to prove a cruel chastisement for her old age. He contemplated his brother with a tenderness easily to be understood. The latter had usurped nothing over him, had cast no shade over his life. He bowed with a friendly air to Saint-Aignan, who was all reverences and smiles, and tremblingly held out his hand to Henrietta, his sister-in-law, whose beauty struck him; but he saw in the eyes of that Princess an expression of coldness which would facilitate, as he thought, their future relations.

"What is your Majesty looking for?" said Henrietta, seeing the King's eyes constantly turning towards the door, and wishing to let fly a little poisoned arrow at his heart, supposing he was so anxiously expecting either La Vallière or a letter from her.

"My sister," said the young man, who had divined her thought, thanks to that marvellous perspicuity of which fortune was from that time about to allow him the exercise, "my sister, I am expecting a most distinguished man, a most able counsellor, whom I wish to present to you all, recommending him to your good graces. Ah! come in then, d'Artagnan."

"What does your Majesty wish?" said d'Artagnan, appearing.

"Where is monsieur the Bishop of Vannes, your friend?"

"Why, sire——"

"I am waiting for him, and he does not come. Let him be sought for."

D'Artagnan remained for an instant stupefied; but soon, reflecting that Aramis had left Vaux secretly with a mission from the King, he concluded that the King wished to preserve the secret of it. "Sire," replied he, "does your Majesty absolutely require M. d'Herblay to be brought to you?"

"Absolutely is not the word," said Philippe; "I do not want him so particularly as that; but if he can be found——"

"I thought so," said d'Artagnan to himself.

"What is all that noise?" said Philippe, turning round towards the door of the second staircase.

And a voice was heard, saying: "This way! this way! A few steps more, sire!"

"The voice of M. Fouquet," said d'Artagnan, who was standing close to the Queen-Mother.

"Then M. d'Herblay cannot be far off," added Philippe.

But he then saw what he little thought to see so near to him. All eyes were turned towards the door at which M. Fouquet was expected to enter; but it was not M. Fouquet who entered. A terrible cry resounded from all corners of the chamber, a painful cry uttered by the King and all present. It is not given to men, even to those whose destiny contains the strangest elements, and accidents the most wonderful, to contemplate a spectacle similar to that which presented itself in the royal chamber at that moment. The half-closed shutters only admitted the entrance of an uncertain light passing through large velvet curtains lined with silk. In this soft shade, the eyes were by degrees dilated, and every one present saw others rather with trust than with positive sight. There could not, however, escape, in these circumstances, one of the surrounding details; and the new object which presented itself appeared as luminous as if it had been enlightened by the sun. So it happened with Louis XIV, when he showed himself pale and frowning in the doorway of the secret stairs. The face of Fouquet appeared behind him, impressed with sorrow and sternness. The Queen-Mother, who perceived Louis XIV, and who held the hand of Philippe, uttered the cry of which we have spoken, as if she had beheld a phantom. Monsieur was bewildered, and kept turning his head in astonishment from one to the other. Madame made a step forward, thinking she saw the form of her brother-in-law reflected in a glass. And, in fact, the illusion was possible. The two princes, both pale as death—for we renounce the hope of being able to describe the fearful state of Philippe—both trembling, and, clenching their hands convulsively, measured each other with their looks, and darted their eyes like poniards, into each other. Mute, panting, bending forward, they appeared as if about to spring upon an enemy. The unheard-of resemblance of countenance, gesture, shape, height, even to the resemblance of costume, produced by chance—for Louis XIV had been to the Louvre and put on a violet-coloured dress—the perfect analogy of the two princes, completed the consternation of Anne of Austria. And yet she did not at once guess the truth. There are misfortunes in life that no one will accept; people would rather believe in the supernatural and the impossible. Suddenly Louis XIV, more impatient and more accustomed to command, ran to one of the shutters, which he opened, tearing the curtains in his eagerness. A flood of living light entered the chamber, and made Philippe draw back to the alcove. Louis seized upon this movement with eagerness, and addressing himself to the Queen,—

"My mother," said he, "do you not acknowledge your son, since every one here has forgotten his King!" Anne of Austria started, and raised her arms towards Heaven, without being able to articulate a single word.

"My mother," said Philippe, with a calm voice, "do you not acknowledge your son?" And this time, in his turn, Louis drew back.

As to Anne of Austria, struck in both head and heart with remorse, she lost her equilibrium. No one aiding her, for all were petrified, she sank back in her chair, breathing a weak, trembling sigh. Louis could not endure this spectacle and this affront. He bounded towards d'Artagnan, upon whom the vertigo was beginning to gain, and who staggered as he caught at the door for support.

"Captain!" said he, "look us in the face and say which is the paler, he or I!"

This cry roused d'Artagnan, and stirred in his heart the fibre of obedience. He shook his head, and, without more hesitation, he walked straight up to Philippe, upon whose shoulder he laid his hand, saying, "Monsieur, you are my prisoner!"

Philippe did not raise his eyes towards Heaven, nor stir from the spot, where he seemed nailed to the floor, his eye intensely fixed upon the King his brother. He reproached him by a sublime silence with all his misfortunes past, with all his tortures to come. Against this language of the soul the King felt he had no power; he cast down his eyes, dragging away precipitately his brother and sister, forgetting his mother, sitting motionless within three paces of the son whom she left a second time to be condemned to death. Philippe approached Anne of Austria, and said to her, in a soft and nobly agitated voice,—

"If I were not your son, I should curse you, my mother, for having rendered me so unhappy."

D'Artagnan felt a shudder pass through the marrow of his bones. He bowed respectfully to the young Prince, and said, as he bent, "Excuse me, monseigneur, I am but a soldier, and my oaths are his who has just left the chamber."

"Thank you, M. d'Artagnan. But what is become of M. d'Herblay?"

"M. d'Herblay is in safety, monseigneur." said a voice behind them; "and no one, while I live and am free, shall cause a hair to fall from his head."

"Monsieur Fouquet!" said the Prince, smiling sadly.

"Pardon me, monseigneur," said Fouquet, kneeling, "but he who is just gone out from hence was my guest."

"Here are," murmured Philippe, with a sign, "brave friends and good hearts. They make me regret the world. On, M. d'Artagnan, I follow you."

At the moment the captain of the musketeers was about to leave the room with his prisoner, Colbert appeared, and, after remitting an order from the King to d'Artagnan, retired. D'Artagnan read the paper, and then crushed it in his hand with rage.

"What is it?" asked the Prince.

"Read, monseigneur," replied the musketeer.

Philippe read the following words, hastily traced by the hand of the King:—"M. d'Artagnan will conduct the prisoner to the Iles Sainte-Marguerite. He will cover his face with an iron visor, which the prisoner cannot raise without peril of his life."

"That is just," said Philippe, with resignation, "I am ready."

"Aramis was right," said Fouquet, in a low voice to the musketeer; "this one is quite as much of a king as the other."

"More!" replied d'Artagnan. "He only wants you and me."

Chapter 38

IN WHICH PORTHOS THINKS HE IS PURSUING A DUCHY

ARAMIS and Porthos, having profited by the time granted them by Fouquet, did honour to the French cavalry by their speed. Porthos did not clearly understand for what kind of mission he was forced to display so much velocity; but as he saw Aramis spurring on furiously, he, Porthos, spurred on in the same manner.

Thus travelled they on for eight long hours, and then arrived at Orleans. It was four o'clock in the afternoon. Aramis, on observing this, judged that nothing demonstrated pursuit to be possible. It would be without example that a troop capable of taking him and Porthos should be furnished with relays sufficient to perform forty leagues in eight hours. Thus, admitting pursuit, which was not at all manifest, the fugitives were five hours in advance of their pursuers.

Aramis thought that there might be no imprudence in taking a little rest, but that to continue would make the matter more certain. Twenty leagues more, performed with the same rapidity, twenty more leagues devoured, and no one, not even d'Artagnan, could overtake the enemies of the King. Aramis felt obliged, therefore, to inflict upon Porthos the pain of mounting on horseback again. They rode on till seven o'clock in the evening, and had only one post more between them and Blois. But here a diabolical accident alarmed Aramis greatly. There were no horses at the post. The prelate asked himself by what infernal machination his enemies had succeeded in depriving him of the means of going farther,—he who never recognised chance as a deity, he who found a cause for every result, he preferred believing that the refusal of the postmaster, at such an hour in such a country, was the consequence of an order emanating from above; an order given with a view of stopping short the king-maker in the midst of his flight. But at the moment he was about to fly into a passion, so as to procure either a horse or an explanation, he was struck with the recollection that the Comte de la Fère lived in the neighbourhood.

"I am not travelling," said he; "I do not want horses for a whole stage. Find me two horses to go and pay a visit to a nobleman of my acquaintance who resides near this place."

"What nobleman?" asked the postmaster.

"M. le Comte de la Fère."

"Oh!" replied the postmaster, uncovering with respect, "a very worthy nobleman. But, whatever may be my desire to make myself agreeable to him, I cannot furnish you with horses, for all mine are engaged by M. le Duc de Beaufort."

"Indeed!" said Aramis, much disappointed.

"Only," continued the postmaster, "if you will put up with a little carriage I have, I will harness an old blind horse, who has still his legs left, and will draw you to the house of M. le Comte de la Fère."

"That is worth a louis," said Aramis.

"No, monsieur, that is never worth more than a crown; that is what M. Grimaud, the Comte's intendant, always pays me when he makes use of that carriage; and I should not wish the Comte de la Fère to have to reproach me with having imposed on one of his friends."

"As you please," said Aramis, "particularly as regards disobliging the Comte de la Fère; only I think I have a right to give you a louis for your idea."

"Oh! doubtless!" replied the postmaster, with delight. And he himself harnessed the old horse to the creaking carriage. In the meanwhile Porthos was curious to behold. He imagined he had discovered the secret, and he felt pleased, because a visit to Athos, in the first place, promised him much satisfaction, and, in the next, gave him the hopes of finding at the same time a good bed and a good supper. The master, having got the carriage ready, ordered one of his men to drive the strangers to La Fère. Porthos took his seat by the side of Aramis, whispering in his ear, "I understand."

"Ah! ah!" said Aramis, "and what do you understand, my friend?"

"We are going, on the part of the King, to make some great proposal to Athos."

"Pooh!" said Aramis.

"You need tell me nothing about it," added the worthy Porthos, endeavouring to place himself so as to avoid the jolting, "you need tell me nothing, I shall guess."

"Well! do, my friend; guess away."

They arrived at Athos's dwelling about nine o'clock in the evening, favoured by a splendid moon. This cheerful light rejoiced Porthos beyond expression; but Aramis appeared annoyed by it in an equal degree. He could not help showing something of this to Porthos, who replied. "Ay, ay! I guess how it is! the mission is a secret one."

These were his last words in the carriage. The driver interrrupted him by saying, "Gentlemen, you are arrived."

Athos and Raoul were, as usual, conversing, and walking backwards and forwards in the long alley of limes in the park, when the bell which served to announce to the Comte either the hour of dinner or the arrival of a visitor was rung; and, without attaching any importance to it, he turned towards the house with his son; and at the end of the alley they found themselves in the presence of Aramis and Porthos.

Chapter 39

THE LAST ADIEUX

RAOUL uttered a cry, and affectionately embraced Porthos. Aramis and Athos embraced like old men; and this embrace itself being a question for Aramis, he immediately said, "My friend, we have not long to remain with you."

"Ah!" said the Comte.

"Only time to tell you of my good fortune," interrupted Porthos.

"Ah!" said Raoul.

Athos looked silently at Aramis, whose sombre air had already appeared to him very little in harmony with the good news Porthos spoke of.

"What is the good fortune that has happened to you? Let us hear it," said Raoul, with a smile.

"The King has made me a duke," said the worthy Porthos, with an air of mystery, in the ear of the young man, "a duke by brevet."

But the asides of Porthos were always loud enough to be heard by everybody. His murmurs were in the diapason of ordinary roaring. Athos heard him, and uttered an exclamation which made Aramis start. The latter took Athos by the arm, and, after having asked Porthos's permission to say a word to his friend in private, "My dear Athos," he began, "you see me overwhelmed with grief."

"With grief, my dear friend?" cried the Comte; "oh, what!"

"In two words. I have raised a conspiracy against the King; that conspiracy has failed, and, at this moment, I am doubtless pursued."

"You are pursued!—a conspiracy! Eh! my friend, what do you tell me?"

"A sad truth. I am entirely ruined."

"Well, but Porthos—this title of duke—what does all that mean?"

"That is the subject of my severest pain; that is the deepest of my wounds. I have, believing in an infallible success, drawn Porthos into my conspiracy. He has thrown himself into it, as you know he would do, with all his strength, without knowing what he was about; and now, he is as much compromised as myself—as completely ruined as I am."

"Good God!" And Athos turned towards Porthos, who was smiling complacently.

"You are taking him away; whither?"

"To Belle-Isle, at first. That is an impregnable place of refuge. Then I have the sea, and a vessel to pass over into England, where I have many relations."

"You? in England?"

"Yes, or else into Spain, where I have still more."

"But, our excellent Porthos! you ruin him, for the King will confiscate all his property."

"All is provided for. I know how, when once in Spain, to reconcile myself with Louis XIV, and restore Porthos to favour."

"You have credit, seemingly, Aramis," said Athos, with a discreet air.

"Much; and at the service of my friends."

These words were accompanied by a warm pressure of the hand.

"Thank you," replied the Comte.

"And while we are on that head," said Aramis, "you also are a malcontent; you also, Raoul, have griefs to lay to the King. Follow our example; pass over into Belle-Isle."

"No; for my part I prefer having something to reproach the King with; it is a pride natural to my race to pretend to a superiority over royal races. Doing what you propose, I should become the obliged of the King; I should certainly be a gainer on that ground, but I should be a loser in my conscience.—No, thank you!"

Raoul was gone out to give orders for the saddling of the horses. The group was already divided. Athos saw his two friends on the point of departure, and something like a mist passed before his eyes, and weighed upon his heart.

"It is strange," thought he; "whence comes the inclination I feel to embrace Porthos once more?" At that moment Porthos turned round, and he came towards his old friend with open arms. This last endearment was tender as in youth, as in times when the heart was warm and life happy. And then Porthos mounted his horse. Aramis came back once more to throw his arms round the neck of Athos. The latter watched them along the high road, elongated by the shade, in their white cloaks. Like two phantoms, they seemed to be enlarged on departing from the earth, and it was not in the mist, but in the declivity of the ground that they disappeared. At the end of the perspective, both seemed to have given a spring with their feet, which made them vanish as if evaporated into the clouds.

Then Athos, with an oppressed heart, returned towards the house, saying to Bragelonne, "Raoul, I don't know what it is that has just told me that I have seen these two men for the last time."

Raoul shook his head sadly, and leant upon the shoulder of the Comte, without either of them finding another word in their hearts, which were ready to overflow.

All at once a noise of horses and voices, from the extremity of the road to Blois, attracted their attention that way. Flambeaux-bearers shook their torches merrily among the trees of their route, and turned round, from time to time, to avoid distancing the horsemen who followed them. These flames, this noise, this dust of a dozen richly caparisoned horses, formed a strange contrast in the middle of the night with the melancholy funeral disappearance of the two shadows of Aramis and Porthos. Athos went towards the house; but he had hardly reached the parterre, when the entrance gate appeared in a blaze; all the flambeaux stopped and appeared to enflame the road. A cry was heard of "M. le Duc de Beaufort"—and Athos sprang towards the door of his house. But the Duc had already alighted from his horse, and was looking around him.

"I am here, monseigneur," said Athos.

"Ah! good evening, dear Comte," said the Prince, with that frank cordiality which won him so many hearts. "Is it too late for a friend?"

"Ah! my dear Prince—come in!" said the Comte.

And, M. de Beaufort leaning on the arm of Athos, they entered the house, followed by Raoul, who walked respectfully and modestly among the officers of the Prince, with several of whom he was acquainted.

Chapter 40

MONSIEUR DE BEAUFORT

The Prince turned round at the moment when Raoul, in order to leave him alone with Athos, was shutting the door, and preparing to go with the other officers into an adjoining apartment.

"Is that the young man I have heard M. le Prince speak so highly of?" asked M. de Beaufort.

"It is, monseigneur."

"*Ma foi!* he is tall and handsome!" continued the Duke. "Will you give him to me, monseigneur, if I ask him of you?"

"How am I to understand you, monseigneur?" said Athos.

"I am going to become an African Prince,—a Bedouin gentleman. The King is sending me to make conquests among the Arabs."

"What do you tell me, monseigneur?"

"Strange, is it not? I, Parisian of the Parisians,—I, who have reigned in the faubourgs, and have been called King of the *Halles*,—I am going to pass from the Place Maubert to the minarets of Gigelli; I become from a *Frondeur* an adventurer!"

"Oh, monseigneur, if you did not yourself tell me that—"

"And can you believe, just and simple man as you are, that if I go into Africa for this ridiculous motive, I will not endeavour to come out of it without ridicule? Will I not give the world cause to speak of me? And to be spoken of, nowadays, when there are M. le Prince, M. de Turenne, and many others, my contemporaries, I, admiral of France, grandson of Henry IV, King of Paris, have I anything left but to get myself killed? *Cordieu!* I will be talked of, I tell you; I shall be killed, whether or not; if not there, somewhere else."

"Why, monseigneur, this is only exaggeration; and hitherto you have demonstrated nothing of that kind but in bravery."

"But, what is this, Comte, only one glass?"

"I should not think of drinking with your Highness, unless your Highness permitted me," replied Athos, with noble humility.

"*Cordieu!* you were right to bring only one glass, we will both drink out of it, like two brothers in arms. Begin, Comte."

"Do me the honour," said Athos, gently putting back the glass.

"You are a charming friend," replied the Duc de Beaufort, who drank, and passed the goblet to his companion. "But that is not all," continued he, "I am still thirsty, and I wish to do honour to this handsome young man who stands here. I carry good luck with me, Vicomte," said he to Raoul; "wish for something while drinking out of my glass, and the plague stifle me if what you wish does not come to pass!" He held the goblet to Raoul, who hastily moistened his lips, and replied with the same promptitude:

"I have wished for something, monseigneur." His eyes sparkled with a gloomy fire, and the blood mounted to his cheeks; he terrified Athos, if only with his smile.

"And what have you wished for?" replied the Duc, sinking back into his chair, whilst with one hand he returned the bottle to Grimaud, and with the other gave him a purse.

"Will you promise me, monseigneur, to grant me what I wish for?"

"*Pardieu!* That is agreed upon!"

"I wished, Monsieur le Duc, to go with you."

"Well! *mordieu!*" cried the Duc, "the young Vicomte is right! What can he do here? He will rot with grief."

Raoul blushed, and the excitable Prince continued: "War is a distraction; we gain everything by it; we can only lose one thing by it: life;—then so much the worse!"

"That is to say, memory," said Raoul eagerly; "and that is to say, so much the better."

"Well, come," said the Duc, "let us see! Shall he go, or shall he not? If he goes, Comte, he shall be my aide-de-camp, my son."

"Monseigneur!" cried Raoul, bending his knee.

"Monseigneur!" cried Athos, taking the hand of the Duc; "Raoul shall do just as he likes."

"Oh! no, monsieur, just as you like," interrupted the young man.

"Comte, I shall set off in two days for Toulon," said M. de Beaufort. "Will you meet me there in a fortnight?"

"I will have the honour of thanking you there, my Prince, for all your kindnesses," replied the Comte.

"Here is your commission," said the Prince to Raoul. "I had prepared it, reckoning upon you. You will go on before me as far as Antibes."

"Yes, monseigneur."

"Here is the order." And de Beaufort gave Raoul the order. "Do you know anything of the sea?"

"Yes, monseigneur; I have travelled with M. le Prince."

"That is well; all these barges and lighters must be in attendance to form an escort, and carry my provisions. The army must be prepared to embark in a fortnight at latest."

"That shall be done, monseigneur."

"The present order gives you the right to visit and search all the isles along the coast; you will there make the enrolments and levies you may want for me."

"Yes, Monsieur le Duc."

"And as you are an active man, and will work freely, you will spend much money."

"I hope not, monseigneur."

"But I reckon you will. My intendant has prepared orders of a thousand livres, drawn upon the cities of the south; he will give you a hundred of them. Now, dear Vicomte, begone."

Athos interrupted the Prince. "I shall go with Raoul; the mission with which you charge him is a troublesome and difficult one. Alone it would be too much for him to execute. You do not observe, monseigneur, you have given him a command of the first order."

"That may be true. But, when people resemble him, do they not do all that is required of them?"

"Monseigneur, I believe you will find nowhere so much zeal and intelligence, so much real bravery, as in Raoul; but if he failed in your embarkation, you would only meet with what you deserve."

Chapter 41

THE SILVER DISH

THE journey passed off pretty well. Athos and his son traversed France at the rate of fifteen leagues per day; sometimes more, sometimes less, according to the intensity of Raoul's grief. Athos learned that d'Artagnan had been seen at Antibes, and the Comte was eager to see his old friend before Raoul was due to embark. Raoul was much affected at not meeting with d'Artagnan. His affectionate heart longed to take a farewell and receive consolation from that heart of steel. Athos knew from experience that d'Artagnan became impenetrable when engaged in any serious affair, whether on his own account, or in the service of the King. He even feared to offend his friend, or thwart him by too pressing inquiries. And yet when Raoul commenced his labour of classing the flotilla, and got together the lighters to send them to Toulon, one of the fishermen told the Comte that his boat had been laid up to refit since a trip he had made on account of a gentleman who was in great haste to embark. Athos, believing that this man was telling a falsehood in order to be left at liberty to fish, and so gain more money when all his companions were gone, insisted upon having the details. The fisherman informed him that six days previously a man had come in the night to hire his boat, for the purpose of visiting the island of St. Honorat. The price was agreed upon, but the gentleman had arrived with an immense carriage case, which he insisted upon embarking, in spite of all the difficulties which opposed themselves to that operation. The fisherman had wished to retract. He had even threatened, but his threats had procured him nothing but a shower of blows from the gentleman's cane, which fell upon his shoulders sharp and long. Swearing and grumbling, he had recourse to the syndic of his brotherhood at Antibes, who administer justice among themselves and protect each other; but the gentleman had exhibited a certain paper, at the sight of which the syndic, bowing to the very ground, had enjoined obedience from the fisherman, and abused him for having been refractory. They then departed with the freight.

"But all this does not tell us," said Athos, "how you have injured your boat."

"This is the way. I was steering towards St. Honorat as the gentleman had desired me; but he changed his mind, and pretended that I could not pass to the south of the abbey."

"And why not?"

"Because, monsieur, there is in front of the square tower of the Benedictines, towards the southern point, the bank of the *Moines.*"

"A rock?" asked Athos.

"Level with the water, and below the water; a dangerous passage, but one I have cleared a thousand times; the gentleman required me to land him at Sainte-Marguerite's."

"Well?"

"Well, monsieur!" cried the fisherman, with his Provençal accent, "a man is a sailor, or he is not; he knows his course, or he is nothing but a fresh-water lubber. I was obstinate, and wished to try the channel. The gentleman took me by the collar, and told me quietly he would strangle me. My mate armed himself with a hatchet, and so did I. We had the affront of the night before to pay him out for. But the gentleman drew his sword, and used it in such an astonishingly rapid manner, that we neither of us could get near him. I was about to hurl my hatchet at his head, and I had a right to do so, hadn't I, monsieur? for a sailor aboard is master, as a citizen is in his chamber; I was going, then, in self-defence, to cut the gentleman in two, when all at once—believe me or not, monsieur—the great carriage case opened of itself, I don't know how, and there came out of it a sort of a phantom, his head covered with a black helmet and a black mask, something terrible to look upon, which came towards me threatening with its fists."

"And that was——" said Athos.

"That was the devil, monsieur; for the gentleman, with great glee, cried out on seeing him: 'Ah! thank you, monseigneur!'"

"A strange story!" murmured the Comte, looking at Raoul.

"And what did you do?" asked the latter of the fisherman.

"You must know, monsieur, that two poor men, such as we are, could be no match for two gentlemen; but when one of them is the devil we had no chance! My companion and I did not stop to consult one another; we made but one jump into the sea, for we were within seven or eight hundred feet of the shore."

"Well, and then?"

"Why, and then, monsieur, as there was a little wind from the south-west, the boat drifted into the sands of Sainte-Marguerite's."

"Oh!—but the two travellers?"

"Bah! you need not be uneasy about them! It was pretty plain that one was the devil, and protected the other; for when we recovered the boat, after she got afloat again, instead of finding these two creatures injured by the shock, we found nothing, not even the carriage or the case."

"We will go to Sainte-Marguerite's, shall we?" said the Comte to Bragelonne, as the man walked away.

"Yes, monsieur, for there is something to be cleared up; that man does not seem to me to have told the truth."

"Nor to me neither, Raoul. The story of the masked man and the carriage having disappeared may be told to conceal some violence these fellows have committed upon their passenger in the open sea, to punish him for his persistence in embarking."

"I formed the same suspicion; the carriage was more likely to contain property than a man."

"We shall see to that, Raoul. This gentleman very much resembles d'Artagnan; I recognise his mode of proceeding. Alas! we are no longer the young invincibles of former days. Who knows whether the hatchet or the iron bar of this miserable coaster has not succeeded in doing that which the best blades of Europe, balls, and bullets have not been able to do in forty years?"

That same day they set out for Sainte-Marguerite's, on board a lugger, come from Toulon under orders. The impression they felt on landing was a singularly pleasing one. The isle was full of flowers and fruits. Flat, offering nothing but a tiny bay for the convenience of embarkation, and under the protection of the governor, who went shares with them, smugglers made use of it as a provisional depot, at the expense of not killing the game or devastating the garden. With this compromise, the governor was in a situation to be satisfied with a garrison of eight men to guard his fortress, in which twelve cannons accumulated their coats of mouldy green. The governor was a sort of happy farmer, harvesting wines, figs, oil, and organes, preserving his citrons and lemons within his sunny casemates.

Athos and Raoul wandered for some time round the fences of the garden without finding any one to introduce them to the governor. They ended by making their own way into the garden. It was at the hottest time of the day. Everything sought shelter beneath grass or stone. Athos saw nothing living but a soldier, upon the terrace between the second and third court, who was carrying a basket of provisions on his head. This man returned almost immediately without his basket, and disappeared in the shade of his sentry-box. Athos supposed this man must have been carrying dinner to some one, and, after having done so, returned to dine himself. All at once they heard some one call out, and raising their heads, perceived in the frame of the bars of a window something of a white colour, like a hand that was waved backwards and forwards—something shining, like a polished weapon struck by the rays of the sun. And before they were able to ascertain what it was they saw, a luminous train, accompanied by a hissing sound in the air, called their attention from the donjon to the ground. A second dull noise was heard from the ditch, and Raoul ran to pick up a silver plate which was rolling along the dry sand. The hand which had thrown this plate made a sign to the two gentlemen, and then disappeared. Athos and Raoul, approaching each other, commenced an attentive examination of the dusty plate, and they discovered, in characters traced upon the bottom of it with the point of a knife, this inscription:

"*I am the brother of the King of France—a prisoner to-day—a madman to-morrow. French gentlemen and Christians, pray to God for the soul and the reason of the son of your masters.*"

The plate fell from the hands of Athos whilst Raoul was endeavouring to make out the meaning of these dismal words. At the same instant they heard a cry from the top of the donjon. As quick as lightning, Raoul bent down his head and forced down that of his father likewise. A musket barrel glittered from the crest of the wall. A white smoke floated like a plume from the mouth of the musket, and a ball was flattened against a stone within six inches of the two gentlemen.

"*Cordieu!*" cried Athos. "What, are people assassinated here? Come down, cowards as you are!"

"Yes, come down!" cried Raoul, furiously shaking his fist at the castle.

One of the assailants—he who was about to fire—replied to these cries by an exclamation of surprise; and, as his companion, who wished to continue the attack, had seized his loaded musket, he who had cried out, threw up the weapon, and the ball flew into the air. Athos and Raoul seeing them disappear from the platform, expected they would come to them, and waited with a firm demeanour. Five minutes had not elapsed, when a stroke upon a drum called the eight soldiers of the garrison to arms, and they showed themselves on the other side of the ditch with their muskets in hand. At the head of these men was an officer, whom Athos and Raoul recognised as the one who had fired the first musket. The man ordered the soldiers to "make ready."

"We are going to be shot!" cried Raoul; "but, sword in hand, at least, let us leap the ditch! We shall kill at least two of these scoundrels when their muskets are empty." And, suiting the action to the word, Raoul was springing forward, followed by Athos, when a well-known voice resounded behind them—"Athos! Raoul!"

"D'Artagnan!" replied the two gentlemen.

"Recover arms! *Mordioux!*" cried the captain to the soldiers, "I was sure I could not be mistaken."

The governor came up, having crossed the ditch upon a plank bridge. "Well!" said he to d'Artagnan, "what stops us?"

"You are Spaniards—you do not understand a word of French," said the captain eagerly, to his friends, in a low vioce.

"Well!" replied he, addressing the governor, "I was right; these gentlemen are two Spanish captains with whom I was acquainted at Ypres, last year; they don't know a word of French."

"Ah!" said the governor sharply. "And yet they were trying to read the inscription on the plate."

D'Artagnan took it out of his hands, effacing the characters with the point of his sword.

"How!" cried the governor—"what are you doing? I cannot read them now!"

"It is a State secret," replied d'Artagnan bluntly; "and as you know that, according to the King's order, it is under the penalty of death any one should penetrate it, I will, if you like, allow you to read it, and have you shot immediately afterwards."

During this apostrophe—half serious, half ironical—Athos and Raoul preserved the coolest, most unconcerned silence.

"But, is it possible," said the governor, "that these gentlemen do not comprehend at least some words?"

"Suppose they do! If they do understand a few spoken words, it does not follow that they should understand what is written. They cannot even read Spanish. A noble Spaniard, remember, ought never to know how to read."

The governor was obliged to be satisfied with these explanations, but he was still tenacious. "Invite these gentlemen to come to the fortress," said he.

"That I will willingly do. I was about to propose it to you." The fact is, the captain had quite another idea, and would have wished his friends a hundred leagues off. But he was obliged to make the best of it. He addressed the two gentlemen in Spanish, giving them a polite invitation, which they accepted. They all turned towards the entrance of the fort, and the incident being exhausted, the eight soldiers returned to their delightful leisure for a moment disturbed by this unexpected adventure.

Chapter 42

CAPTIVE AND JAILERS

WHEN they had entered the fort, and whilst the governor was making some preparations for the reception of his guests—"Come," said Athos, "let us have a word of explanation whilst we are alone."

"It is simply this," replied the musketeer. "I have conducted hither a prisoner, who the King commands shall not be seen. You came here, he has thrown something to you through the lattice of his window; I was at dinner with the governor, I saw the object thrown, and I saw Raoul pick it up. It does not take long to understand this. I understood it; and I thought you in intelligence with my prisoner. And then——"

"And then—you commanded us to be shot."

"*Ma foi!* I admit it; but if I was the first to seize a musket, fortunately I was the last to take aim at you."

"If you had killed me, d'Artagnan, I should have had the good fortune to die for the royal house of France, and it would be an honour to die by your hand—you, its noblest and most loyal defender."

"What the devil, Athos, do you mean by the royal house?" stammered d'Artagnan. "You don't mean that you, a well-informed and sensible man, can place any faith in the nonsense written by an idiot?"

"I do believe in it."

"With so much the more reason, my dear Chevalier, from your having orders to kill all those who do believe in it," said Raoul.

"That is because," replied the captain of the musketeers,—"because every calumny, however absurd it may be, has the almost certain chance of becoming popular."

"No, d'Artagnan," replied Athos promptly; "but because the King is not willing that the secret of his family should transpire among the people, and cover with shame the executioners of the son of Louis XIII."

"Do not talk in such a childish manner, Athos, or I shall begin to think you have lost your senses. Besides, explain to me how it is possible Louis XIII should have a son in the Isle of Sainte-Marguerite?"

"A son whom you have brought hither masked, in a fishing boat," said Athos. "Why not?"

D'Artagnan was brought to a pause.

"Ah! ah!" said he; "whence do you know that a fishing boat——"

"Brought you to Sainte- Marguerite's with the carriage containing the prisoner—with a prisoner whom you styled monseigneur. Oh! I am acquainted with all that," resumed the Comte. D'Artagnan bit his moustache.

"If it were true," said he, "that I had brought hither in a boat, and with a carriage, a masked prisoner, nothing proves that this prisoner must be a prince—a prince of the house of France?"

"Oh! ask that of Aramis," replied Athos coolly.

"Of Aramis!" cried the musketeer, quite at a stand. "Have you seen Aramis?"

"After his discomfiture at Vaux, yes; I have seen Aramis, a fugitive, pursued, ruined; and Aramis has told me enough to make me believe in the complaints that this unfortunate young man cut upon the bottom of the plate."

D'Artagnan's head sank upon his breast with confusion. "This is the way," said he, "in which God turns to nothing that which men call their wisdom! A fine secret must that be of which twelve or fifteen persons hold the tattered fragments! Athos, cursed be the chance which has brought you face to face with me in this affair! for now——"

"Well!" said Athos, with his customary mild severity, "is your secret lost because I know it? Consult your memory, my friend. Have I not borne secrets as heavy as this?"

"You have never borne one so dangerous," replied d'Artagnan, in a tone of sadness. "I have something like a sinister idea that all who are concerned with this secret will die, and die unfortunately."

"The will of God be done!" said Athos, "but here is your governor."

D'Artagnan and his friends immediately resumed their parts. The governor, suspicious and hard, behaved towards d'Artagnan with a politeness almost amounting to obsequiousness. With respect to the travellers, he contented himself with offering them good cheer, and never taking his eye from them. Athos and Raoul observed that he often tried to embarrass them by sudden attacks, or to catch them off their guard; but neither the one nor the other gave him the least advantage. What d'Artagnan had said was probable, if the governor did not believe it to be quite true. They rose from table to repose awhile.

"What is this man's name? I don't like the looks of him," said Athos to d'Artagnan, in Spanish.

"De Saint-Mars," replied the captain.

"Ask these gentlemen," interrupted the governor, "what was their purpose in coming to Sainte-Marguerite?"

"They came from learning there was a convent of Benedictines at Sainte-Honorat which is considered curious; and from being told there was excellent shooting in the island."

M. de Saint-Mars went to make his rounds, and left d'Artagnan alone with the pretended Spaniards.

"And now," said the musketeer, "answer me the question put to you by that black-looking Saint-Mars: 'What did you come to do at the Lerin Isles?'"

"To bid you farewell."

"Bid me farewell! What do you mean by that? Is Raoul going anywhere?"

"Yes."

"Then I will lay a wager it is with M. de Beaufort?"

"With M. de Beaufort it is, my dear friend; you always guess rightly."

"From habit."

As they were passing over the ramparts to a gallery of which d'Artagnan had the key, they saw M. de Saint-Mars directing his steps towards the chamber inhabited by the prisoner. Upon a sign from d'Artagnan they concealed themselves in an angle of the staircase.

"What is it?" said Athos.

"You will see. Look. The prisoner is returning from chapel."

And they saw, by the red flashes of the lightning against the violet fog which the wind stamped upon the bankward sky, they saw pass gravely, at six paces behind the governor, a man clothed in black, and masked by a visor of polished steel, soldered to a helmet of the same nature, which altogether enveloped the whole of his head. The fire of the heavens cast red reflections upon the polished surface, and these reflections, flying off capriciously, seemed to be angry looks launched by this unfortunate, instead of imprecations. In the middle of the gallery the prisoner stopped for a moment, to contemplate the infinite horizon, to respire the sulphurous perfumes of the tempest, to drink in thirstily the hot rain, and to breathe a sigh resembling a smothered roar.

"Come on, monsieur," said Saint-Mars sharply to the prisoner, for he had already become uneasy at seeing him look so long beyond the walls. "Monsieur, come on!"

"Say monseigneur!" cried Athos, from his corner, with a voice so solemn and terrible, that the governor trembled from head to foot. Athos insisted upon respect being paid to fallen majesty. The prisoner turned round.

"Who spoke?" asked Saint-Mars.

"It was I," replied d'Artagnan, showing himself promptly. "You know that is the order."

"Call me neither Monsieur nor Monseigneur," said the prisoner in his turn, in a voice that penetrated to the very soul of Raoul; "call me ACCURSED!" He passed on, and the iron door creaked after him.

"That is truly an unfortunate man!" murmured the musketeer in a hollow whisper, pointing out to Raoul the chamber inhabited by the Prince.

Chapter 43

PROMISES

SCARCELY had d'Artagnan re-entered his apartment with his two friends, than one of the soldiers of the fort came to inform him that the governor was seeking for him. The barque which Raoul had perceived at sea, and which appeared so eager to gain the port, came to Sainte-Marguerite with an important despatch for the captain of the musketeers. On opening it, d'Artagnan recognised the writing of the King: "I should think," said Louis XIV, "you will have completed the execution of my orders, Monsieur d'Artagnan; return then immediately to Paris, and join me at the Louvre."

"There is the end of my exile," cried the musketeer with joy; "God be praised, I am no longer a jailer!" And he showed the letter to Athos.

Athos and Raoul returned to Toulon, which began to be filled with the noise of carriages, with the noise of arms, with the noise of neighing horses. The trumpeters sounded their spirited marches; the drummers signalised their strength; the streets were overflowing with soldiers, servants, and trades-people. The Duc de Beaufort was everywhere, superintending the embarkation with the zeal and interest of a good captain. He encouraged even the most humble of his companions; he scolded his lieutenants, even those of the highest rank. Artillery, provisions, baggage, he insisted upon seeing all himself. He examined the equipment of every soldier; he assured himself of the health and soundness of every horse. It was plain that, light, boastful, egotistical in his hotel, the gentleman became the soldier again—the high noble, a captain—in face of the responsibility he had accepted. And yet, it must be admitted that, whatever was the care with which he presided over the preparations for departure, it was easy to perceive careless precipitation, and the absence of all the precaution which make the French soldier the first soldier in the world, because in that world, he is the one most abandoned to his own physical and moral resources. All things having satisfied, or appearing to have satisfied, the admiral, he paid his compliments to Raoul, and gave the last orders for sailing, which was ordered the next morning at daybreak. He invited the Comte and his son to dine with him; but they, under a pretext of the service, kept themselves apart. Gaining their hostelry, situated under the trees of the great Place, they took their repast in haste, and Athos led Raoul to the rocks which dominate the city, vast grey mountains, whence the view is infinite, and embraces a liquid horizon, which appears, so remote is it, on a level with the rocks themselves. The night was fine, as it always is in these happy climates. The moon, rising behind the rocks, unrolled, like a silver sheet, upon the blue carpet of the sea. In the road manœuvred silently the vessels which had just taken their rank to facilitate the embarkation. The sea, loaded with phosphoric light, opened beneath the hulls of the barques which transported the baggage and munitions; every dip of the prow ploughed up this gulf of white flames; and from every oar dropped liquid diamonds. The sailors, rejoicing in the largesses of the admiral, were heard murmuring their slow and artless songs. Sometimes, the grinding of the chains was mixed with the dull noise of shot falling into the holds. These harmonies, and this spectacle, oppress the heart like fear, and dilate it like hope. All this life speaks of death. Athos had seated himself with his son, upon the moss, among the brambles of the promontory. Around their heads passed and repassed large bats, carried along in the fearful whirl of their blind chase. The feet of Raoul were across the edge of the cliff, and bathed in that void which is peopled by vertigo, and provokes to annihilation.

At that moment the drums suddenly rolled, and the clarions filled the air with their inspiring notes. The regiments destined for the expedition began to debouch from the city. They advanced to the number of five, each composed of forty companies. Royals marched first, distinguished by their white uniform, faced with blue. The regimental colours, quartered crosswise, violet and dead-leaf, with a sprinkling of golden fleurs-de-lis, left the white-coloured flag, with its fleur-de-lised cross, to dominate over the whole. Musketeers, at the wings, with their forked sticks and their muskets on their shoulders; pikemen in the centre, with their lances, fourteen feet in length, marched gaily towards the transports, which carried them in detail to the ships. The regiments of Picardy, Navarre, Normandy, and Royal Vaisseau followed after. M. de Beaufort had known well how to select his troops. He himself was seen closing the march with his staff—it would take a full hour before he could reach the sea. Raoul with Athos turned his steps slowly towards the beach, in order to take his place when the Prince embarked. Grimaud, boiling with the ardour of a young man, superintended the embarkation of Raoul's baggage in the admiral's vessel. Athos, with his arm passed through that of the son he was about to lose, absorbed in melancholy meditation, was deaf to the noise around him. An officer came quickly towards them to inform Raoul that M. de Beaufort was anxious to have him by his side.

"Have the kindness to tell the Prince," said Raoul, "that I request he will allow me this hour to enjoy the company of my father."

"No, no," said Athos, "an aide-de-camp ought not thus to quit his general. Please to tell the Prince, monsieur, that the Vicomte will join him immediately." The officer set off at a gallop.

"Whether we part here or part there," added the Comte, "it is no less a separation." He carefully brushed the dust off his son's coat, and passed his hand over his hair as they walked along. "But, Raoul," said he, "you want money. M. de Beaufort's train will be splendid, and I am certain it will be agreeable to you to purchase horses and arms, which are very dear things in Africa. Now, as you are not actually in the service of the King, or M. de Beaufort, and are simply a volunteer, you must not reckon upon either pay or largesses. But I should not like you to want for anything at Gigelli. Here are two hundred pistoles; if you would please me, Raoul, spend them."

Raoul pressed the hand of his father, and, at the turning of a street, they saw M. de Beaufort, mounted upon a magnificent white horse, which replied by graceful curvets to the applauses of the women of the city. The Duc called Raoul, and held out his hand to the Comte. He spoke to him for some time, with such a kindly expression, that the heart of the poor father even felt a little comforted. It was, however, evident to both father and son that their walk was directed to nothing less than a punishment. There was a terrible moment—that at which, in quitting the sands of the shore, the soldiers and sailors exchanged the last kisses with their families and friends; a supreme moment, in which, notwithstanding the clearness of the heavens, the warmth of the sun, the perfumes of the air, and the rich life that was circulating in their veins, everything appeared black, everything appeared bitter, everything created doubts of a God, whilst speaking by the mouth, even, of God. It was customary for the admiral and his suite to embark the last; the cannon waited to announce, with its formidable voice, that the leader had placed his foot on board his vessel. Athos, forgetful of both the admiral and the fleet, and of his own dignity as a strong man, opened his arms to his son, and pressed him, convulsively, to his heart.

"Accompany us on board," said the Duc, very much affected; "you will gain a good half-hour."

"No," said Athos, "my farewell is spoken. I do not wish to speak a second."

"Then, Vicomte, embark—embark quickly!" added the Prince, wishing to spare the tears of these two men, whose hearts were bursting. And paternally, tenderly, very much as Porthos might have done, he took Raoul in his arms and placed him in the boat; the oars of which at a signal immediately were dipped in the waves. Himself, forgetful of ceremony, he jumped into his boat, and pushed it off with a vigorous foot. "Adieu!" cried Raoul.

Towards midday, when the sun devoured space, and scarcely the tops of the masts dominated the incandescent line of the sea, Athos perceived a soft aerial shadow rise, and vanish as soon as seen. This was the smoke of a cannon, which M. de Beaufort ordered to be fired as a last salute to the coast of France. The point was buried in its turn beneath the sky, and Athos returned painfully and slowly to his hostelry.

Chapter 44

AMONG WOMEN

D'ARTAGNAN, riding fast, thinking as constantly, alighted from his horse in Paris, fresh and tender in his muscles as the athlete preparing for the gymnasium. The King did not expect him so soon, and had just departed for the chase towards Meudon. D'Artagnan, instead of riding after the King, as he would formerly have done, took off his boots, had a bath, and waited till His Majesty should return dusty and tired. He occupied the interval of five hours in taking, as people say, the air of the house, and in arming himself against all ill chances. He learned that the King, during the last fortnight, had been gloomy; that the Queen-Mother was ill and much depressed; that Monsieur, the King's brother, was exhibiting a devotional turn; that Madame had the vapours; and that M. de Guiche was gone to one of his estates. He learned that M. Colbert was radiant; that M. Fouquet consulted a fresh physician every day, who still did not cure him, and that his principal complaint was one which physicians do not usually cure, unless they are political physicians. The King, d'Artagnan was told, behaved in the kindest manner to M. Fouquet, and did not allow him ever to be out of his sight; but the Surintendant, touched to the heart, like one of those fine trees which a worm has punctured, was declining daily, in spite of the royal smile, that sun of court trees. D'Artagnan learned that Mademoiselle de la Vallière had become indispensable to the King; that the King, during his sporting excursions, if he did not take her with him, wrote to her frequently—no longer verses, but, what was much worse, prose, and that whole pages at a time. Thus, as the poetical Pleiad of the day said, the *first King in the world* was seen descending from his horse *with an ardour beyond compare,* and on the crown of his hat scrawling bombastic phrases, which M. de Saint-Aignan, aide-de-camp in perpetuity, carried to La Vallière at the risk of foundering his horses. During this time, deer and pheasants were left to the free enjoyments of their nature, hunted so lazily, that, it was said, the art of venery ran great risk of degenerating at the court of France. D'Artagnan then thought of the wishes of poor Raoul, and as he loved to philosophise a little occasionally, he resolved to profit by the absence of the King to have a minute's talk with Mademoiselle de la Vallière. This was a very easy affair: while the King was hunting, Louise was walking with some other ladies in one of the galleries of the Palais Royal, exactly where the captain of the musketeers had some guards to inspect. D'Artagnan did not doubt, that if he could but open the conversation upon Raoul, Louise might give him grounds for writing a consolatory letter to the poor exile; and hope, or at least consolation for Raoul, in the state of heart in which he had left him, was the sun, was life, to two men who were very dear to our captain. He directed his course, therefore, to the spot where he knew he should find Mademoiselle de la Vallière. D'Artagnan found La Vallière the centre of a circle. In her apparent solitude, the King's favourite received, like a queen, more perhaps than the Queen, a homage of which Madame had been so proud, when all the King's looks were directed to her and commanded the looks of the courtiers. D'Artagnan, although no squire of dames, received, nevertheless, civilities and attentions from the ladies; he was polite, as a brave man always is, and his terrible reputation had conciliated as much friendship among the men as admiration among the women. On seeing him enter, therefore, they immediately accosted him: and, as is not infrequently the case with fair ladies, opened the attack by questions: "Where *had* he been? What *had* become of him so long? Why had they not seen him as usual make his fine horse curvet in such beautiful style, to the delight and astonishment of the curious, from the King's balcony?"

He replied that he had just come from the land of oranges. This set all the ladies laughing. Those were times in which everybody travelled, but in which, notwithstanding, a journey of a hundred leagues was a problem often solved by death.

"Have we any of us any friends there?" said Mademoiselle de Tonnay-

Charente coldly, but in a manner to attract attention to a question that was not without a calculated aim.

"Why," replied d'Artagnan, "yes; there were M. de la Guillitière, M. de Manchy, M. de Bragelonne——"

La Vallière became pale. "M. de Bragelonne!" cried the perfidious Athenaïs. "Eh, what!—is he gone to the wars?—he!"

Montalais trod upon her toe, but in vain.

"Do you know what my opinion is?" continued she, addressing d'Artagnan.

"No, mademoiselle; but I should like very much to know it."

"My opinion is, then, that all the men who go to this war, are desperate, desponding men, whom love has treated ill; and who go to try if they cannot find black women more kind than fair ones have been."

Some of the ladies laughed. La Vallière was evidently confused. Montalais coughed loud enough to waken the dead.

"Mademoiselle," interrupted d'Artagnan, "you are in error when you speak of black women at Gigelli; the women there are not black; it is true, they are not white—they are yellow."

"Yellow!" exclaimed the bevy of fair beauties.

"Eh! do not disparage it. I have never seen a finer colour to match with black eyes and a coral mouth."

"So much the better for M. de Bragelonne," said Mademoiselle de Tonnay-Charente, with persistent malice. "He will make amends for his loss. Poor fellow!"

Louise, half-dead, caught at the arm of the captain of the musketeers, whose face betrayed unusual emotion. "You wished to speak with me, Monsieur d'Artagnan," said she, in a voice broken by anger and pain. "What had you to say to me?"

D'Artagnan made several steps along the gallery, holding Louise on his arm; then, when they were far enough removed from the others—"What I had to say to you, mademoiselle," replied he, "Mademoiselle de Tonnay-Charente has just expressed; roughly, and unkindly, it is true, but still in its entirety."

She uttered a faint cry; and, struck to the heart by this new wound, she went on her way, like one of those poor birds which, struck to death, seeks the shade of the thicket to die in. She disappeared at one door, at the moment the King was entering by another. The first glance of the King was directed towards the empty seat of his mistress. Not perceiving La Vallière, a frown came over his brow; but as soon as he saw d'Artagnan, who bowed to him—"Ah! monsieur!" cried he, "you *have* been diligent! I am much pleased with you." This was the superlative expression of royal satisfaction. Many men would have been ready to lay down their lives for such a speech from the King. The maids of honour and the courtiers, who had formed a respectful circle round the King on his entrance, drew back, on observing he wished to speak privately with the captain of the musketeers. The King led the way out of the gallery, after having again, with his eyes, sought everywhere for La Vallière, whose absence he could not account for. The moment they were out of the reach of curious ears, "Well! Monsieur d'Artagnan," said he, "the prisoner?"

"Is in his prison, sire."

The King perceived that he was unwilling to speak. "I have sent for you, captain, to desire you to go and prepare my lodgings at Nantes."

"At Nantes!" cried d'Artagnan.

"In Bretagne."

"Yes, sire, it is in Bretagne. Will your Majesty make so long a journey as to Nantes?"

"The States are assembled there," replied the King. "I have two demands to make of them: I wish to be there."

D'Artagnan bowed as if to take his leave; but, perceiving the King very much embarrassed, "Will your Majesty," said he, stepping two paces forward, "take the court with you?"

"Certainly I shall."

"Then your Majesty will, doubtless, want the musketeers?" And the eye of the King sank beneath the penetrating glance of the captain.

"Take a brigade of them," replied Louis.

"Is that all? Has your Majesty no other orders to give me?"

"No—ah—yes."

"I am all attention, sire."

"At the castle of Nantes, which I hear is very ill arranged, you will adopt the practice of placing musketeers at the door of each of the principal dignitaries I shall take with me."

"Of the principal?"

"Yes."

"For instance, at the door of M. de Lyonne?"

"Yes."

"And of Monsieur le Surintendant?"

"Without doubt."

"Very well, sire. By to-morrow I shall have set out."

"Oh, yes; but one more word, Monsieur d'Artagnan. At Nantes you will meet with M. le Duc de Gesvres, captain of the guards. Be sure that your musketeers are placed before his guards arrive. Precedence always belongs to the first comer."

"Yes, sire."

"And if M. de Gesvres should question you?"

"Question me, sire! Is it likely that M. de Gesvres should question me?" And the musketeer, turning cavalierly on his heel, disappeared. "To Nantes!" said he to himself, as he descended the stairs. "Why did he not dare to say, from thence to Belle-Isle?"

Chapter 45

HOW KING LOUIS XIV PLAYED HIS LITTLE PART

FOUQUET, on his arrival at Nantes, got into a carriage which the city sent to him, we know not why or how, and he repaired to *la Maison de Nantes*, escorted by a vast crowd of people, who for several days had been boiling with the expectation of a convocation of the States. Scarcely was he installed, when Gourville went out to order horses upon the route to Poitiers and Vannes, and a boat at Paimbœuf. He performed these various operations with so much mystery, activity, and generosity, that never was Fouquet, then labouring under an access of fever, more near being saved, except for the co-operation of that immense disturber of human projects—chance. A report was spread during the night, that the King was coming in great haste upon post horses, and that he would arrive within ten or twelve hours at latest. The people, while waiting for the King, were greatly rejoiced to see the musketeers, freshly arrived with Monsieur d'Artagnan, their captain, and quartered in the castle, of which they occupied all the posts, in quality of guard of honour.

The King was entering the city, which soon resounded with the cannon from the ramparts, and from a vessel which replied from the lower part of the river. Fouquet's brow darkened; he called his *valets de chambre*, and dressed in ceremonial costume. From his window, behind the curtains, he could see the eagerness of the people, and the movement of a large troop, which had followed the Prince, without its being to be guessed how. The King was conducted to the castle in great pomp, and Fouquet saw him dismount under the portcullis, and speak something in the ear of d'Artagnan, who held his stirrup. D'Artagnan, when the King had passed under the arch, directed his steps towards the house Fouquet was in, but so slowly, and stopping so frequently to speak to his musketeers, drawn up as a hedge, that it might be said he was counting the seconds, or the steps, before accomplishing his message. Fouquet opened the window to speak to him in the court.

"Ah!" cried d'Artagnan, on perceiving him, "are you still there, monseigneur?"

The Surintendant sighed deeply. "Good Heavens! yes, monsieur," replied he. "The arrival of the King has interrupted me in the projects I had formed."

"Oh! then you know that the King has arrived?"

"Yes, monsieur, I have seen him; and this time you come from him—"

"To inquire after you, monseigneur; and, if your health is not too bad, to beg you to have the kindness to repair to the castle."

"Directly, Monsieur d'Artagnan, directly?"

"Ah!" said the captain, "now the King is come, there is no more walking for anybody—no more free-will; the pass-word governs all now, you as well as me, me as well as you."

Fouquet heaved a last sigh, got into his carriage, so great was his weakness, and went to the castle, escorted by d'Artagnan.

It was two o'clock in the afternoon. The King, full of impatience, went to his cabinet on the terrace, and kept opening the door of the corridor, to see what his secretaries were doing. M. Colbert, seated in the same place M. Saint-Aignan had so long occupied in the morning, was chatting, in a low voice, with M. de Brienne. The King opened the door suddenly, and addressing them, "What do you say?" asked he.

"We were speaking of the first sitting of the States," said M. de Brienne, rising.

He had not finished these words when a much rougher voice than that of the King was heard.

"D'Artagnan!" cried the King, with evident joy. "In the first place, let me see the result of your commission, monsieur; you may repose afterwards."

D'Artagnan, who was just passing through the door, stopped at the voice of the King. "I have arrested M. Fouquet, sire."

"You took plenty of time about it," said the King sharply.

D'Artagnan looked at the King.

"Where is M. Fouquet at this moment?" asked Louis, after a short silence.

"M. Fouquet, sire," replied d'Artagnan, "is in the iron cage that M. Colbert had prepared for him, and is going, as fast as four vigorous horses can drag him, towards Angers."

"Why did you leave him on the road?"

"Because your Majesty did not tell me to go to Angers. The proof, the best proof of what I advance is, that the King desired me to be sought for but this minute."

"Monsieur d'Artagnan," said the King, "give twenty of your musketeers to M. de Saint-Aignan, to form a guard for M. Fouquet. And from Angers," continued the King, "they will conduct the prisoner to the Bastille, in Paris."

D'Artagnan was about to retire; but the King stopped him.

"Monsieur," said he, "you will go immediately, and take possession of the isle and fief of Belle-Isle-en-Mer."

"Yes, sire. Alone?"

"You will take a sufficient number of troops to prevent delay, in case the place should be contumacious."

A murmur of adulatory incredulity arose from the group of courtiers. "That is to be done," said d'Artagnan.

"I saw the place in my infancy," resumed the King, "and I do not wish to see it again. You have heard me? Go, monsieur, and do not return without the keys of the place."

Colbert went up to d'Artagnan. "A commission which, if you carry it out well," said he, "will be worth a marshal's baton to you."

"Why do you employ the words, 'if you carry it out well'?"

"Because it is difficult."

"Ah! in what respect?"

"You have friends in Belle-Isle, Monsieur d'Artagnan; and it is not an easy thing for men like you to march over the bodies of their friends to obtain success."

D'Artagnan hung down his head, whilst Colbert returned to the King. A quarter of an hour after, the captain received the written order from the King, to blow up the fortress of Belle-Isle, in case of resistance, with the power of life and death over all the inhabitants or refugees, and an injunction not to allow one to escape.

"Colbert was right," thought d'Artagnan; "my baton of a marshal of France will cost the lives of my two friends. Only they seem to forget that my friends are not more stupid than the birds, and that they will not wait for the hand of the fowler to extend their wings. I will show them that hand so plainly, that they will have quite time enough to see it. Poor Porthos! Poor Aramis. No; my fortune shall not cost your wings a feather."

Chapter 46

BELLE-ISLE-EN-MER

AT THE extremity of the mole, which the furious sea beats at evening tide, two men, holding each other by the arm, were conversing in an animated and expansive tone. Every one has already perceived that those two men were our proscribed heroes, Porthos and Aramis, who had taken refuge in Belle-Isle since the ruin of their hopes, since the discomfiture of the vast plan of M. d'Herblay.

"It is of no use you saying anything to the contrary, my dear Aramis," repeated Porthos, inhaling vigorously the saline air with which he filled his powerful chest. "It is of no use, Aramis. The disappearance of all the fishing-boats that went out two days ago, is not an ordinary circumstance. There has been no storm at sea; the weather has been constantly calm, not even the lightest gale; and even if we had had a tempest, all our boats would not have foundered. I repeat, it is strange. This complete disappearance astonishes me, I tell you."

"True," murmured Aramis. "You are right, friend Porthos; it is true, there is something strange in it."

"And, further," added Porthos, whose ideas the assent of the Bishop of Vannes seemed to enlarge; "and, further, have you remarked, that if the boats have perished, not a single plank has been washed ashore?"

"I have remarked that as well as you."

"Have you remarked, besides, that the two boats which I sent in search of the others——"

"Porthos, what is that yonder?" interrupted Aramis, rising suddenly, and pointing out to his friend a black spot upon the empurpled line of the water.

"A bark!" said Porthos; "yes, it is a bark! Ah! we shall have some news at last."

"There are two!" cried the Bishop, on discovering another mast; "two! three! four!"

"Five!" said Porthos, in his turn. "Six! seven! Ah! *mon Dieu! mon Dieu!* It is a whole fleet!"

An old fisherman passed. "Are those our barks yonder?" asked Aramis. The old man looked steadily into the horizon.

"No, monseigneur," replied he, "they are lighter boats in the King's service."

Aramis leant his head upon his hands, and made no reply. Then, all at once,—"Porthos," said he, "have the alarm sounded."

"The alarm! do you think of such a thing?"

"Yes, and let the cannoniers mount to their batteries, let the artillerymen be at their pieces, and be particularly watchful of the coast batteries."

Porthos opened his eyes to their widest extent. He looked attentively at his friend, to convince himself he was in his proper senses.

"I will do it, my dear Porthos," continued Aramis, in his most bland tone; "I will go and have these orders executed myself, if you do not go, my friend."

"Well! I will go instantly!" said Porthos, who went to execute the orders, casting all the while looks behind him, to see if the Bishop of Vannes were not deceived; and if, on returning to more rational ideas, he would not recall him. The alarm was sounded, the trumpets brayed, the drums rolled; the great bell of the belfry was put in motion. The dikes and moles were quickly filled with the curious and soldiers; the matches sparkled in the hands of the artillerymen, placed behind the large cannon bedded in their stone carriages. When every man was at his post, when all the preparations for the defence were made: "Permit me, Aramis, to try and comprehend," whispered Porthos timidly, in Aramis's ear.

"My dear friend, you will comprehend but too soon," murmured M. d'Herblay, in reply to this question of his lieutenant.

"The fleet which is coming yonder, with sails unfurled, straight towards the port of Belle-Isle, is a royal fleet, is it not?"

"But as there are two kings in France, Porthos, to which of these two kings does this fleet belong?"

"Oh! you open my eyes," replied the giant, stunned by this argument.

And Porthos, for whom the reply of his friend had just opened the eyes, or rather thickened the bandage which covered his sight, went with his best speed to the batteries to overlook his people, and exhort every one to do his duty. It was quite night when one of these vessels, which had created such a sensation among the inhabitants of Belle-Isle, was moored within cannon-shot of the place. It was soon seen, notwithstanding the darkness, that a sort of agitation reigned on board this vessel, from the side of which a skiff was lowered, of which the three rowers, bending to their oars, took the direction of the port, and in a few instants struck land at the foot of the fort. The commander of this yawl jumped on shore. He had a letter in his hand, which he waved in the air, and seemed to wish to communicate with somebody. This man was soon recognised by several soldiers, as one of the pilots of the island. He was the skipper of one of the two barques kept back by Aramis, and which Porthos, in his anxiety with regard to the fate of the fishermen who had disappeared for two days, had sent in search of the missing boats. He asked to be conducted to M. d'Herblay. Two soldiers, at a signal from the sergeant, placed him between them, and escorted him. Aramis was upon the quay. The envoy presented himself before the Bishop of Vannes. The darkness was almost complete, notwithstanding the flambeaux borne at a small distance by the soldiers who were following Aramis in his rounds.

Aramis eagerly read the following lines:

"Order of the King to take Belle-Isle; or to put the garrison to the sword, if they resist; order to make prisoners of all the men of the garrison; signed, D'ARTAGNAN, who, the day before yesterday, arrested M. Fouquet, for the purpose of his being sent to the Bastille."

Aramis turned pale, and crushed the paper in his hands.

"What is it?" asked Porthos.

"Nothing, my friend, nothing."

"What shall I do?" asked Jonathan.

"You will return on board this captain's vessel."

"Yes, monseigneur."

"And tell him that we beg he will himself come into the island."

"Ah! I comprehend!" said Porthos.

"Yes, monseigneur," replied Jonathan; "but if the captain should refuse to come to Belle-Isle?"

"If he refuses, as we have cannon, we will make use of them."

"What! against d'Artagnan?"

"If it is d'Artagnan, Porthos, he will come. Go, Jonathan, go!"

"*Ma foi!* I no longer comprehend anything," murmured Porthos.

"I will make you comprehend all, my dear friend; the time for it is come; sit down upon this gun-carriage, open your ears, and listen well to me."

"Oh! *pardieu!* I shall listen, no fear of that."

"May I depart, monseigneur?" cried Jonathan.

"Yes, begone, and bring back an answer. Allow the canoe to pass, you men there!" And the canoe pushed off to regain the fleet.

Aramis took Porthos by the hand, and explained all to him.

Chapter 47

THE EXPLANATIONS OF ARAMIS

"So THEN," said Porthos, when Aramis had concluded his narrative, "so then, it seems, I have quite fallen out with Louis XIV?"

"My dear friend," said Aramis, smiling with a strong shade of sadness, "do not let us reason like children; let us be men in council and execution— But, hark! I hear a hail for landing at the port. Attention, Porthos, serious attention!"

"It is d'Artagnan, no doubt," said Porthos, in a voice of thunder, approaching the parapet.

"Yes, it is I," replied the captain of the musketeers, running lightly up the steps of the mole, and gaining rapidly the little esplanade upon which his two friends waited for him. As soon as he came towards them, Porthos and Aramis observed an officer who followed d'Artagnan, treading apparently in his very steps. The captain stopped upon the stairs of the mole, when half-way up. His companion imitated him.

"Make your men draw back," cried d'Artagnan to Porthos and Aramis; "let them retire out of hearing." The order being given by Porthos, was executed immediately. Then d'Artagnan, turning towards him who followed him:

"Monsieur," said he, "we are no longer here on board the King's fleet, where, in virtue of your order, you spoke so arrogantly to me just now."

"Monsieur," replied the officer, "I did not speak arrogantly to you; I simply, but rigorously, obeyed what I had been commanded. I have been directed to follow you. I follow you. I am directed not to allow you to communicate with any one without taking cognisance of what you do; I mix myself, therefore, with your communications."

D'Artagnan trembled with rage, and Porthos and Aramis, who heard this dialogue, trembled likewise, but with uneasiness and fear. D'Artagnan, biting his moustache with that vivacity which denoted in him the state of an exasperation closely to be followed by a terrible explosion, approached the officer.

"Monsieur," said he, in a low voice, so much the more impressive, that affecting a calm it threatened a tempest—"monsieur, when I sent a canoe hither, you wished to know what I wrote to the defenders of Belle-Isle. You produced an order to that effect; and, in my turn, I instantly showed you the note I had written. When the skipper of the boat sent by me returned, when I received the reply of these two gentlemen (and he pointed to Aramis and Porthos), you heard every word of what the messenger said. All that was plainly in your orders, all that was well executed, very punctually, was it not?"

"Yes, monsieur," stammered the officer; "yes, without doubt, but——"

"Monsieur," continued d'Artagnan, growing warm—"Monsieur, when

I manifested the intention of quitting my vessel to cross to Belle-Isle, you required to accompany me; I did not hesitate; I brought you with me. You are now at Belle-Isle, are you not?"

"Yes, monsieur, but—"

"But—the question no longer is of M. Colbert, who has given you that order, or of whomsoever in the world you are following the instructions: the question now is of a man who is a clog upon M. d'Artagnan, and who is alone with M. d'Artagnan upon steps whose feet are bathed by thirty feet of salt water; a bad position for that man, a bad position, monsieur! I warn you."

The officer did not stir; he became pale under this terrible threat, but replied with simplicity, "Monsieur, you are wrong in acting against my orders."

Porthos and Aramis, mute and trembling at the top of the parapet, cried to the musketeer, "Dear d'Artagnan, take care!"

D'Artagnan made them a sign to keep silence, raised his foot with a terrifying calmness to mount the stairs, and turned round, sword in hand, to see if the officer followed him. The officer made a sign of the cross and stepped up. Porthos and Aramis, who knew their d'Artagnan, uttered a cry, and rushed down to prevent the blow they thought they already heard. But, d'Artagnan, passing his sword into his left hand,—

"Monsieur," said he to the officer, in an agitated voice, "you are a brave man. You ought better to comprehend what I am going to say to you now than that which I have just said to you."

"Speak, Monsieur d'Artagnan, speak," replied the brave officer.

"These gentlemen we have just seen, and against whom you have orders, are my friends."

"I know they are, monsieur."

"You can understand if I ought to act towards them as your instructions prescribe."

"I understand your reserves."

"Very well; permit me, then, to converse with them without a witness."

"Monsieur d'Artagnan, if I yielded to your request, if I did that which you beg me to do, I should break my word; but if I do not do it, I shall disoblige you. I prefer the one to the other. Converse with your friends, and do not despise me, monsieur, for doing for the sake of you, whom I esteem and honour; do not despise me for committing for you, and you alone, an unworthy act." D'Artagnan, much agitated, passed his arms rapidly round the neck of the young man, and went up to his friends. The officer, enveloped in his cloak, sat down on the damp weed-covered steps.

"Well!" said d'Artagnan to his friends, "such is my position; judge for yourselves." They all three embraced. All three pressed each other in their arms as in the glorious days of their youth.

"What is the meaning of all these rigours?" said Porthos.

"You ought to have some suspicions of what it is," said d'Artagnan.

"Not much, I assure you, my dear captain; for, in fact, I have done nothing, no more has Aramis," hastened the worthy baron to say.

D'Artagnan darted a reproachful look at the prelate, which penetrated that hardened heart.

"Dear Porthos!" cried the Bishop of Vannes.

"You see what has been done against you," said d'Artagnan; "interception of all that is coming to or going from Belle-Isle. Your boats are all seized. If you had endeavoured to fly, you would have fallen into the hands of the cruisers which plough the sea in all directions on the watch for you. The King wants you to be taken, and he will take you." And d'Artagnan tore several hairs from his grey moustache. Aramis became sombre, Porthos angry.

"My idea was this," continued d'Artagnan; "to make you both come on board, to keep you near me, and restore you your liberty. But now, who can say that when I return to my ship, I may not find a superior; that I may not find secret orders which will take from me my command, and give it to another, who will dispose of me and you without hopes of help?"

D'Artagnan came to the parapet, leaned over towards the steps of the mole, and called the officer, who immediately came up. "Monsieur," said d'Artagnan, after having exchanged the most cordial courtesies, natural between gentlemen, who know and appreciate each other worthily—"monsieur, if I wished to take away these gentlemen, what would you do?"

"I should not oppose it, monsieur; but having direct orders, formal orders to take them under my guard, I should detain them."

"Ah!" said d'Artagnan.

"That's all over," said Aramis gloomily. Porthos did not stir.

"But still take Porthos," said the Bishop of Vannes; "he can prove to the King, I will help him in doing so, and you also can, Monsieur d'Artagnan, that he has had nothing to do in this affair."

"Hum!" said d'Artagnan. "Will you come? Will you follow me, Porthos? The King is merciful."

"I beg to reflect," said Porthos nobly.

"You will remain here, then?"

"Until fresh orders," cried Aramis, with vivacity.

"Until we have had an idea," resumed d'Artagnan; "and I now believe that will not be long first, for I have one already."

"Let us say adieu, then," said Aramis; "but in truth, my good Porthos, you ought to go."

"No!" said the latter laconically.

"As you please," replied Aramis, a little wounded in his nervous susceptibility at the morose tone of his companion. "Only I am reassured by the promise of an idea from d'Artagnan, an idea I fancy I have divined."

"Let me see," said the musketeer, placing his ear near Aramis's mouth. The latter spoke several words rapidly to which d'Artagnan replied, "That is it, precisely."

"Infallible, then!" cried Aramis.

D'Artagnan having tenderly embraced his two old friends, left Belle-Isle with the inseparable companion M. Colbert had given him. Thus, with the exception of the explanation with which the worthy Porthos had been willing to be satisfied, nothing had changed in appearance in the fate of the one or the other. "Only," said Aramis, "there is d'Artagnan's idea."

D'Artagnan did not return on board without examining to the bottom the idea he had discovered. Now, we know that when d'Artagnan did examine, according to custom, daylight pierced through. As to the officer, become mute again, he left him full measure to meditate. Therefore, on putting his foot on board his vessel, moored within cannon-shot of the island, the captain of the musketeers had already got together all his means, offensive and defensive.

He immediately assembled his council, which consisted of the officers serving under his orders. These were eight in number: a chief of the maritime forces; a major directing the artillery; an engineer, the officer we are acquainted with, and four lieutenants. Having assembled them in the chamber of the poop, d'Artagnan arose, took off his hat, and addressed them thus:

"Gentlemen, I have been to reconnoitre Belle-Isle-en-Mer, and I have found it a good and solid garrison; moreover, preparations are made for a defence that may prove troublesome. I therefore intend to send for two of the principal officers of the place, that we may converse with them. Having separated them from their troops and their cannon, we shall be better able to deal with them; particularly with good reasoning. Is this your opinion, gentlemen?"

The officers looked at each other as if to read their opinions in their eyes, with the intention of evidently acting, after they should have agreed, according to the desire of d'Artagnan. And already the latter saw with joy that the result of their consent would be sending a barque to Porthos and Aramis, when the King's officer drew from his pocket a folded paper, which he placed in the hands of d'Artagnan.

D'Artagnan, full of mistrust, unfolded the paper, and read these words:

"Prohibition to M. d'Artagnan to assemble any council whatever, or to deliberate in any way before Belle-Isle be surrendered and the prisoners shot. Signed, Louis."

D'Artagnan repressed the movement of impatience that ran through his whole body, and, with a gracious smile,—

"That is well, monsieur," said he; "the King's orders shall be complied with."

Chapter 48

RESULT OF THE IDEAS OF THE KING, AND THE IDEAS OF D'ARTAGNAN

THE BLOW was direct. It was severe, mortal. D'Artagnan, furious at having been anticipated by an idea of the King's, did not, however, yet despair; and, reflecting upon the idea he had brought back from Belle-Isle, he augured from it a new means of safety for his friends.

"Gentlemen," said he suddenly, "since the King has charged some other than myself with his secret orders, it must be because I no longer possess his confidence, and I should be really unworthy of it, if I had the courage to hold a command subject to so many injurious suspicions. I will go then immediately and carry my resignation to the King. I give it before you all, enjoining you all to fall back with me upon the coast of France, in such a way as not to compromise the safety of the forces His Majesty has confided to me. For this purpose, return all to your posts; within an hour we shall have the ebb of the tide. To your posts, gentlemen! I suppose," added he, on seeing that all prepared to obey him, except the surveillant officer, "you have no orders to object, this time?"

And d'Artagnan almost triumphed while speaking these words. This plan was the safety of his friends. The blockade once raised, they might embark immediately and set sail for England or Spain, without fear of being molested. Whilst they were making their escape, d'Artagnan would return to the King; would justify his return by the indignation which the mistrusts of Colbert had raised in him; he would be sent back with full powers, and he would take Belle-Isle, that is to say, the cage, after the birds had flown. But to this plan the officer opposed a second order of the King's. It was thus conceived:

"From the moment M. d'Artagnan shall have manifested the desire of giving in his resignation, he shall no longer be reckoned leader of the expedition, and every officer placed under his orders shall be held to no longer obey him. Moreover, the said Monsieur d'Artagnan having lost that quality of leader of the army sent against Belle-Isle, shall set out immediately for France, in company of the officer who will have remitted the message to him, and who will consider him as a prisoner for whom he is answerable."

Brave and careless as he was, d'Artagnan turned pale. Everything had been calculated with a depth which, for the first time in thirty years, had recalled to him the solid foresight and the inflexible logic of the great Cardinal. He leant his head on his hand, thoughtful, scarcely breathing. "If I were to put this order into my pocket," thought he, "who would know it, or who would prevent my doing it? Before the King had had time to be informed, I should have saved those poor fellows yonder. Let us exercise a little audacity! My head is not one of those which the executioner strikes off for disobedience. We will disobey!" But at the moment he was about to adopt this plan, he saw the officers around him reading similar orders which the infernal agent of the thoughts of Colbert had just distributed to them. The case of disobedience had been foreseen, as the others had been.

"Monsieur," said the officer, coming up to him, "I await your good pleasure to depart."

"I am ready, monsieur," replied d'Artagnan, grinding his teeth.

The officer immediately commanded a canoe to receive M. d'Artagnan and himself. At sight of this he became almost mad with rage.

"How," stammered he, "will you carry on the direction of the different corps?"

"When you are gone, monsieur," replied the commander of the fleet, "it is to me the direction of the whole is committed."

"Then, monsieur," rejoined Colbert's man, addressing the new leader, "it is for you that this last order that has been remitted to me is intended. Let us see your powers."

"Here they are," said the sea officer, exhibiting a royal signature.

"Here are your instructions," replied the officer, placing the folded paper in his hands; and turning towards d'Artagnan, "Come, monsieur," said he in an agitated voice (such despair did he behold in that man of iron), "do me the favour to depart at once."

"Immediately!" articulated d'Artagnan feebly, subdued, crushed by implacable impossibility.

And he let himself slide down into the little boat, which started, favoured by wind and tide, for the coast of France. The King's guards embarked with him. The musketeer still preserved the hope of reaching Nantes quickly, and of pleading the cause of his friends eloquently enough to incline the King to mercy. The barque flew like a swallow. D'Artagnan distinctly saw the land of France profiled in black against the white clouds of night.

"Ah! monsieur," said he, in a low voice, to the officer, to whom, for an hour, he had ceased speaking, "what would I give to know the instructions for the new commander! They are all pacific, are they not? and——"

He did not finish; the sound of a distant cannon rolled over the waters, then another, and two or three still louder. D'Artagnan shuddered.

"The fire is opened upon Belle-Isle," replied the officer. The canoe had just touched the soil of France.

Chapter 49

THE ANCESTORS OF PORTHOS

WHEN d'Artagnan had quitted Aramis and Porthos, the latter returned to the principal fort to converse with the greater liberty. Porthos, still thoughtful, was a constraint upon Aramis, whose mind had never felt itself more free.

"Dear Porthos," said he suddenly, "I will explain d'Artagnan's idea to you."

"What idea, Aramis?"

"An idea to which we shall owe our liberty within twelve hours."

"Ah! indeed!" said Porthos, much astonished. "Let us see it."

"Did you remark, in the scene our friend had with the officer that certain orders restrained him with regard to us?"

"Yes, I did remark that."

"Well! d'Artagnan is going to give in his resignation to the King, and during the confusion which will result from his absence, we will get away, or rather you will get away, Porthos, if there is a possibility of flight only for one."

Here Porthos shook his head and replied: "We will escape together, Aramis, or we will remain here together."

"You are a generous heart," said Aramis, "only your melancholy uneasiness afflicts me."

"I am not uneasy," said Porthos.

"Then you are angry with me."

"I am not angry with you."

"Then why, my friend, do you put on such a dismal countenance?"

"I will tell you: I feel fatigued. It is the first time, and there is a custom in our family."

"What is it, my friend?"

"My grandfather was a man twice as strong as I am."

"Indeed!" said Aramis; "then your grandfather must have been Samson himself."

"No; his name was Antoine. Well! he was about my age, when setting out one day for the chase, he felt his legs weak, he who had never known this before."

"What was the meaning of that fatigue, my friend?"

"Nothing good, as you will see; for having set out, complaining still of the weakness of his legs, he met a wild boar, which made head against him; he missed him with his arquebuse, and was ripped up by the beast, and died directly."

"There is no reason in that why you should alarm yourself, dear Porthos."

"Oh! you will see. My father was as strong again as I am. He was a rough soldier, under Henry III and Henry IV; his name was not Antoine, but Gaspard, the same as M. de Coligny. Always on horseback, he had never known what lassitude was. One evening, as he rose from table, his legs failed him."

"He had supped heartily, perhaps," said Aramis, "and that was why he staggered."

"Bah! A friend of M. de Bassompierre, nonsense! No, no, he was astonished at feeling this lassitude, and said to my mother, who laughed at him, 'Would not she believe I was going to meet with a wild boar, as the late M. du Vallon, my father, did?' "

"Well?" said Aramis.

"Well! having this weakness, my father insisted upon going down into the garden instead of going to bed; his foot slipped on the first stair; the staircase was steep; my father fell against a stone angle in which an iron hinge was fixed. The hinge opened his temple; and he lay dead upon the spot."

Aramis raised his eyes to his friend: "These are two extraordinary circumstances," said he; "let us not infer that there may succeed a third. It is not becoming in a man of your strength to be superstitious, my brave Porthos. Besides, when were your legs seen to fail? Never have you been so firm, so superb; why, you could carry a house on your shoulders."

"At this moment," said Porthos, "I feel myself pretty active; but at times I vacillate, I sink; and lately this phenomenon, as you say, has occurred four times. I will not say that this frightens me, but it annoys me. Life is an agreeable thing. I have money; I have fine estates; I have horses that I love; I have also friends I love: d'Artagnan, Athos, Raoul, and you."

The admirable Porthos did not even take the trouble to dissimulate to Aramis the rank he gave him in his friendship. Aramis pressed his hand: "We will still live many years," said he, "to preserve in the world specimens of rare men. Trust yourself to me, my friend; we have no reply from d'Artagnan; that is a good sign. He must have given orders to get the vessels together and clear the seas. On my part I have just issued directions that a barque should be rolled upon rollers to the mouth of the great cavern of Locmaria, which you know, where we have so often laid wait for foxes."

"Yes, and which terminates at the little creek by a trench which we discovered the day that splendid fox escaped that way."

"Precisely. In case of misfortunes, a barque is to be concealed for us in that cavern; indeed, it must be there by this time. We will wait for a favourable moment, and, during the night, to sea!"

"That is a good idea; what shall we gain by it?"

"We shall gain by it—that nobody knows that grotto, or rather its issue, except ourselves and two or three hunters of the island; we shall gain by it—that if the island is occupied, the scouts, seeing no barque upon the shore, will never imagine we can escape, and will cease to watch."

All at once a cry resounded in their ears: "To arms! to arms!"

This cry, repeated by a hundred voices, brought to the chamber where the two friends were conversing, surprise to the one, and uneasiness to the other. Aramis opened the window; he saw a crowd of people running with flambeaux. Women were seeking places of safety, the armed population were hastening to their posts.

"The fleet! the fleet!" cried a soldier, who recognised Aramis.

"The fleet?" repeated the latter.

"Within half cannon-shot," continued the soldier.

"To arms!" cried Aramis.

"To arms!" repeated Porthos formidably. And both rushed forth towards the mole, to place themselves within the shelter of the batteries. Boats, laden with soldiers, were seen approaching; they took three directions, for the purpose of landing at three points at once.

"What must be done?" said an officer of the guard.

"Stop them; and if they persist, fire!" said Aramis.

Five minutes after the cannonade commenced. These were the shots that d'Artagnan had heard as he landed in France. But the boats were too near the mole to allow the cannon to aim correctly. They landed, and the combat commenced hand to hand.

"What's the matter, Porthos?" said Aramis to his friend.

"Nothing! nothing!—only my legs; it is really incomprehensible!—they will be better when we charge." In fact, Porthos and Aramis did charge with such vigour; they so thoroughly animated their men, that the royalists re-embarked precipitately, without gaining anything but the wounds they carried away.

"Eh! but, Porthos," cried Aramis, "we must have a prisoner, quick! quick!" Porthos bent over the stair of the mole, and seized by the nape of the neck one of the officers of the royal army who was waiting to embark till all his people should be in the boat. The arm of the giant lifted up his prey, which served him as a buckler, as he recovered himself, without a shot being fired at him.

"Here is a prisoner for you," said Porthos coolly to Aramis.

"Well!" cried the latter, laughing, "have you not calumniated your legs?"

"It was not with my legs I took him," said Porthos; "it was with my arms."

Chapter 50

THE SON OF BISCARRAT

THE Bretons of the Isle were very proud of this victory; Aramis did not encourage them in the feeling.

"What will happen," said he to Porthos, when everybody was gone home, "will be that the anger of the King will be roused by the account of the resistance, and that these brave people will be decimated or shot when they are taken, which cannot fail to take place."

"From which it results then," said Porthos, "that what we have done is of no use."

"For the moment it may be of some," replied the Bishop, "for we have a prisoner from whom we shall learn what our enemies are preparing to do."

"Yes, let us interrogate the prisoner," said Porthos, "and the means of making him speak are very simple. We are going to supper; we will invite him to join us; when he drinks he will talk."

This was done. The officer was at first rather uneasy, but became reassured on seeing what sort of men he had to deal with. He gave, without having any fear of compromising himself, all the details imaginable of the resignation and departure of d'Artagnan. He explained how, after that departure, the new leader of the expedition had ordered a surprise upon Belle-Isle. There his explanations stopped. Aramis and Porthos exchanged a glance which evinced their despair. No more dependence to be placed upon the brave imagination of d'Artagnan; consequently, no more resources in the event of defeat. Aramis, continuing his interrogations, asked the prisoner what the leaders of the expedition contemplated doing with the leaders of Belle-Isle.

"The orders are," replied he, "to kill during the combat, and hang afterwards."

Porthos and Aramis looked at each other again, and the colour mounted to their faces.

"One more cup of wine to your health," said Porthos, drinking himself. From one subject to another the chat with the officer was prolonged. He was an intelligent gentleman, and suffered himself to be led away by the charm of Aramis's wit, and Porthos's cordial *bonhomie*.

"Do you know what my name is?"

"*Ma foi!* no, monsieur; but you can tell us, and——"

"I am called Georges de Biscarrat."

"Oh!" cried Porthos in his turn, "Biscarrat! Do you remember that name, Aramis?"

"Biscarrat!" reflected the Bishop. "It seems to me——"

"Try to recollect, monsieur," said the officer.

"*Pardieu!* that won't take me long," said Porthos. "Biscarrat—called Cardinal—one of the four who interrupted us the day on which we formed our friendship with d'Artagnan, sword in hand."

"Precisely, gentlemen."

"The only one," cried Aramis eagerly, "we did not wound."

"Consequently, a good blade," said the prisoner.

"That's true! very true!" exclaimed both the friends together. "*Ma foi!* Monsieur Biscarrat, we are delighted to make the acquaintance of such a brave man's son."

Biscarrat pressed the hands held out to him by the two ancient musketeers. Aramis looked at Porthos as much as to say—Here is a man who will help us, and without delay,—"Confess, monsieur," said he, "that it is good to have once been a good man."

"My father always said so, monsieur."

"Confess, likewise, that it is a sad circumstance in which you find yourself, of falling in with men destined to be shot or hung, and to learn that these men are old acquaintances—old hereditary acquaintances."

"Oh! you are not reserved for such a frightful fate as that, messieurs and friends!" said the young man warmly.

"In that you are perfectly right, my worthy friend," replied Aramis, constantly consulting with his looks the countenance of Biscarrat, who was silent and constrained. "You wish, Monsieur de Biscarrat, to say something to us, to make us some overture, and you dare not—is not that true?"

"Ah! gentlemen and friends! it is because in speaking I betray my duty. But, hark! I hear a voice which liberates mine by dominating over it."

"Cannon!" said Porthos.

"Cannon and musketry too!" cried the Bishop.

"What is that?"

"The attack made by you was nothing but a feint; is not that true, monsieur? And whilst your companions allowed themselves to be repulsed, you were certain of effecting a landing on the other side of the island."

"Oh! several, monsieur."

"Monsieur de Biscarrat," said the Bishop of Vannes, with a singular accent of nobleness and courtesy, "Monsieur de Biscarrat, be kind enough to resume your liberty."

The worthy officer, then jumping upon a horse given him by Aramis, departed in the direction of the sound of the cannon, and which, by bringing the crowd into the fort, had interrupted the conversation of the two friends and their prisoner. Aramis watched his departure, and when left alone with Porthos, "Well, do you comprehend?" said he.

"*Ma foi!* no."

"Did not Biscarrat inconvenience you here?"

"No; he is a brave fellow."

"Yes; but the grotto of Locmaria—is it necessary all the world should know it?"

"Ah! that is true, that is true; I comprehend. We are going to escape by the cavern."

"If you please" replied Aramis joyously. "Forward, my friend, Porthos; our boat awaits us, and the King has not caught us yet."

Chapter 51

THE GROTTO OF LOCMARIA

THE cavern of Locmaria was sufficiently distant from the mole to render it necessary for our friends to husband their strength to arrive there. Besides, night was advancing; midnight had struck at the fort. Porthos and Aramis were loaded with money and arms. They walked then, across the heath, which is between the mole and the cavern, listening to every noise, and endeavouring to avoid ambushes. At length, after a rapid course, frequently interrupted by prudent stoppages, they reached the deep grottos, into which the foreseeing Bishop of Vannes had taken care to have rolled upon cylinders a good barque capable of keeping the sea at this fine season.

"My good friend," said Porthos, after having respired vigorously, "we are arrived, it seems. But I thought you spoke of three men, three servants who were to accompany us. I don't see them—where are they?"

"Why should you see them, dear Porthos?" replied Aramis. "They are certainly waiting for us in the cavern, and, no doubt, are resting for a moment, after having accomplished their rough and difficult task."

Aramis stopped Porthos, who was preparing to enter the cavern. "Will you allow me, my friend," said he to the giant, "to pass in first? I know the signal I have given to these men; who, not hearing it, would be very likely to fire upon you or slash away with their knives in the dark."

"Go on, then, Aramis; go on—go first; you are all wisdom and prudence; go on. Ah! there is that fatigue again, of which I spoke to you. It has just seized me again."

Aramis left Porthos sitting at the entrance of the grotto, and bowing his head, he penetrated into the interior of the cavern, imitating the cry of the owl. A little plaintive cooing, a scarcely distinct cry, replied from the depths of the cave. Aramis pursued his way cautiously, and soon was stopped by the same kind of cry as he had first uttered, and this cry sounded within ten paces of him.

"Are you there, Yves?" said the Bishop.

"Yes, monseigneur; Goenne is here likewise. His son accompanies us."

"That is well. Are all things ready?"

"Yes, monseigneur."

"Go to the entrance of the grottos my good Yves, and you will there find the Seigneur de Pierrefonds, who is resting after the fatigue of our journey. And if he should happen not to be able to walk, lift him up, and bring him hither to me."

The three men obeyed. But the recommendation given to his servants was useless. Porthos, refreshed, had already himself commenced the descent, and his heavy step resounded amongst the cavities, formed and supported by columns of silex and granite. As soon as the Seigneur de Bracieux had rejoined the Bishop, the Bretons lighted a lantern with which they were furnished, and Porthos assured his friend that he felt as strong as ever.

"Let us visit the canoe," said Aramis, "and satisfy ourselves at once what it will hold."

"Do not go too near with the light," said Yves; "for, as you desired me, monseigneur, I have placed under the bench of the poop, in the coffer you know of, the barrel of powder, and the musket charges that you sent me from the fort."

"Very well," said Aramis; and, taking the lantern himself, he examined minutely all parts of the canoe, with the precautions of a man who is neither timid nor ignorant in the face of danger. The canoe was long, light, drawing little water, thin of keel; in short, one of those which have always been so well constructed at Belle-Isle; a little high in its sides, solid upon the water, very manageable, furnished with planks, which, in uncertain weather, form a sort of bridge over which the waves glide and which protect the rowers. In two well-closed coffers, placed beneath the benches of the prow and the poop, Aramis found bread biscuit, dried fruits, a quarter of bacon, a good provision of water in leathern bottles; the whole forming rations sufficient for people who did not mean to quit the coast, and would be able to revictual, if necessity commanded. The arms, eight muskets, and as many horse pistols, were in good condition, and all loaded. There were additional oars, in case of accident, and a little lug sail, which assists the speed of the canoe at the same time the boatmen row, and is so useful when the breeze is slack. When Aramis had seen all these things, and appeared satisfied with the result of his inspection, "Let us consult, Porthos," said he, "to know if we must endeavour to get the barque out by the unknown extremity of the grotto, following the descent and the shade of the cavern, or whether it be better in the open air, to make it slide upon the rollers, through the bushes, levelling the road of the little beach, which is but twenty feet high, and gives at its foot, in the tide, three or four fathoms of good water upon as sound bottom."

"It must be as you please, monseigneur," replied Yves, respectfully; "but I don't believe that by the slope of the cavern, and in the dark, in which we shall be obliged to manœuvre our boat, the road will be so convenient as in the open air. I know the beach well, and can certify that it is as smooth as a grass plat in a garden; the interior of the grotto, on the contrary, is rough; without again reckoning, monseigneur, that at the extremity we shall come to the trench which leads to the sea, and perhaps the canoe will not pass down it."

"I have made my calculations," said the Bishop, "and I am certain it would pass."

"So be it; I wish it may, monseigneur," continued the skipper; "but your greatness knows very well that to make it reach the extremity of the trench, there is an enormous stone to be lifted—that under which the fox always passes, and which closes the trench up like a door."

"That can be raised," said Porthos, "that is nothing."

And the three robust Bretons went to the boat, and were beginning to place their rollers underneath it to put it in motion, when the distant barking of dogs was heard, proceeding from the interior.

"It is a pack of hounds," said Porthos; "the dogs are upon a scent."

"Who can be hunting at such a moment as this?" said Aramis.

"And this way particularly," continued Porthos, "this way, where they may expect the army of the royalists."

"In common prudence," said Aramis, "let us go back into the grotto; the voices evidently draw nearer; we shall soon know what we have to trust to."

They re-entered, but had scarcely proceeded a hundred steps in the darkness, when a noise like the hoarse sigh of a creature in distress resounded through the cavern, and breathless, rapid, terrified, a fox passed like a flash of lightning before the fugtives, leaped over the boat and disappeared, leaving behind it its sour scent, which was perceptible for several seconds under the low vaults of the cave.

"The fox!" cried the Bretons, with the joyous surprise of hunters.

"Accursed chance!" cried the Bishop, "our retreat is discovered."

As if to confirm the words of Aramis, they heard the yelping pack come with frightful swiftness upon the trail of the animal. Six foxhounds burst out at once upon the little heath, with a cry resembling the noise of a triumph.

"There are the dogs plain enough!" said Aramis, posted on the lookout behind a chink between two rocks; "now, who are the huntsmen?"

Porthos applied his eye to the slit, and saw at the summit of a hillock a dozen horsemen urging on their horses in the track of the dogs, shouting "*Taïaut! taïaut!*"

"The guards!" said he.

"Yes, my friend, the King's guards."

"The King's guards! do you say, monseigneur!" cried the Bretons, becoming pale in their turns.

"And Biscarrat at their head, mounted upon my grey horse," continued Aramis.

The hounds at the same moment rushed into the grotto like an avalanche, and the depths of the cavern were filled with their deafening cries.

"Ah! the devil!" said Aramis, resuming all his coolness at the sight of this certain, inevitable danger. "I am perfectly satisfied we are lost, but we have at least one chance left. If the guards who follow their hounds happen to discover there is an issue to the grotto, there is no more help for us, for on entering they must see both us and our boat. The dogs must not go out of the cavern. The masters must not enter."

"That is clear," said Porthos.

"You understand," added Aramis, with the rapid precision of command; "there are six dogs which will be forced to stop at the great stone under which the fox has glided—but at the too narrow opening of which they shall be themselves stopped and killed."

The Bretons sprang forward knife in hand. In a few minutes there was a lamentable concert of growls, and mortal howlings—and then, nothing.

"That's well!" said Aramis, coolly, "now for the masters!"

"What is to be done with them?" said Porthos.

"Wait their arrival, conceal ourselves, and kill them."

"Kill them!" replied Porthos.

"There are sixteen," said Aramis, "at least, up at present."

"And well armed," added Porthos, with a smile of consolation.

"It will last about ten minutes," said Aramis. "To work!"

And with a resolute air he took up a musket, and placed his hunting knife between his teeth.

"Yves, Goenne, and his son," continued Aramis, "will pass the muskets to us. You, Porthos, will fire when they are close. We shall have brought down eight before the others are aware of anything—that is certain; then, all, there are five of us; we will despatch the other eight, knife in hand."

"And poor Biscarrat?" said Porthos.

Aramis reflected a moment—"Biscarrat the first," replied he coolly; "He knows us."

Chapter 52

THE GROTTO

BISCARRAT, better mounted than his companions, arrived the first at the opening of the grotto, and comprehended that the fox and the dogs were all engulfed in it.

"Well?" asked the young man, coming up out of breath and unable to understand the meaning of his inaction.

"Well! I cannot hear the dogs; they and the fox must be all engulfed in this cavern."

"What the devil can have become of them?" asked the young men in chorus.

And every master called his dog by name, whistled to him in his favourite note, without a single one replying to either the call or the whistle.

"It is perhaps an enchanted grotto," said Biscarrat; "let us see." And jumping from his horse, he made a step into the grotto.

"Stop! stop! I will accompany you," said one of the guards, on seeing Biscarrat disappear in the shade of the cavern's mouth.

"No," replied Biscarrat, "there must be something extraordinary in the place—don't let us risk ourselves all at once. If in ten minutes you do not hear of me you can come in, but not all at once."

Biscarrat entered then alone, and advanced through the darkness till he came in contact with the muzzle of Porthos's musket. The resistance which his chest met with astonished him. He naturally raised his hand and laid hold of the icy barrel. At the same instant, Yves lifted a knife against the young man which was about to fall upon him with all the force of a Breton's arm, when the iron wrist of Porthos stopped it half-way. Then, like low, muttering thunder, his voice growled in the darkness; "I will not have him killed."

Biscarrat found himself between a protection and a threat, the one almost as terrible as the other. However brave the young man might be, he could not prevent a cry escaping him, which Aramis immediately suppressed by placing a handkerchief over his mouth.

"Monsieur Biscarrat," said he, "you would be already dead if we had not had regard for your youth and our ancient association with your father; but you may yet escape from the place by swearing that you will not tell your companions what you have seen."

"I will not only swear that I will not speak of it," said Biscarrat, "but I still further swear that I will do everything in the world to prevent my companions from setting foot in the grotto."

"Biscarrat! Biscarrat!" cried several voices from the outside, coming like a whirlwind into the cave.

"Reply," said Aramis.

"Here am I!" cried Biscarrat.

"Now, begone; we depend upon your loyalty." And he left his hold of the young man, who hastily returned towards the light.

"Biscarrat! Biscarrat!" cried the voices, still nearer. And the shadows of several human forms projected into the interior of the grotto.

Biscarrat rushed to meet his friends, in order to stop them, and met them just as they were adventuring into the cave.

Biscarrat made a last effort to stop his friends, but it was useless. In vain he threw himself before the most rash; in vain he clung to the rocks to bar the passage; the crowd of young men rushed into the cave, in the steps of the officer who had spoken last, but who had sprung in first, sword in hand, to face the unknown danger. Biscarrat, repulsed by his friends, not able to accompany them without passing in the eyes of Porthos and Aramis for a traitor and a perjurer, with painfully attentive ear and still supplicating hands leant against the rough side of a rock which he thought must be exposed to the fire of the musketeers. As to the guards, they penetrated farther and farther, with cries that grew weaker as they advanced. All at once, a discharge of musketry, growling like thunder, exploded beneath the vault. Two or three balls were flattened against the rock where Biscarrat was leaning. At the same instant, cries, howlings, and imprecations burst forth, and the little troop of gentlemen reappeared—some pale, some bleeding—all enveloped in a cloud of smoke, which the outward air seemed to draw from the depths of the cavern. "Biscarrat! Biscarrat!" cried the fugitives, "you knew that was an ambuscade in that cavern, and you have not warned us! Biscarrat, you are the cause that four of us have been killed! Woe be to you, Biscarrat!"

Biscarrat, with hair on end, haggard eyes, and bewildered head, advanced towards the interior of the cavern, saying, "You are right. Death to me, who have allowed my companions to be assassinated. I am a base wretch!" And throwing away his sword, for he wished to die without defending himself, he rushed head foremost into the cavern. The others followed him. The eleven who remained out of sixteen imitated his example; but they did not go farther than the first. A second discharge laid five upon the icy sand; and, as it was impossible to see whence this murderous thunder issued, the others fell back with a terror that can be better imagined than expressed. But, far from flying, as the others had done, Biscarrat remained safe and sound, seated on a fragment of rock, and waited. There were only six gentlemen left.

"Where is Biscarrat?" The young men looked round them, and saw that Biscarrat did not answer.

"He is dead!" said two or three voices.

"Oh! no," replied another; "I saw him through the smoke, sitting quietly on a rock. He is in the cavern; he is waiting for us."

"He must know who are there."

"And how should he know them?"

"He was taken prisoner by the rebels."

"Good!" said an officer. "We have no longer any need of him; here are reinforcements coming."

In fact, a company of the guards, left in the rear by their officers, whom the ardour of the chase had carried away—from seventy-five to eighty men —arrived in good order, led by their captain and the first lieutenant. The five officers hastened to meet their soldiers; and, in a language, the eloquence of which may be easily imagined, they related the adventure, and asked for aid. The captain interrupted them: "Where are your companions?" demanded he.

"Dead!"

"But there were sixteen of you."

"Ten are dead. Biscarrat is in the cavern, and we are five."

"Biscarrat is then a prisoner?"

"Probably."

"No, for here he is—look." In fact, Biscarrat appeared at the opening of the grotto.

"He makes us a sign to come on," said the officer. "Come on!"

"Come on!" cried all the troop. And they advanced to meet Biscarrat.

"Monsieur," said the captain, addressing Biscarrat, "I am assured that you know who the men are in that grotto, and who make such a desperate defence. In the King's name I command you to declare what you know."

"Captain," said Biscarrat, "you have no need to command me; my word has been restored to me this very instant; and I come in the name of these men."

"To tell me who they are?"

"To tell you they are determined to defend themselves to the death, unless you grant them good terms."

"How many are there of them, then?"

"There are two," said Biscarrat.

"Two men—and they have killed ten in two discharges! That is impossible, Monsieur Biscarrat!"

And he marched first as far as the opening of the grotto. There he halted. The object of this halt was to give to Biscarrat and his companions time to describe to him the interior of the grotto. Then, when he believed he had a sufficient acquaintance with the places, he divided his company into three bodies, which were to enter successively, keeping up a sustained fire in all directions.

"Captain," said Biscarrat, "I beg to be allowed to march at the head of the first platoon."

"So be it," replied the captain; "you have all the honour of it. That is a present I make you."

"Thanks!" replied the young man, with all the firmness of his race.

"Take your sword, then."

"I shall go as I am, captain," said Biscarrat, "for I do not go to kill, I go to be killed."

And placing himself at the head of the first platoon with his head uncovered and his arms crossed,—"March, gentlemen!" said he.

Chapter 53

AN HOMERIC SONG

It is time to pass into the other camp, and to describe at once the combatants and the field of battle. Aramis and Porthos had gone to the grotto of Locmaria with the expectation of finding there their canoe ready armed, as well as the three Bretons, their assistants; and they at first hoped to make the barque pass through the little issue of the cavern, concealing in that fashion both their labours and their flight. The arrival of the fox and the dogs had obliged them to remain concealed. The grotto extended the space of about two hundred yards, to that little slope dominating a creek. The first entrance to the cavern was by a moderate descent, above which heaped-up rocks formed a low arcade; the interior, very unequal as to the ground, dangerous from the rocky inequalities of the vault, was subdivided into several compartments which commanded each other and joined each other by means of several rough, broken steps, fixed right and left, in enormous natural pillars. At the third compartment, the vault was so low, the passage so narrow, the barque would scarcely have passed without touching the two sides; nevertheless, in a moment of despair, wood softens and stone becomes compliant under the breath of human will. Such was the thought of Aramis, when, after having fought the fight, he decided upon flight—a flight certainly dangerous, since all the assailants were not dead; and that, admitting the possibility of putting the barque to sea, they would have to fly in open day, before the conquered, to interested on recognising their small number, in pursuing their conquerors. Then the two discharges had killed ten men. Aramis, habituated to the windings of the cavern, went to reconnoitre them one by one—counted them, for the smoke prevented seeing outside; and he immediately commanded that the canoe should be rolled as far as the great stone, the closure of the liberating issue. Porthos collected all his strength, took the canoe up in his arms and raised it up, whilst the Bretons made it run rapidly along the rollers. They had descended into the third compartment; they had arrived at the stone which walled up the outlet. Porthos seized this gigantic stone at its base, applied to it his robust shoulder, and gave a heave which made this wall crack. A cloud of dust fell from the vault with the ashes of ten thousand generations of sea-birds, whose nests stuck like cement to the rock. At the third shock the stone gave way; it oscillated for a minute. Porthos, placing his back against the neighbouring rock, made an arch with his foot, which drove the block out of the calcareous masses which served for hinges and cramps. The stone fell, and daylight was visible, brilliant, radiant, which rushed into the cavern by the opening, and the blue sea appeared to the delighted Bretons. They then began to lift the barque over the barricade. Twenty more yards, and it might glide into the ocean. It was during this time, that the company arrived, was drawn up by the captain, and disposed for either an escalade or an assault. Aramis watched over everything, to favour the labours of his friends. He saw the reinforcements, he counted the men, he convinced himself at a single glance of the insurmountable peril to which a fresh combat would expose them. To escape by sea, at the moment the cavern was about to be invaded, was impossible. In fact, the daylight which had just been admitted to the last two compartments had exposed to the soldiers the barque being rolled towards the sea, the two rebels within musket shot, and one of their discharges would riddle the boat if it did not kill the five navigators. Aramis, digging his hands into his grey hair with rage, invoked the assistance of God and the assistance of the demon. Calling to Porthos, who was working alone more than all the rollers—whether of flesh or of wood— "My friend," said he, "our enemies have just received a reinforcement."

"Ah! ah!" said Porthos quietly, "what is to be done, then?"

"We two will keep the powder, the balls, and the muskets here."

"But only two, my dear Aramis—we shall never fire three shots together," said Porthos innocently, "the defence by musketry is a bad one."

"Find a better, then."

"I have found one," said the giant eagerly; "I will place myself in ambuscade behind the pillar with this iron bar, and invisible, unattackable if they come on in floods, I can let my bar fall upon their skulls, thirty times in a minute. *Hein!* what do you think of the project? You smile!"

"Excellent, dear friend, perfect! I approve it greatly; only you will frighten them, and half of them will remain outside to take us by famine. What we want my good friend, is the entire destruction of the troop; a single man left standing ruins us."

"You are right, my friend, but how can we attract them, pray?"

"By not stirring, my good Porthos."

"Well! we won't stir, then; but when they shall be all together——"

"Then leave it to me! I have an idea."

"If it is thus, and your idea be a good one—and your idea is most likely to be good—I am satisfied."

"To your ambuscade, Porthos, and count how many enter."

"But you, what will you do?"

"Don't trouble yourself about me; I have a task to perform."

"I think I can hear cries."

"It is they. To your post. Keep within reach of my voice and hand."

Porthos took refuge in the second compartment, which was absolutely black with darkness. Aramis glided into the third; the giant held in his hand an iron bar of about fifty pounds weight. Porthos handled this lever, which had been used in rolling the barque, with marvellous facility. During this time, the Bretons had pushed the barque to the beach. In the enlightened compartment, Aramis, stooping and concealed, was busied in some mysterious manœuvre. A command was given in a loud voice. It was the last order of the captain commandant. Twenty-five men jumped from the upper rocks into the first compartment of the grotto, and having taken their ground, began to fire. The echoes growled, the hissing of the balls cut the air, an opaque smoke filled the vault.

"To the left! to the left!" cried Biscarrat, who, in his first assault, had seen the passage to the second chamber, and who, animated by the smell of powder, wished to guide his soldiers in that direction. The troop accordingly precipitated themselves to the left—the passage gradually growing narrower. Biscarrat, with his hands stretched forward, devoted to death, marched in advance of the muskets. "Come on!" exclaimed he, "I see daylight!"

"Strike, Porthos!" cried the sepulchral voice of Aramis.

Porthos heaved a heavy sigh—but he obeyed. The iron bar fell full and direct upon the head of Biscarrat, who was dead before he had ended his cry. Then the formidable lever rose ten times in ten seconds, and made ten corpses. The soldiers could see nothing; they heard sighs and groans; they stumbled over dead bodies, but as they had no conception of the cause of all this, they came forward jostling each other. The implacable bar, still falling, annihilated the first platoon, without a single sound having warned the second which was quietly advancing, only this second platoon, commanded by the captain, had broken a thin fir, growing on the shore, and, with its resinous branches twisted together, the captain had made a flambeau. On arriving at the compartment where Porthos, like the exterminating angel had destroyed all he touched, the first rank drew back in terror. No firing had replied to that of the guards, and yet their way was stopped by a heap of dead bodies—they literally walked in blood. Porthos was still behind his pillar. The captain, on enlightening with the trembling flame of the fir this frightful carnage, of which he in vain sought the cause, drew back towards the pillar, behind which Porthos was concealed. Then a gigantic hand issued from the shade, and fastened on the throat of the captain, who uttered a stifled rattle; his outstretched arms beating the air, the torch fell and was extinguished in blood. A second after the corpse of the captain fell close to the extinguished torch, and added another body to the heap of dead which blocked up the passage. From an unreflective, instinctive, mechanical feeling, the lieutenant cried,—"Fire!"

Immediately a volley of musketry flamed, thundered, roared in the cavern, bringing down enormous fragments from the vaults. The cavern was lighted for an instant by this discharge, and then immediately returned to a darkness rendered still thicker by the smoke. To this succeeded a profound silence, broken only by the steps of the third brigade, now entering the cavern.

Chapter 54

THE DEATH OF A TITAN

AT THE moment when Porthos, more accustomed to the darkness than all these men coming from open daylight, was looking round him to see if in this night Aramis were not making him some signal, he felt his arm gently touched, and a voice low as a breath murmured in his ear, "Come."

And amidst the noise of the third brigade, which continued to advance, amidst the imprecations of the guards left alive, of the dying, rattling their last sigh, Aramis and Porthos glided imperceptibly along the granite walls of the cavern. Aramis led Porthos into the last but one compartment, and showed him, in a hollow of the rocky wall, a barrel of powder weighing from seventy to eighty pounds, to which he had just attached a match. "My friend," said he to Porthos, "you will take this barrel, the match of which I am going to set fire to, and throw it amidst our enemies; can you do so?"

"*Parbleu!*" replied Porthos; and he lifted the barrel with one hand. "Light it!"

"Stop," said Aramis, "till they are all massed together, and then, my Jupiter, hurl your thunder-bolt among them."

"Light it," repeated Porthos.

"On my part," continued Aramis, "I will join our Bretons, and help them to get the canoe to the sea. I will wait for you on the shore; launch it strongly, and hasten to us."

"Light it," said Porthos, a third time.

"But do you understand me?"

"*Parbleu!*" said Porthos again, with laughter that he did not even attempt to restrain; "when a thing is explained to me I understand it; begone, and give me the light."

Aramis gave the burning match to Porthos, who held out his arm to him, his hands being engaged. Aramis pressed the arm of Porthos with both his hands, and fell back to the outlet of the cavern where the three rowers awaited him.

Porthos, left alone, applied the spark bravely to the match. The spark—a feeble spark, first principle of a conflagration—shone in the darkness like a fire-fly, then was deadened against the match which it enflamed, Porthos enlivening the flame with his breath. The smoke was a little dispersed, and by the light of the sparkling match, objects might, for two seconds, be distinguished.

Then the arm of the giant swung round; then was seen to pass through the air, like a falling star, the train of fire. The barrel, hurled a distance of thirty feet, cleared the barricade of dead bodies, and fell amidst a group of shrieking soldiers, who threw themselves on their faces. The officer had followed the brilliant train in the air; he endeavoured to precipitate himself upon the barrel and tear out the match before it reached the powder it contained. Useless devotedness! the air had made the flame attached to the conductor more active; the match, which at rest might have burnt five minutes, was consumed in thirty seconds, and the infernal work exploded. Furious vortices, hissings of sulphur and nitre, devouring ravages of the fire which caught to objects, the terrible thunder of the explosion, this is what the second which followed the two seconds we have described, disclosed in that cavern, equal in horrors to a cavern of demons. The rock split like planks of deal under the axe. A jet of fire, smoke, and debris sprang up from the middle of the grotto, enlarging as it mounted. The large walls of silex tottered and fell upon the sand, and the sand itself, an instrument of pain when launched from its hardened bed, riddled the face with its myriads of cutting atoms. Cries, howlings, imprecations, and existences—all were extinguished in one immense crash.

As to Porthos, after having hurled the barrel of powder amidst his enemies, he had fled as Aramis had directed him to do, and had gained the last compartment, into which air, light, and sunshine penetrated through the opening. Therefore, scarcely had he turned the angle which separated the third compartment from the fourth when he perceived at a hundred paces from him the barque dancing on the waves; there were his friends, there was liberty, there was life after victory. Six more of his formidable strides, and he would be out of the vault; out of the vault! two or three vigorous springs and he would reach the canoe. Suddenly he felt his knees give way; his knees appeared powerless, his legs to yield under him.

"Oh! oh!" murmured he, "there is my fatigue seizing me again! I can walk no further! What is this?"

Aramis perceived him through the opening, and unable to conceive what could induce him to stop thus—"Come on, Porthos! come on!" cried he; "come quickly."

"Oh!" replied the giant, making an effort which acted upon every muscle of his body—"oh, but I cannot." While saying these words he fell upon his knees, but with his robust hands he clung to the rocks, and raised himself up again.

"Quick! quick!" repeated Aramis, bending forward towards the shore, as if to draw Porthos towards him with his arms.

"Here I am," stammered Porthos, collecting all his strength to make one step more.

"In the name of Heaven! Porthos, make haste! the barrel will blow up!"

"Make haste, monseigneur!" shouted the Bretons to Porthos, who was floundering as in a dream.

But there was no longer time; the explosions resounded, the earth gaped, the smoke which rushed through the large fissures obscured the sky.

This frightful shock seemed to restore to Porthos the strength he had lost; he arose, himself a giant among these giants. But at the moment he was flying between the double hedge of granite phantoms, these latter, which were no longer supported by the corresponding links, began to roll with a crash around this Titan, who looked as if precipitated from heaven amidst rocks which he had just been launching at it. Porthos felt the earth beneath his feet shaken by this long rending. He extended his vast hands to the right and left to repulse the falling rocks. A gigantic block was held back by each of his extended hands; he bent his head and a third granite mass sank between his two shoulders. For an instant the arms of Porthos had given way, but the Hercules united all his forces, and the two walls of the prison in which he was buried fell back slowly and gave him place. For an instant he appeared in this frame of granite like the ancient angel of chaos, but in pushing back the lateral rocks, he lost his point of support for the monolith, which weighed upon his strong shoulders, and the monolith, weighing upon him with all its weight, brought the giant down upon his knees. The lateral rocks, for an instant pushed back, drew together again, and added their weight to the primitive weight which would have been sufficient to crush ten men. The giant fell without crying for help; he fell while answering Aramis with words of encouragement and hope, and, thanks to the powerful arch of his hands, for an instant, he might believe that, like Enceladus, he should shake off the triple load. But, by degrees, Aramis saw the block sink; the hands strung for an instant, the arms stiffened for a last effort, gave way, the extended shoulders sank wounded and torn, and the rock continued to lower gradually.

"Porthos! Porthos!" cried Aramis, tearing his hair. "Porthos! where are you? Speak!"

"There, there!" murmured Porthos, with a voice growing evidently weaker, "Patience! patience!"

Scarcely had he pronounced these words, when the impulse of the fall augmented the weight; the enormous rock sank down, pressed by the two others which sank in from the sides, and, as it were, swallowed up Porthos in a sepulchre of broken stones. On hearing the dying voice of his friend, Aramis had sprung to land. Two of the Bretons followed him, with each a lever in his hand—one being sufficient to take care of the barque. The last rattles of the valiant struggler guided them amidst the ruins. Aramis, animated, active, and young, as at twenty, sprang towards the triple mass, and with his hands, delicate as those of a woman, raised by a miracle of vigour a corner of the immense sepulchre of granite. Then he caught a glimpse, in the darkness of that grave, of the still brilliant eye of his friend, to whom the momentary lifting of the mass restored that moment of respiration. The two men came rushing in, grasped their iron levers, united their triple strength, not merely to raise it, but to sustain it. All was useless. The three men slowly gave way with cries of grief, and the rough voice of Porthos, seeing them exhaust themselves in a useless struggle, murmured in a jeering tone those supreme words which came to his lips with the last respiration, "Too heavy."

After which the eye darkened and closed, the face became pale, the hand whitened, and the Titan sank quite down, breathing his last sigh. With him sank the rock, which, even in his agony, he had still held up.

The three men dropped the levers, which rolled upon the tumulary stone. Then, breathless, pale, his brow covered with sweat, Aramis listened, his breast oppressed, his heart ready to break.

Nothing more! The giant slept the eternal sleep, in the sepulchre which God had made to his measure.

Chapter 55

THE EPITAPH OF PORTHOS

ARAMIS, silent, icy, trembling like a timid child, arose shivering from the stone. A Christian does not walk upon tombs. But though capable of standing, he was not capable of walking. It might be said that something of dead Porthos had just died within him. His Bretons surrounded him; Aramis yielded to their kind exertions, and the three sailors, lifting him up, carried him into the canoe. Then having laid him down upon the bench near the rudder, they took to their oars, preferring to get off by rowing to hoisting a sail, which might betray them.

Aramis, still pale, still icy, his heart upon his lips, Aramis looked, even till with the last ray of daylight, the shore faded on the horizon. Not a word escaped his lips, not a sigh rose from his deep breast. The superstitious Bretons looked at him trembling. That silence was not of a man, it was of a statue. In the meantime, with the first grey lines that descended from the heavens, the canoe had hoisted its little sail, which, swelling with the kisses of the breeze, and carrying them rapidly from the coast, made brave way with its head towards Spain, across the terrible gulf of Gascony, so rife with tempests. But scarcely half an hour after the sail had been hoisted, the rowers became inactive, reclining upon their benches, and making an eyeshade with their hands, pointed out to each other a white spot which appeared on the horizon as motionless as is in appearance a gull rocked by the insensible respiration of the waves. But that which might have appeared motionless to ordinary eyes was moving at a quick rate to the experienced eye of the sailor; that which appeared stationary on the ocean was cutting a rapid way through it. For some time, seeing the profound torpor in which their master was plunged, they did not dare to rouse him, and satisfied themselves with exchanging their conjectures in a low, disturbed voice. Aramis, in fact, so vigilant, so active—Aramis, whose eye, like that of the lynx, watched without ceasing, and saw better by night than by day—Aramis seemed to sleep in the despair of his soul. An hour passed thus, during which daylight gradually disappeared, but during which also the sail in view gained so swiftly on the barque, that Goenne, one of the three sailors, ventured to say aloud,—

"Monseigneur, we are being chased!"

Aramis made no reply; the ship still gained upon them. Then, of their own accord, two of the sailors, by the direction of the skipper Yves, lowered the sail, in order that that single point which appeared above the surface of the waters should cease to be a guide to the eye of the enemy who was pursuing them. On the part of the ship in sight, on the contrary, two more small sails were run up at the extremities of the masts. Unfortunately, it was the time of the finest and longest days of the year, and the moon in all her brilliancy succeeded to this inauspicious daylight. The corvette, which was pursuing the little barque before the wind, had then still half an hour of twilight, and a whole night almost as light as day.

The oars dropped from the hands of the sailors, and the barque, ceasing to make way, rocked motionless on the summits of the waves. Night came on, but the vessel still approached nearer. It might be said it redoubled its speed with the darkness. From time to time, as a bloody-necked vulture rears its head out of its nest, the formidable Greek fire darted from its sides, and cast its flame into the ocean like an incandescent snow. At last it came within musket-shot. All the men were on deck, arms in hand; the cannoniers were at their guns, and matches were burning. It might be thought they were about to board a frigate and to combat a crew superior in number to their own, and not to take a canoe manned by four people.

"Surrender!" cried the commander of the corvette, with the aid of the speaking trumpet.

The sailors looked at Aramis. Aramis made a sign with his head. Yves waved a white cloth at the end of a gaff. This was like striking their flag. The vessel came on like a racehorse. It launched a fresh Greek fire which fell within twenty paces of the little canoe, and threw a stronger light upon them than the most ardent ray of the sun could have done.

"At the first sign of resistance," cried the commander of the corvette, "fire!" And the soldiers brought their muskets to the present.

"Did not we say we surrendered?" said Yves.

"Living! living, captain!" cried some highly excited soldiers. "They must be taken living."

"Well, yes—living," said the captain. Then turning towards the Bretons, "Your lives are all safe, my friends!" cried he, "except the Chevalier d'Herblay."

"We accept," repeated the sailors: "but what security have we?"

"The word of a gentleman," said the officer. "By my rank and by my name I swear, that all but M. le Chevalier d'Herblay shall have their lives spared. I am lieutenant of the King's frigate the *Pomona*, and my name is Louis Constant de Pressigny."

With a rapid gesture, Aramis—already bent over the side of the barque towards the sea—with a rapid gesture, Aramis raised his head, drew himself up, and with a flashing eye, and a smile upon his lips, "Throw out the ladder, messieurs," said he, as if the command had belonged to him. He was obeyed. Then Aramis, seizing the ropeladder, instead of the terror which was expected to be displayed upon his countenance, the surprise of the sailors of the corvette was great, when they saw him walk straight up to the commander, with a firm step, look at him earnestly, make a sign to him with his hand, a mysterious and unknown sign, at the sight of which the officer turned pale, trembled, and bowed his head. Without saying a word, Aramis then raised his hand close to the eyes of the commander, and showed him the collet of a ring which he wore on the ring-finger of his left hand. And while making this sign, Aramis, draped in cold, silent, and haughty majesty, had the air of an emperor giving his hand to be kissed. The commandant, who for a moment had raised his head, bowed a second time with marks of the most profound respect. Then stretching his hand out towards the poop, that is to say, towards his own cabin, he drew back to allow Aramis to go first. The three Bretons, who had come on board after their Bishop, looked at each other, stupefied. The crew were struck with silence. Five minutes after, the commander called the second lieutenant, who returned immediately, and gave directions for the head to be put towards Corunna. Whilst the order was being executed Aramis reappeared upon the deck, and took a seat near the bulwarks. The night had fallen, the moon had not yet risen, and yet Aramis looked incessantly towards Belle-Isle. Yves then approached the captain, who had returned to take his post in the stern, and said, in a low and humble voice, "What course are we to follow, captain?"

"We take what course monseigneur pleases," replied the officer.

Aramis passed the night leaning upon the bulwarks. Yves, on approaching him the next morning, remarked, that "the night must have been very humid, for the wood upon which the Bishop's head had rested, was soaked with dew." Who knows!—that dew was, perhaps, the first tears that had ever fallen from the eyes of Aramis!

What epitaph would have been worth that? Good Porthos!

Chapter 56

KING LOUIS XIV

D'ARTAGNAN was not accustomed to resistances like that he had just experienced. He returned, profoundly irritated, to Nantes. Irritation with this vigorous man vented itself in an impetuous attack, which few people, hitherto, were they King, were they giants, had been able to resist. D'Artagnan, trembling with rage, went straight to the castle, and asked to speak to the King.

The King was seated in his cabinet, with his back turned towards the door of entrance. In front of him was a mirror, in which, while turning over his papers, he could see with a glance those who came in. He did not take any notice of the entrance of d'Artagnan, but laid over his letters and plans the large silk cloth which he made use of to conceal his secrets from the importunate. D'Artagnan understood his play, and kept in the background; so that, at the end of a minute, the King, who heard nothing and saw nothing but with the corner of his eye, was obliged to cry, "Is not M. d'Artagnan there?"

"I am here, sire," replied the musketeer, advancing.

"Well, monsieur," said the King, fixing his clear eye upon d'Artagnan, "what have you to say to me?"

"I, sire!" replied the latter, who watched the first blow of his adversary to make a good retort; "I have nothing to say to your Majesty, unless it be that you have caused me to be arrested, and here I am."

The King was going to reply that he had not had d'Artagnan arrested, but the sentence appeared too much like an excuse, and he was silent. D'Artagnan likewise preserved an obstinate silence.

"Monsieur," at length resumed the King, "what did I charge you to go and do at Belle-Isle? Tell me, if you please."

"Well! sire, I know nothing about it; it is not of me that question should be asked, but of that infinite number of officers of all kinds, to whom have been given an infinite number of orders of all kinds, whilst to me, head of the expedition, nothing precise was ordered."

The King was wounded; he showed it by his reply. "Monsieur," said he, "orders have only been given to such as were judged faithful. You have ill-served me, monsieur, by taking part with my enemies against me."

"Who are your enemies, sire?"

"The men I sent you to fight with."

"Two men the enemies of the whole of your Majesty's army! That is incredible!"

"You have no power to judge of my will."

"But I have to judge of my own friendships, sire."

"He who serves his friends, does not serve his master."

"For one bad servant your Majesty loses," said the musketeer, with bitterness, "there are ten who have, on that same day, gone through their ordeal. Listen to me, sire; I am not accustomed to that service. Mine is a rebel sword when I am required to do ill. It was ill to send me in pursuit of two men whose lives M. Fouquet, your Majesty's preserver, had implored you to save. Still further, these men were my friends. They did not attack your Majesty, they succumbed to a blind anger. Besides, why were they not allowed to escape? What crime had they committed?"

Almost at the same moment an officer entered and placed a despatch in the hands of the King, who, in his turn, changed colour while reading it.

"Monsieur," said he, "what I learn here you would know later; it is better I should tell you, and that you should learn it from the mouth of your King. A battle has taken place at Belle-Isle."

"Oh! ah!" said d'Artagnan, with a calm air, though his heart beat enough to break through his chest. "Well, sire!"

"Well, monsieur—and I have lost a hundred and ten men."

A beam of joy and pride shone in the eyes of d'Artagnan. "And the rebels?" said he.

"The rebels have fled," said the King.

D'Artagnan could not restrain a cry of triumph. "Only," added the King, "I have a fleet which closely blockades Belle-Isle, and I am certain no barque can escape."

"So that," said the musketeer, brought back to his dismal ideas, "if these two gentlemen are taken——"

"They will be hanged," said the King quietly.

"And do they know it?" replied d'Artagnan, repressing his trembling.

"They know it, because you must have told them yourself; and all the country knows it."

"Then, sire, they will never be taken alive, I will answer for that." D'Artagnan wiped the sweat which flowed from his brow.

"I have told you," pursued Louis XIV, "that I would one day be an affectionate, generous, and constant master. You are now the only man of former times worthy of my anger or my friendship. I will not be sparing of either to you, according to your conduct. Could you serve a king, Monsieur d'Artagnan, who should have a hundred kings his equals in the kingdom? Could I, tell me, do with such weakness, the great things I meditate? Have you ever seen an artist effect solid works with a rebellious instrument? Far from us, monsieur, these old leavens of feudal abuses! The Fronde which threatened to ruin the monarchy, has emancipated it. I am master at home, Captain d'Artagnan, and I shall have servants who, wanting, perhaps, your genius, will carry devotedness and obedience up to heroism. Of what consequence, I ask you, of what consequence is it that God has given no genius to arms and legs? It is to the head he has given it, and the head, you know, all the rest obey. I am the head."

D'Artagnan started. Louis XIV continued as if he had seen nothing, although this emotion had not at all escaped him. "Now let us conclude between us two that bargain which I promised to make with you one day when you found me very little at Blois. Do me justice, monsieur, when you think that I do not make any one pay for the tears of shame I then shed. Look around you; lofty heads have bowed. Bow yours, or choose the exile that will best suit you. Perhaps, when reflecting upon it, you will find that this king is a generous heart, who reckons sufficiently upon your loyalty to allow you to leave him dissatisfied, when you possess a great state secret. You are a brave man; I know you to be so. Why have you judged me prematurely? Judge me from this day forward, d'Artagnan, and be as severe as you please."

"Oh!" replied d'Artagnan in a melancholy tone, "that is difficult, but I have got over greater difficulties than that. I will do it. Why should I do it? Because I love money?—I have enough. Because I am ambitious?—my career is bounded. Because I love the court? No. I will remain because I have been accustomed for thirty years to go and take the orderly word of the King, and to have said to me, 'Good-evening, d'Artagnan,' with a smile I did not beg for! That smile I will beg for! Are you content, sire?" And d'Artagnan bowed his silvered head, upon which the smiling King placed his white hand, with pride.

"Thanks, my old servant, my faithful friend," said he. "As reckoning from this day, I have no longer any enemies in France; it remains with me to send you to a foreign field to gather your marshal's baton. Depend upon me for finding you an opportunity. In the meanwhile, eat of my best bread, and sleep tranquilly."

"That is all kind and well!" said d'Artagnan, much agitated. "But those poor men at Belle-Isle? One of them, in particular—so good! so brave! so true!"

"Do you ask their pardon of me?"

"Upon my knees, sire."

"Well, then, go and take it to them, if it be still time. But do you answer for them?"

"With my life, sire!"

And, with a heart swelling with joy, he rushed out of the castle on his way to Belle-Isle.

Chapter 57

D'ARTAGNAN'S NEWS

THE KING had returned to Paris, and with him d'Artagnan, who, in twenty-four hours, having made with the greatest care all possible inquiries at Belle-Isle, had learned nothing of the secret so well kept by the heavy rock of Locmaria, which had fallen on the heroic Porthos.

Louis, satisfied with his success, Louis—more mild and more affable since he felt himself more powerful—had not ceased for an instant to ride close to the carriage door of Mademoiselle de la Vallière. Everybody had been anxious to amuse the two Queens, so as to make them forget this abandonment of the son and husband. Everything breathed of the future; the past was nothing to anybody. Only that past came like a painful and bleeding wound to the hearts of some tender and devoted spirits. Scarcely was the King reinstalled in Paris, when he received a touching proof of this. Louis XIV had just risen and taken his first repast, when his captain of the musketeers presented himself before him. D'Artagnan was pale and looked unhappy. The King, at the first glance, perceived the change in a countenance generally so unconcerned. "What is the matter, d'Artagnan?" said he.

"Sire, a great misfortune has happened to me."

"Good heavens! what is that?"

"Sire, I have lost one of my friends, M. du Vallon, in the affair of Belle-Isle."

And while speaking these words, d'Artagnan fixed his falcon eye upon Louis XIV to catch the first feeling that would show itself.

"I knew it," replied the King quietly.

"You knew it, and did not tell me!" cried the musketeer.

"To what good? Your grief, my friend, is so respectable. It was my duty to treat it kindly. To have informed you of this misfortune, which I knew would pain you so greatly, d'Artagnan, would have been, in your eyes, to have triumphed over you. Yes, I knew that M. du Vallon had buried himself beneath the rocks of Locmaria; I knew that M. d'Herblay had taken one of my vessels with its crew, and had compelled it to convey him to Bayonne. But I was willing you should learn these matters in a direct manner, in order that you might be convinced my friends are with me respected and sacred; that always in me the man will immolate himself to men, whilst the King is so often found to sacrifice men to his majesty and power."

"But, sire, how could you know?"

"How do you yourself know, d'Artagnan?"

"By this letter, sire, which M. d'Herblay, free and out of danger, writes me from Bayonne."

"Look here," said the King, drawing from a casket placed upon the table close to the seat upon which d'Artagnan was leaning, "here is a letter copied exactly from that of M. d'Herblay. Here is the very letter which Colbert placed in my hands a week before you received yours. I am well served, you may perceive."

"Yes, sire," murmured the musketeer, "you were the only man whose fortune was capable of dominating the fortunes and strength of my two friends. You have used it, sire, but you will not abuse it, will you?"

"D'Artagnan," said the King, with a smile beaming with kindness, "I could have M. d'Herblay carried off from the territories of the King of Spain, and brought here alive to inflict justice upon him. But, d'Artagnan, be assured I will not yield to this first and natural impulse. He is free; let him continue free."

"Oh, sire! you will not always remain so clement, so noble, so generous as you have shown yourself with respect to me and M. d'Herblay; you will have about you counsellors who will cure you of that weakness."

"No, d'Artagnan, you are mistaken when you accuse my council of urging me to pursue rigorous measures. The advice to spare M. d'Herblay comes from Colbert himself."

"Oh, sire!" said d'Artagnan, extremely surprised.

"As for you," continued the King, with a kindness very uncommon with him, "I have several pieces of good news to announce to you; but you shall know them, my dear captain, the moment I have made my accounts all straight. I have said that I wished to make, and would make, your fortune; that promise will soon be a reality."

"A thousand times thanks, sire!"

Chapter 58

THE VISION OF ATHOS

WHILE all these affairs were separating for ever the four musketeers, formerly bound together in a manner that seemed indissoluble, Athos, left alone after the departure of Raoul, began to pay his tribute to that anticipated death which is called the absence of those we love. Returned to his house at Blois, no longer having even Grimaud to receive a poor smile when he passed through the parterre, Athos daily felt the decline of the vigour of a nature which for so long a time had appeared infallible. Age, which had been kept back by the presence of the beloved object, now came on, with its attendant pains and inconveniences. The Comte de la Fère, who had remained a young man up to his sixty-second year; the warrior who had preserved his strength in spite of fatigues, his freshness of mind in spite of misfortunes, his mild serenity of soul and body in spite of malady, in spite of Mazarin, in spite of La Vallière: Athos had become an old man in a week, from the moment at which he had lost the support of his latter youth. Still handsome, though bent; noble, but sad; gentle, and tottering under his grey hairs, he sought, since his solitude, the glades where the rays of the sun penetrated through the foliage of the walks. He discontinued all the strong exercises he had enjoyed through life, when Raoul was no longer with him.

He did not even desire that all letters that came should be brought to him directly. He knew very well that every distraction which should arrive would be a joy, a hope, which his servants would have paid with their blood to procure him. Sleep had become rare. By intense thinking, Athos forgot himself, for a few hours at most, in a reverie more profound, more obscure than other people would have called a dream. This momentary repose which this forgetfulness afforded the body, fatigued the soul, for Athos lived a double life during these wanderings of his understanding. One night, he dreamt that Raoul was dressing himself in a tent, to go upon an expedition commanded by M. de Beaufort in person. The young man was sad; he clasped his cuirass slowly, and slowly he girded on his sword.

"What is the matter?" asked his father tenderly.

"What afflicts me is the death of Porthos, ever so dear a friend," replied Raoul. "I suffer here of the grief you will feel at home."

And the vision disappeared with the slumber of Athos. At daybreak one of his servants entered his master's apartment, and gave him a letter which came from Spain.

"The writing of Aramis," thought the Comte; and he read.

"Porthos is dead!" cried he, after the first lines. "Oh! Raoul, Raoul! thanks! thou keepest thy promise; thou warnest me!"

And Athos, seized with a mortal sweat, fainted in his bed, without any other cause than his weakness.

Then commenced for Athos a strange, indefinable state. Free to think, his mind turned towards Raoul, that beloved son. His imagination painted the fields of Africa in the environs of Gigelli, where M. de Beaufort must have landed his army. There were grey rocks, rendered green in certain parts by the waters of the sea, when it lashed the shore in storms and tempests. Beyond, the shore, strewn over with these rocks like tombs, ascended, in form of an amphitheatre, among mastick-trees and cacti, a sort of small town, full of smoke, confused noises and terrified movements.

Night then came over the scene; a night dark upon the earth, brilliant in the firmament. The large, blazing stars which sparkled in the African sky shone without lighting anything even around them.

Then, while his eye was wandering over the plain, turning on all sides, he saw a white form appear behind the resinous myrtles. This figure was clothed in the costume of an officer: it held in its hand a broken sword: it advanced slowly towards Athos, who, stopping short and fixing his eyes upon it, neither spoke nor moved, but wished to open his arms, because, in this silent and pale officer, he had just recognised Raoul.

At length he gained the crest of the hill, and saw, thrown out in black, upon the horizon, whitened by the moon, the elongated aerial form of Raoul. Athos stretched out his hand to get closer to his beloved son upon the plateau, and the latter also stretched out his; but suddenly, as if the young man had been drawn away in spite of himself, still retreating, he left the earth, and Athos saw the clear blue sky shine between the feet of his child and the ground of the hill. Raoul rose insensibly into the void, still smiling, still calling with a gesture:—he departed towards heaven. Athos uttered a cry of terrified tenderness. He looked below again. He saw a camp destroyed and all those white bodies of the royal army, like so many motionless atoms. And then, when raising his head, he saw still, still, his son beckoning him to ascend with him.

Chapter 59

THE ANGEL OF DEATH

ATHOS was at this part of his marvellous vision, when the charm was suddenly broken by a great noise rising from the outward gates of the house. A horse was heard galloping over the hard gravel of the great alley, and the sound of most noisy and animated conversations ascended to the chamber in which the Comte was dreaming. Athos did not stir from the place he occupied; he scarcely turned his head towards the door to ascertain the sooner what these noises could be. A heavy step ascended the stairs; the horse which had recently galloped, departed slowly towards the stables. Great hesitation appeared in the steps, which by degrees approached the chamber of Athos. A door then was opened, and Athos, turning a little towards the part of the room the noise came from, cried in a weak voice:

"It is a courier from Africa, is it not?"

"No, Monsieur le Comte," replied a voice which made the father of Raoul start upright in his bed.

"Grimaud!" murmured he. And the sweat began to pour down his cheeks. "Raoul is dead, is he not?"

Behind Grimaud, the other servants listened breathlessly with their eyes fixed upon the bed of their sick master. They heard the terrible question, and an awful silence ensued.

"Yes," replied the old man, heaving up the monosyllable from his chest with a hoarse, broken sigh.

Then arose voices of lamentation, which groaned without measure, and filled with regrets and prayers the chamber where the agonised father sought with his eyes for the portrait of his son. This was for Athos like the transition which led to his dream. Without uttering a cry, without shedding a tear, patient, mild, resigned as a martyr, he raised his eyes towards heaven, in order to there see again, rising above the mountain of Gigelli, the beloved shade which was leaving him at the moment of Grimaud's arrival. Without doubt, while looking towards the heavens, when resuming his marvellous dream, he repassed by the same road by which the vision, at once so terrible and so sweet, had led him before, for, after having gently closed his eyes, he reopened them and began to smile: he had just seen Raoul, who had smiled upon him. With his hands joined upon his breast, his face turned towards the window, bathed by the fresh air of night, which brought to his pillow the aroma of the flowers and the woods, Athos entered, never again to come out of it, into the contemplation of that paradise which the living never see. God willed, no doubt, to open to this elect the treasures of eternal beatitude, at the hour when other men tremble with the idea of being severely received by the Lord, and cling to this life they know, in the dread of the other life of which they get a glimpse by the dismal, murky torches of death. Athos was guided by the pure and serene soul of his son, which aspired to be like the paternal soul. Everything for this just man was melody and perfume in the rough road which souls take to return to the celestial country. After an hour of this ecstasy, Athos softly raised his hands, as white as wax; the smile did not quit his lips, and he murmured low, so low as scarcely to be audible, these three words addressed to God or to Raoul:

"HERE I AM!"

And his hands fell down slowly, as if he himself had laid them on the bed.

Death had been kind and mild to this noble creature. It had spared him the tortures of the agony, the convulsions of the last departure; it had opened with an indulgent finger the gates of eternity to that noble soul, worthy of every respect. But Grimaud, fatigued as he was, refused to leave the room. He sat himself down upon the threshold, watching his master with the vigilance of a sentinel, and jealous to receive either his first waking look, or his last dying sigh. The noises were all quieted in the house, and every one respected the slumber of their lord. But Grimaud, by anxiously listening, perceived that the Comte no longer breathed. Fear seized him; he rose completely up, and, at the very moment, heard some one coming up the stairs. A noise of spurs knocking against a sword—a warlike sound, familiar to his ears—stopped him as he was going towards the bed of Athos. A voice still more sonorous than brass or steel resounded within three paces of him.

"Athos! Athos! my friend!" cried this voice, agitated even to tears.

"Monsieur le Chevalier d'Artagnan!" faltered out Grimaud.

"Where is he? Where is he?" continued the musketeer.

Grimaud seized his arm in his bony fingers, and pointed to the bed, upon the sheets of which the livid tint of the dead already showed.

A choked respiration, the opposite to a sharp cry, swelled the throat of d'Artagnan. He advanced on tip-toe, trembling, frightened at the noise his feet made upon the floor, and his heart rent by a nameless agony. He placed his ear to the breast of Athos, his face to the Comte's mouth. Neither noise, nor breath! D'Artagnan drew back.

All at once, the bitter flood which mounted from minute to minute invaded his heart, and swelled his breast almost to bursting. Incapable of mastering his emotion, he arose, and tearing himself violently from the chamber where he had just found dead him to whom he came to report the news of the death of Porthos, he uttered sobs so heart-rending that the servants who seemed only to wait for an explosion of grief, answered to it by their lugubrious clamours, and the dogs of the late Comte by their lamentable howlings. Grimaud was the only one who did not lift up his voice. Even in the paroxysm of his grief he would not have dared to profane the dead, or for the first time disturb the slumber of his master. Athos had accustomed him never to speak.

Chapter 60

THE LAST CANTO OF THE POEM

ON THE morrow, all the nobility of the provinces, of the environs, and wherever messengers had carried the news, were seen to arrive.

D'Artagnan was struck at seeing two open coffins in the hall. In reply to the mute invitation of Grimaud, he approached, and saw in one of them Athos, still handsome in death, and, in the other, Raoul with his eyes closed, his cheeks pearly as those of the Pallas of Virgil, with a smile on his violet lips. He shuddered at seeing the father and son, those two departed souls, represented on earth by two silent, melancholy bodies, incapable of touching each other, however close they might be.

At length arrived the moment when the cold remains of these two gentlemen were to be returned to the earth. There was such an affluence of military and other people that up to the place of sepulchre, which was a chapel in the plain, the road from the city was filled with horsemen and pedestrians in mourning habits. Athos had chosen for his resting-place the little enclosure of a chapel erected by himself near the boundary of his estates. He had had the stones, cut in 1550, brought from an old Gothic manor-house in Berry, which had sheltered his early youth. The chapel, thus re-edified, thus transported, was pleasant beneath its wood of poplars and sycamores.

It was to this place the two coffins were brought, attended by a silent and respectful crowd. The office of the dead being celebrated, the last adieux paid to the noble departed, the assembly dispersed, talking, along the roads, of the virtues and mild death of the father, of the hopes the son had given, and of his melancholy end upon the coast of Africa.

By little and little, all noises were extinguished, like the lamps illumining the humble nave. The minister bowed for a last time to the altar and the still fresh graves, then, followed by his assistant, who rang a hoarse bell, he slowly took the road back to the presbytery. D'Artagnan, left alone, perceived that night was coming on. He had forgotten the hour, while thinking of the dead. He arose from the oaken bench on which he was seated in the chapel, and wished, as the priest had done, to go and bid a last adieu to the double grave which contained his two lost friends.

A woman was praying, kneeling on the moist earth. D'Artagnan stopped at the door of the chapel, to avoid disturbing this woman, and also to endeavour to see who was the pious friend who performed this sacred duty with so much zeal and perseverance. The unknown concealed her face in her hands, which were white as alabaster. From the noble simplicity of her costume, she must be a woman of distinction. Outside the enclosure were several horses mounted by servants, and a travelling carriage waiting for this lady. D'Artagnan in vain sought to make out what caused her delay. She continued praying, she frequently passed her handkerchief over her face, by which d'Artagnan perceived she was weeping. He saw her strike her breast with the pitiless compunction of a Christian woman. He heard her several times proffer, as if from a wounded heart: "Pardon! pardon!" And as she appeared to abandon herself entirely to her grief, as she threw herself down, almost fainting, amidst complaints and prayers, d'Artagnan, touched by his love for his so much regretted friends, made a few steps towards the grave, in order to interrupt the melancholy colloquy of the penitent with the dead. But as soon as his step sounded on the gravel the unknown raised her head, revealing to d'Artagnan a face inundated with tears, but a well-known face. It was Mademoiselle de la Vallière! "Monsieur d'Artagnan!" murmured she.

"You!" replied the captain, in a stern voice—"you here!—oh! madame, I should better have liked to see you decked with flowers in the mansion of the Comte de la Fère. You would have wept less—they too—I too!"

"Monsieur!" she said, sobbing.

"For it is you," added this pitiless friend of the dead,—"it is you have laid these two men in the grave."

"Oh! spare me!"

"God forbid, madame, that I should offend a woman, or that I should make her weep in vain; but I must say that the place of the murderer is not upon the grave of her victims." She wished to reply.

"What I now tell you," added he coldly, "I told the King."

She clasped her hands. "I know," said she, "I have caused the death of the Vicomte de Bragelonne."

"Ah! you know it?"

"The news arrived at court yesterday. I have travelled during the night forty leagues to come and ask pardon of the Comte, whom I supposed to be still living, and to supplicate God, upon the tomb of Raoul, that He would send me all the misfortunes I have merited, except a single one. Now, monsieur, I know that the death of the son has killed the father; I have two crimes to reproach myself with; I have two punishments to look for from God."

"I will repeat to you, Mademoiselle," said d'Artagnan, "what M. de Bragelonne said of you at Antibes, when he already meditated death: 'If pride and coquetry have misled her, I pardon her while despising her. If love has produced her error, I pardon her, swearing that no one could have loved her as I have done.'"

"You know," interrupted Louise, "that for my love I was about to sacrifice myself; you know whether I suffered when you met me lost, dying, abandoned. Well! never have I suffered so much as now; because then I hoped, I desired—now I have nothing to wish for; because this death drags away all my joy into the tomb; because I can no longer dare to love without remorse, and I feel, that he whom I love—oh! that is the law—will repay me with the tortures I have made others undergo."

D'Artagnan made no reply; he was too well convinced she was not mistaken.

"Well! then," added she, "dear Monsieur d'Artagnan, do not over-whelm me to-day, I again implore you. I am like the branch torn from the trunk, I no longer hold to anything in this world, and a current drags me on, I cannot say whither. I love madly, I love to the point of coming to tell it, impious as I am, over the ashes of the dead; and I do not blush for it—I have no remorse on account of it. This love is a religion. Only, as hereafter you will see me alone, forgotten, disdained; as you will see me punished with that with which I am destined to be punished, spare me in my ephemeral happiness, leave it to me for a few days, for a few minutes. Now even, at the moment I am speaking to you, perhaps it no longer exists. My God! this double murder is perhaps already expiated!"

While she was speaking thus, the sound of voices and the steps of horses drew the attention of the captain. M. de Saint-Aignan came to seek La Vallière. "The King," he said, "was a prey to jealousy and uneasiness." Saint-Aignan did not see d'Artagnan, half concealed by the trunk of a chestnut-tree which shaded the two graves. Louise thanked Saint-Aignan, and dismissed him with a gesture. He rejoined the party outside the enclosure.

"You see, madam," said the captain bitterly to the young woman,—"you see that your happiness still lasts."

The young woman raised her head with a solemn air. "A day will come," said she, "when you will repent of having so ill-judged me. On that day it is I who will pray God to forgive you for having been unjust towards me. Besides, I shall suffer so much that you will be the first to pity my sufferings. Do not reproach me with that happiness, Monsieur d'Artagnan; it costs me dear, and I have not paid all my debt." Saying these words, she again knelt down, softly and affectionately.

"Pardon me, the last time, my affianced Raoul!" said she. "I have broken our chain; we are both destined to die of grief. It is thou who departest the first; fear nothing, I shall follow thee. See, only, that I have not been base, and that I have come to bid thee this last adieu. The Lord is my witness, Raoul, that if with my life I could have redeemed thine, I would have given that life without hesitation. I could not give my love. Once more, pardon!"

She gathered a branch and stuck it into the ground; then, wiping the tears from her eyes, she bowed to d'Artagnan, and disappeared.

The captain watched the departure of the horses, horsemen, and carriage, then crossing his arms upon his swelling chest, "When will it be my turn to depart?" said he, in an agitated voice. "What is there left for man after youth, after love, after glory, after friendship, after strength, after riches? That rock, under which sleeps Porthos, who possessed all I have named; this moss, under which repose Athos and Raoul, who possessed still much more!"

He hesitated a moment, with a dull eye; then, drawing himself up: "Forward! still forward!" said he. "When it shall be time, God will tell me, as he has told the others."

He touched the earth, moistened with the evening dew, with the ends of his fingers, signed himself as if he had been at the fount of a church, and retook alone—ever alone—the road to Paris.

EPILOGUE

FOUR years after the scene we have just described, two horsemen, well mounted, traversed Blois early in the morning, for the purpose of arranging a birding party which the King intended to make in that uneven plain which the Loire divides in two, and which borders on the one side on Meung, on the other on Amboise. These were the captain of the King's harriers and the governor of the falcons, personages greatly respected in the time of Louis XIII, but rather neglected by his successor. These two horsemen, having reconnoitred the ground, were returning, their observations made, when they perceived some little groups of soldiers here and there whom the sergeants were placing at distances at the openings of the enclosures. These were the King's musketeers. Behind them came, upon a good horse, the captain, known by his richly embroidered uniform. His hair was grey, his beard was becoming so. He appeared a little bent, although sitting and handling his horse gracefully. He was looking about him watchfully.

"M. d'Artagnan does not get any older," said the captain of the harriers to his colleague the falconer; "with ten years more than either of us, he has the seat of a young man on horseback."

"That is true," replied the falconer. "I don't see any change in him for the last twenty years."

But this officer was mistaken; d'Artagnan in the last four years had lived twelve years. Age imprinted its pitiless claws at each angle of his eyes; his brow was bald; his hands, formerly brown and nervous, were getting white as if the blood began to chill there.

D'Artagnan accosted the officers with the shade of affability which distinguishes superior men, and received in return for his courtesy two most respectful bows.

"Ah! what a lucky chance to see you here, Monsieur d'Artagnan!" cried the falconer.

"It is rather I who should say that, messieurs," replied the captain, "for nowadays the King makes more frequent use of his musketeers than of his falcons."

"Ah! it is not as it was in the good old times," sighed the falconer. "Do you remember, Monsieur d'Artagnan, when the late King flew the pie in the vineyards beyond Beaugence? Ah! you were not captain of the musketeers at that time, Monsieur d'Artagnan."

"And you were nothing but under-corporal of the tiercelets," replied d'Artagnan, laughing. "Never mind that; it was a good time, seeing that it was always a good time when we are young. Good day, monsieur the captain of the harriers."

"You do me honour, Monsieur le Comte," said the latter. D'Artagnan made no reply. The title of Comte had not struck him; d'Artagnan had been a Comte for four years.

They could already catch glimpses of the huntsmen at the issues of the wood, the feathers of the outriders passing like shooting-stars across the clearings, and the white horses cutting with their luminous apparitions the dark thickets of the copses.

"But," resumed d'Artagnan, "will the sport be long? Pray give us a good swift bird, for I am very tired. Is it a heron or a swan?"

"Both, Monsieur d'Artagnan," said the falconer; "but you need not be alarmed; the King is not much of a sportsman; he does not sport on his own account; he only wishes to give amusement to the ladies."

The words "to the ladies," were so strongly accented, that it set d'Artagnan listening.

"Ah!" said he, looking at the falconer with surprise.

The captain of the harriers smiled.

"Oh! you may safely laugh," said d'Artagnan; "I know nothing of current news; I only arrived yesterday, after a month's absence. I left the court mourning the death of the Queen-Mother. The King was not willing to take any amusement after receiving the last sigh of Anne of Austria; but everything has an end in this world. Well; then he is no longer sad? So much the better."

"And everything commences as well as ends," said the captain of the dogs, with a coarse laugh.

"Ah!" said d'Artagnan a second time—he burned to know, but dignity would not allow him to interrogate people below him,—"there is something beginning, then, it appears?"

The captain gave him a significant wink; but d'Artagnan was unwilling to learn anything from this man.

"Shall we see the King early?" asked he of the falconer.

"At seven o'clock, monsieur, I shall fly the birds."

"Who comes with the King? How is madame? How is the Queen?"

"Better, monsieur."

"Has she been ill, then?"

"Monsieur, since the last chagrin she had, Her Majesty has been unwell."

"What chagrin? You need not fancy your news is old. I am but just returned."

"It appears that the Queen, a little neglected since the death of her mother-in-law, complained to the King, who replied to her,—'Do I not sleep with you every night, madame? What more do you want?'"

"Ah!" said d'Artagnan,—"poor woman! She must heartily hate Mademoiselle de la Vallière."

"Oh, no! not Mademoiselle de la Vallière," replied the falconer.

"Who then——?" The horn interrupted this conversation. It summoned the dogs and the hawks. The falconer and his companion set off immediately, leaving d'Artagnan alone in the midst of the suspended sentence. The King appeared at a distance, surrounded by ladies and horsemen. D'Artagnan, with an eye a little weakened, distinguished behind the group three carriages. The first was intended for the Queen; it was empty. D'Artagnan, who did not see Mademoiselle de la Vallière by the King's side, on looking about for her, saw her in the second carriage. She was alone with two of her women, who seemed as dull as their mistress. On the left hand of the King, upon a high-spirited horse, restrained by a bold and skilful hand, shone a lady of the most dazzling beauty. The King smiled upon her, and she smiled upon the King. Loud laughter followed every word she spoke.

"I must know that woman," thought the musketeer; "who can she be?" And he stooped towards his friend the falconer, to whom he addressed the question he had put to himself. The falconer was about to reply, when the King, perceiving d'Artagnan, "Ah, Comte!" said he, "you are returned, then! why have I not seen you?"

"Sire," replied the Captain; "because your Majesty was asleep when I arrived; and not awake when I resumed my duties this morning."

"Still the same!" said Louis in a loud voice, denoting satisfaction. "Take some rest, Comte; I command you to do so. You will dine with me to-day."

The King passed a few steps in advance, and d'Artagnan found himself in the midst of a fresh group, among whom shone Colbert.

"Good day, Monsieur d'Artagnan," said the minister, with affable politeness; "have you had a pleasant journey?"

"Yes, monsieur," said d'Artagnan, bowing to the neck of his horse.

"I heard the King invite you to his table for this evening," continued the minister; "you will meet an old friend there."

"An old friend of mine?" asked d'Artagnan, plunging painfully into the dark waves of the past, which had swallowed up for him so many friendships and so many hatreds.

"M. le Duc d'Alméda, who is arrived this morning from Spain."

"The Duc d'Alméda?" said d'Artagnan, reflecting in vain.

"I!" said an old man, white as snow, sitting bent in his carriage, which he caused to be thrown open to make room for the musketeer.

"Aramis!" cried d'Artagnan, struck with perfect stupor. And he left, inert as it was, the thin arm of the old nobleman hanging round his neck.

Colbert, after having observed them in silence for a minute, put his horse forward, and left the two old friends together.

"And so," said the musketeer, taking the arm of Aramis, "you, the exile, the rebel, are again in France!"

"Ah! and I shall dine with you at the King's table," said Aramis smiling. "Yes; will you not ask yourself what is the use of fidelity in this world? Stop! let us allow poor La Vallière's carriage to pass. Look, how uneasy she is! How her eye, dimmed with tears, follows the King, who is riding on horseback yonder!"

"With whom?"

"With Mademoiselle de Tonnay-Charente, now become Madame de Montespan," replied Aramis.

"She is jealous; is she then deserted?"

"Not quite yet, but it will not be long."

They chatted together, while following the sport, and Aramis's coachman drove them so cleverly that they got up at the moment when the falcon, attacking the bird, beat him down, and fell upon him. The King alighted, Madame de Montespan followed his example. They were in front of an isolated chapel, concealed by large trees, already despoiled of their leaves by the first winds of autumn. Behind this chapel was an enclosure, closed by a latticed gate. The falcon had beat down his prey in the enclosure belonging to this little chapel, and the King was desirous of going in to take the first feather, according to custom. The *cortège* formed a circle round the building and the hedges, too small to receive so many. D'Artagnan held back Aramis by the arm, as he was about, like the rest, to alight from his carriage, and in a hoarse, broken voice, "Do you know, Aramis," said he, "whither chance has conducted us?"

"No," replied the Duke.

"Here repose people I have known," said d'Artagnan, much agitated.

Aramis without divining anything, and with a trembling step, penetrated into the chapel by a little door which d'Artagnan opened for him. "Where are they buried?" said he.

"There, in the enclosure. There is a cross, you see, under that little cypress. The little cypress is planted over their tomb; don't go to it; the King is going that way; the heron has fallen just there."

Aramis stopped and concealed himself in the shade. They then saw, without being seen, the pale face of La Vallière, who, neglected in her carriage, had at first looked on, with a melancholy heart, from the door, and then, carried away by jealousy, she had advanced into the chapel, whence, leaning against a pillar, she contemplated in the enclosure the King smiling and making signs to Madame de Montespan to approach, as there was nothing to be afraid of. Madame de Montespan complied; she took the hand the King held out to her, and he, plucking out the first feather from the heron, which the falconer had strangled, placed it in the hat of his beautiful companion. She, smiling in her turn, kissed the hand tenderly which made her this present. The King blushed with pleasure; he looked at Madame de Montespan with all the fire of love.

"What will you give me in exchange?" said he.

She broke off a little branch of cypress and offered it to the King, who looked intoxicated with hope.

"Humph!" said Aramis to d'Artagnan; "the present is but a sad one, for that cypress shades a tomb."

"Yes, and the tomb is that of Raoul de Bragelonne," said d'Artagnan aloud; "of Raoul, who sleeps under that cross with his father."

A groan resounded behind them. They saw a woman fall fainting to the ground. Mademoiselle de la Vallière had seen all, and heard all.

"Poor woman!" muttered d'Artagnan, as he helped the attendants to carry back to her carriage her who from that time was to suffer.

That evening d'Artagnan was seated at the King's table, near M. Colbert and M. le Duc d'Alméda. The King was very gay. He paid a thousand little attentions to the Queen, a thousand kindnesses to Madame, seated at his left hand, and very sad. It might have been supposed to be that calm time when the King used to watch the eyes of his mother for the avowal or disavowal of what he had just done.

Of mistresses there was no question at this dinner. The King addressed Aramis two or three times, calling him M. l'Ambassadeur, which increased the surprise already felt by d'Artagnan at seeing his friend the rebel so marvellously well received at court.

The King, on rising from table, gave his hand to the Queen, and made a sign to Colbert, whose eye watched that of his master. Colbert took d'Artagnan and Aramis on one side. The King began to chat with his sister, whilst Monsieur, very uneasy, entertained the Queen with a pre-occupied air, without ceasing to watch his wife and brother from the corner of his eye. The conversation between Aramis, d'Artagnan, and Colbert turned upon indifferent subjects. They spoke of preceding ministers; Colbert related the feats of Mazarin, and required those of Richelieu to be related to him. D'Artagnan could not overcome his surprise at finding this man, with heavy eyebrows and a low forehead, contain so much sound knowledge and cheerful spirits. Aramis was astonished at that lightness of character which permitted a serious man to retard with advantage the moment for a more important conversation, to which nobody made any allusion, although all three interlocutors felt the imminence of it. It was very plain from the embarrassed appearance of Monsieur, how much the conversation of the King and Madame annoyed him. The eyes of Madame were almost red; was she going to complain? Was she going to commit a little scandal in open court? The King took her on one side, and in a tone so tender that it must have reminded the Princess of the time when she was loved for herself,—

"Sister," said he, "why do I see tears in those beautiful eyes?"

"Why—sire——" said she.

"Monsieur is jealous, is he not, sister?"

She looked towards Monsieur, an infallible sign that they were talking about him.

"Yes," said she.

"Listen to me," said the King; "if your friends compromise you, it is not Monsieur's fault."

He spoke these words with so much kindness, that Madame, encouraged, she, who had had so many griefs for so long a time, was near bursting, so full was her heart.

"Come, come, dear little sister," said the King, "tell me your griefs; by the word of a brother, I pity them; by the word of a King, I will terminate them."

She raised her fine eyes, and in a melancholy tone,—

"It is not my friends who compromise me," said she; "they are either absent or concealed; they have been brought into disgrace with your Majesty; they, so devoted, so good, so loyal!"

"You say this on account of Guiche, whom I have exiled, at the desire of Monsieur?"

"And who, since that unjust exile, has endeavoured to get himself killed every day!"

"Unjust, do you say, sister?"

"So unjust, that if I had not had the respect mixed with friendship that I have always entertained for your Majesty——"

"Well?"

"Well! I would have asked my brother Charles, upon whom I can always——"

The King started. "What then?"

"I would have asked him to have represented to you that Monsieur and his favourite, M. le Chevalier de Lorraine, ought not with impunity to constitute themselves the executioners of my honour and my happiness."

"The Chevalier de Lorraine," said the King; "that dismal face?"

"Is my mortal enemy. Whilst this man lives in my household, where Monsieur retains him and delegates his powers to him, I shall be the most miserable woman in this kingdom."

"So," said the King slowly, "you call your brother of England a better friend than I am?"

"Actions speak for themselves, sire."

"And you would prefer going to ask assistance there."

"To my own country!" said she, with pride; "yes, sire."

"You are the grandchild of Henry IV as well as myself, my friend. Cousin and brother-in-law, does not that amount pretty well to the title of brother-germain?"

"Then," said Henrietta, "act!"

"Let us form an alliance."

"Begin."

"I have, you say, unjustly exiled Guiche."

"Oh! yes," said she, blushing.

"Guiche shall return."

"So far, well."

"And now you say that I am wrong in having in your household the Chevalier de Lorraine, who gives Monsieur ill-advice respecting you."

"Remember well what I tell you, sire; the Chevalier de Lorraine some day—Observe, if ever I come to an ill end, I beforehand accuse the Chevalier de Lorraine; he has a soul capable of any crime."

"The Chevalier de Lorraine shall no longer annoy you—I promise you that."

"Then that will be a true preliminary of alliance, sire—I sign; but since you have done your part, tell me what shall be mine."

"Instead of embroiling me with your brother Charles, you must make him my more intimate friend than ever."

"To the effect that I must go to London, my dear brother."

"I fancy you already on your road, my dear little sister, and consoled for all your griefs."

"I will go, on two conditions. The first is, that I shall know what I am negotiating about."

"This is it. The Dutch, you know, insult me daily in their gazettes, and by their republican attitude. I don't like republics."

"That may easily be conceived, sire."

"I see with pain that these kings of the sea—they call themselves so—keep trade from France in the Indies, and that their vessels will soon occupy all the ports of Europe. Such a power is too near me, sister. Your second condition for going, if you please, sister?"

"The consent of Monsieur, my husband."

"You shall have it."

"Then consider me gone, my brother."

On hearing these words, Louis XIV turned round towards the corner of the room in which d'Artagnan, Colbert and Aramis stood, and made an affirmative sign to his minister.

Colbert then broke the conversation at the point it happened to be at, and said to Aramis,—

"Monsieur l'Ambassadeur, shall we talk about business?"

D'Artagnan immediately withdrew, from politeness.

"Monsieur," said Colbert to Aramis, "this is the moment for us to come to an understanding. I have made your peace with the King, and I owed that clearly to a man of your merit; but as you have often expressed friendship for me, an opportunity presents itself for giving me a proof of it. You are, besides, more a Frenchman than a Spaniard. Shall we have, answer me frankly, the neutrality of Spain, if we undertake anything against the United Provinces?"

"Monsieur," replied Aramis, "the interest of Spain is very clear. To embroil Europe with the United Provinces, against which subsists the ancient malice of their conquered liberty, is our policy, but the King of France is allied with the United Provinces. You are not ignorant, besides, that it would be a maritime war, and that France is not in a state to make such a one with advantage."

Colbert, turning round at this moment, saw d'Artagnan. He called him, at the same time saying in a low voice to Aramis, "We may talk with M. d'Artagnan, I suppose?"

"Oh! certainly," replied the ambassador.

"We were saying, M. d'Alméda and I," said Colbert, "that war with the United Provinces would be a maritime war."

"That's evident enough," replied the musketeer.

"That is why I told Monsieur l'Ambassadeur," said Colbert, "that Spain promising its neutrality, England helping us——"

"If England assists you," said Aramis, "I engage for the neutrality of Spain."

"I take you at your word," hastened Colbert to reply with blunt good humour. "And talking of Spain, you have not the *Golden Fleece*, Monsieur d'Alméda. I heard the King say the other day that he should like to see you wear the Grand Cordon of St. Michael."

Aramis bowed. "Oh!" thought d'Artagnan, "and Porthos is no longer here! What ells of ribbon would there be for him in these decorations! Good Porthos!"

"Monsieur d'Artagnan," resumed Colbert, "between us two, you will have, I would wager, an inclination to lead your musketeers into Holland. Can you swim?" And he laughed like a man in a very good humour.

"Like an eel," replied d'Artagnan.

"Ah! but there are some rough passages of canals and marshes yonder, and the best swimmers are sometimes drowned there."

"It is my profession to die for His Majesty," said the musketeer. "Only, as it is seldom that in war much water is met with without a little fire, I declare to you beforehand that I will do my best to choose fire. I am getting old; water freezes me—fire warms, Monsieur Colbert."

And d'Artagnan looked so handsome in juvenile vigour and pride as he pronounced these words, that Colbert, in his turn, could not help admiring him. D'Artagnan perceived the effect he had produced. He remembered that the best tradesman is he who fixes a high price upon his goods when they are valuable. He prepared then his price in advance.

"So, then," said Colbert, "we go into Holland?"

"Yes," replied d'Artagnan; "only——"

"Only?" said M. Colbert.

"Only," repeated d'Artagnan, "there is in everything the question of interest and the question of self-love. It is a very fine title, that of captain of the musketeers; but observe this: we have now the King's guards and the military household of the King. A captain of musketeers ought either to command all that, and then he would absorb a hundred thousand livres a year for expenses of representation and table——"

"Well! but do you suppose, by chance, that the King would haggle with you?" said Colbert.

"Eh! monsieur, you have not understood me," replied d'Artagnan, sure of having carried the question of interest; "I was telling you that I, an old captain, formerly chief of the King's guard, having precedence of the marshals of France—I saw myself one day in the trenches with two other equals, the captain of the guards and the colonel commanding the Swiss. Now, at no price will I suffer that. I have old habits; I will stand to them."

Colbert felt this blow, but he was prepared for it.

"I have been thinking of what you said just now," replied he.

"About what, monsieur?"

"We were speaking of canals and marshes in which people are drowned."

"Well?"

"Well! if they are drowned, it is for want of a boat, a plank, or a stick."

"Of a stick, however short it may be," said d'Artagnan.

"Exactly," said Colbert. "And, therefore, I never heard of an instance of a marshal of France being drowned."

D'Artagnan became pale with joy, and in a not very firm voice: "People would be very proud of me in my country," said he, "if I were a marshal of France; but a man must have commanded an expedition in chief to obtain the baton."

"Monsieur!" said Colbert, "here is in this pocket-book, which you will study, a plan of a campaign you will have to lead a body of troops to carry out in the next spring."

D'Artagnan took the book tremblingly, and his fingers meeting with those of Colbert, the minister pressed the hand of the musketeer loyally.

"Monsieur," said he, "we had both a revenge to take, one over the other. I have begun; it is now your turn."

"I will do you justice, monsieur," replied d'Artagnan, "and implore you to tell the King that the first opportunity that shall offer, he may depend upon a victory or seeing me dead."

"Then I will have the fleur-de-lis for your marshal's baton prepared immediately," said Colbert.

On the morrow of this day, Aramis, who was setting out for Madrid, to negotiate the neutrality of Spain, came to embrace d'Artagnan at his hotel.

"Let us love each other for four," said d'Artagnan, "we are now but two."

"And you will, perhaps, never see me again, dear d'Artagnan," said Aramis;—"if you knew how I have loved you! I am old, I am extinguished, I am dead."

"My friend," said d'Artagnan, "you will live longer than I shall: diplomacy commands you to live; but for my part, honour condemns me to die."

"Bah! such men as we are, Monsieur le Marshal," said Aramis, "only die satiated with joy or glory."

"Ah!" replied d'Artagnan, with a melancholy smile, "I assure you, Monsieur le Duc, I feel very little appetite for either."

They once more embraced, and, two hours after, they were separated.

THE DEATH OF D'ARTAGNAN

CONTRARY to what always happens, whether in politics or morals, each kept his promise, and did honour to his engagements.

The King recalled M. de Guiche, and banished M. le Chevalier de Lorraine; so that Monsieur became ill in consequence. Madame set out for London, where she applied herself so earnestly to her brother, Charles II, that the alliance between England and France was signed, and the English vessels, ballasted by a few millions of French gold, made a terrible campaign against the fleets of the United Provinces. Colbert had promised the King vessels, munitions, and victories. He kept his word, as is well known. At length Aramis, upon whose promises there was least dependence to be placed, wrote Colbert the following letter, on the subject of the negotiations which he had undertaken at Madrid:

"MONSIEUR COLBERT,—I have the honour to expedite to you the R. P. d'Oliva, general *ad interim* of the Society of Jesus, my provisional successor. The reverend father will explain to you, Monsieur Colbert, that I preserve to myself the direction of all the affairs of the Order which concern France and Spain; but that I am not willing to retain the title of general, which would throw too much light upon the march of the negotiations with which His Catholic Majesty wishes to entrust me. I shall resume that title by the command of His Majesty, when the labours I have undertaken in concert with you, for the great glory of God and his Church, shall be brought to a good end. The R. P. d'Oliva will inform you likewise, monsieur, of the consent which His Catholic Majesty gives to the signature of a treaty which assures the neutrality of Spain, in the event of a war between France and the United Provinces. The consent will be valid, even if England, instead of being active, should satisfy herself with remaining neutral. As to Portugal, of which you and I have spoken, monsieur, I can assure you it will contribute with all its resources to assist the most Christian King in his war. I beg you, Monsieur Colbert, to preserve to me your friendship, as also to believe in my profound attachment, and to lay my respect at the feet of His Most Christian Majesty.

(Signed) LE DUC D'ALMEDA."

Aramis had then performed more than he had promised; it remained to be known how the King, M. Colbert, and d'Artagnan would be faithful to each other. In the spring, as Colbert had predicted, the land army entered on its campaign. It preceded, in magnificent order, the court of Louis XIV, who, setting out on horseback, surrounded by carriages filled with ladies and courtiers, conducted the *élite* of his kingdom to this sanguinary fête. The officers of the army, it is true, had no other music but the artillery of the Dutch forts; but it was enough for a great number, who found in this war honours, advancement, fortune, or death.

The army commanded by d'Artagnan took twelve small places within a month. He was engaged in besieging the thirteenth, which had held out five days. D'Artagnan caused the trenches to be opened without appearing to suppose that these people would ever allow themselves to be taken. The pioneers and labourers were, in the army of this man, a body full of emulation, ideas, and zeal, because he treated them like soldiers, knew how to render their work glorious, and never allowed them to be killed if he could prevent it. It should have been seen then, with what eagerness the marshy glebes of Holland were turned over. Those turf-heaps, those mounds of potter's clay melted at the word of the soldiers like butter in the vast frying-pans of the Friesland housewives.

M. d'Artagnan despatched a courier to the King to give him an account of the last successes, which redoubled the good humour of His Majesty and his inclination to amuse the ladies. These victories of M. d'Artagnan gave so much majesty to the Prince, that Madame de Montespan no longer called him anything but Louis the Invincible. So that Mademoiselle de la Vallière, who only called the King Louis the Victorious, lost much of His Majesty's favour. Besides, her eyes were frequently red, and for an Invincible nothing is more disagreeable than a mistress who weeps while everything is smiling around her. The star of Mademoiselle de la Vallière was being drowned in the horizon in clouds and tears. But the gaiety of Madame de Montespan redoubled with the successes of the King, and consoled him for every other unpleasant circumstance. It was to d'Artagnan the King owed this; and His Majesty was anxious to acknowledge these services; he wrote to M. Colbert:

"Monsieur Colbert, we have a promise to fulfil with M. d'Artagnan, who so well keeps his. This is to inform you that the time is come for performing it. All provisions for this purpose you shall be furnished with in due time,—Louis."

In consequence of this, Colbert, who detained the envoy of d'Artagnan, placed in the hands of that messenger a letter from himself for d'Artagnan, and a small coffer of ebony inlaid with gold, which was not very voluminous in appearance, but which, without doubt, was very heavy, as a guard of five men was given to the messenger, to assist him in carrying it. These people arrived before the place which d'Artagnan was besieging towards daybreak and presented themselves at the lodgings of the general. They were told that M. d'Artagnan, annoyed by a sortie which the governor, an artful man, had made the evening before, and in which the works had been destroyed, seventy-seven men killed, and the reparation of the breaches commenced, had just gone, with half a score companies of grenadiers, to reconstruct the works.

M. Colbert's envoy had orders to go and seek M. d'Artagnan wherever he might be, or at whatever hour of the day or night. He directed his course, therefore, towards the trenches, followed by his escort, all on horseback. They perceived M. d'Artagnan in the open plain with his gold-laced hat, his long cane, and his large gilded cuffs. He was biting his white moustache, and wiping off, with his left hand, the dust which the passing balls threw up from the ground they ploughed near him. They also saw, amidst this terrible fire, which filled the air with its hissing whistle, officers handling the shovel, soldiers rolling barrows, and vast fascines, rising by being either carried or dragged by from ten to twenty men, cover the front of the trench, re-opened to the centre by this extraordinary effort of the general animating his soldiers. In three hours, all had been reinstated. D'Artagnan began to speak more mildly; and he became quite calm, when the captain of the pioneers approached him, hat in hand, to tell him that the trench was again lodgeable. This man had scarcely finished speaking when a ball took off one of his legs, and he fell into the arms of d'Artagnan. The latter lifted up his soldier, and quietly, with soothing words, carried him into the trench, amidst the enthusiastic applause of the two regiments. From that time, it was no longer ardour: it was delirium; two companies stole away up the advanced posts, which they destroyed instantly.

When their comrades, restrained with great difficulty by d'Artagnan, saw them lodged upon the bastions, they rushed forward likewise; and soon a furious assault was made upon the counterscarp, upon which depended the safety of the place. D'Artagnan perceived there was only one means left of stopping his army, and that was to lodge it in the place. He directed all his force to two breaches, which the besieged were busy in repairing. The shock was terrible; eighteen companies took part in it, and d'Artagnan went with the rest, within half cannonshot of the place, to support the attack by *échelons*. The cries of the Dutch, who were being poniarded upon their guns by d'Artagnan's grenadiers, were distinctly audible. The struggle grew fiercer with the despair of the governor, who disputed his position foot by foot. D'Artagnan, to put an end to the affair, and silence the fire, which was unceasing, sent a fresh column, which penetrated like a wimble through the posts that remained solid; and he soon perceived upon the ramparts, through the fire, the terrified flight of the besieged, pursued by the besiegers.

It was at this moment, the general, breathing freely and full of joy, heard a voice behind him, saying, "Monsieur, if you please, from M. Colbert."

He broke the seal of a letter which contained these words:

"Monsieur d'Artagnan,—The King commands me to inform you that he has nominated you Marshal of France, as a reward of your good services, and the honour you do to his arms. The King is highly pleased, monsieur, with the captures you have made; he commands you, in particular, to finish the siege you have commenced, with good fortune to you and success for him."

D'Artagnan was standing with a heated countenance and a sparkling eye. He looked up to watch the progress of his troops upon the walls, still enveloped in red and black volumes of smoke. "I have finished," replied he to the messenger; "the city will have surrendered in a quarter of an hour." He then resumed his reading:

"The accompanying box, Monsieur d'Artagnan, is my own present. You will not be sorry to see that, whilst you warriors are drawing the sword to defend the King, I am animating the pacific arts to ornament the recompenses worthy of you. I commend myself to your friendship, Monsieur le Marshal, and beg you to believe in all mine.—COLBERT."

D'Artagnan, intoxicated with joy, made a sign to the messenger, who approached, with his box in his hands. But at the moment the marshal was going to look at it, a loud explosion resounded from the ramparts, and called his attention towards the city. "It is strange," said d'Artagnan, "that I don't see the King's flag upon the walls, or hear the drums beat." He launched three hundred fresh men, under a high-spirited officer, and ordered another breach to be beaten. Then, being more tranquil, he turned towards the box which Colbert's envoy held out to him. It was his treasure, he had won it.

D'Artagnan was holding out his hand to open the box, when a ball from the city crushed the box in the arms of the officer, struck d'Artagnan full in the chest, and knocked him down upon a sloping heap of earth, whilst the fleur-de-lised baton, escaping from the broken sides of the box, came rolling under the powerless hand of the marshal. D'Artagnan endeavoured to raise himself up. It was thought he had been knocked down without being wounded. A terrible cry broke from the group of his terrified officers; the marshal was covered with blood; the paleness of death ascended slowly to his noble countenance. Leaning upon the arms which were held out on all sides to receive him, he was able once more to turn his eyes towards the place, and to distinguish the white flag at the crest of the principal bastion; his ears, already deaf to the sounds of life, caught feebly the rolling of the drum which announced the victory. Then, clasping in his nerveless hand the baton ornamented with its fleur-de-lis, he cast down upon it his eyes, which had no longer the power of looking upwards towards heaven, and fell back, murmuring those strange words, which appeared to the soldiers cabalistic words,—words which had formerly represented so many things upon earth, and which none but the dying man longer comprehended.

"Athos—Porthos, farewell till we meet again! Aramis, adieu for ever!"

Of the four valiant men whose history we have related, there now no longer remained but one single body; God had resumed the souls.

Printed in Germany